"Describe him,"
Ryan demanded

The one-eyed man's heart was pounding in his chest. It was impossible. This could not be happening.

The brothers exchanged a glance. "The Trader? Hell, I dunno," Sparrow said. "Never saw the guy. He was always inside a big-ass tank, stays behind a blister of the mil glass."

"How many wags?" J.B. pressed him. "Describe them!"

Sparrow scrunched his face. "Well, there were three, one big wag and two others, each plated with metal and covered with blasters. Big stuff. Baron Gaza was scared to death of the guy. Hell, who wouldn't be with all his weapons?"

"More," Ryan said through clenched teeth.

Fumbling for a reply, Jed scratched his head. "Well, I heard Kate call the big truck War Wag One. That help any?"

The universe seemed to go still at those simple words, as if it were breaking apart and rejoining in a new pattern, reorganizing itself on a most basic of levels.

"He made it," Ryan said quietly. "Trader's alive!"

**Other titles in the
Deathlands saga:**

Pilgrimage to Hell
Red Holocaust
Neutron Solstice
Crater Lake
Homeward Bound
Pony Soldiers
Dectra Chain
Ice and Fire
Red Equinox
Northstar Rising
Time Nomads
Latitude Zero
Seedling
Dark Carnival
Chill Factor
Moon Fate
Fury's Pilgrims
Shockscape
Deep Empire
Cold Asylum
Twilight Children
Rider, Reaper
Road Wars
Trader Redux
Genesis Echo
Shadowfall
Ground Zero
Emerald Fire
Bloodlines
Crossways
Keepers of the Sun
Circle Thrice

Eclipse at Noon
Stoneface
Bitter Fruit
Skydark
Demons of Eden
The Mars Arena
Watersleep
Nightmare Passage
Freedom Lost
Way of the Wolf
Dark Emblem
Crucible of Time
Starfall
Encounter:
  Collector's Edition
Gemini Rising
Gaia's Demise
Dark Reckoning
Shadow World
Pandora's Redoubt
Rat King
Zero City
Savage Armada
Judas Strike
Shadow Fortress
Sunchild
Breakthrough
Salvation Road
Amazon Gate
Destiny's Truth
Skydark Spawn
Damnation Road Show

For my buddy, Rich Tucholka

First edition September 2003

ISBN 0-373-62573-1

DEVIL RIDERS

Printed in U.S.A.

JAMES AXLER

DEATH LANDS®

Devil Riders

Scorpion
God
Book I

A GOLD EAGLE BOOK FROM
WORLDWIDE®

TORONTO • NEW YORK • LONDON
AMSTERDAM • PARIS • SYDNEY • HAMBURG
STOCKHOLM • ATHENS • TOKYO • MILAN
MADRID • WARSAW • BUDAPEST • AUCKLAND

The sun and the moon and the stars would
have disappeared long ago...had they
happened to be within the reach of predatory
human hands.
—Havelock Ellis, *The Dance of Life* (1923)

THE DEATHLANDS SAGA

This world is their legacy, a world born in the violent nuclear spasm of 2001 that was the bitter outcome of a struggle for global dominance.

There is no real escape from this shockscape where life always hangs in the balance, vulnerable to newly demonic nature, barbarism, lawlessness.

But they are the warrior survivalists, and they endure—in the way of the lion, the hawk and the tiger, true to nature's heart despite its ruination.

Ryan Cawdor: The privileged son of an East Coast baron. Acquainted with betrayal from a tender age, he is a master of the hard realities.

Krysty Wroth: Harmony ville's own Titian-haired beauty, a woman with the strength of tempered steel. Her premonitions and Gaia powers have been fostered by her Mother Sonja.

J. B. Dix, the Armorer: Weapons master and Ryan's close ally, he, too, honed his skills traversing the Deathlands with the legendary Trader.

Doctor Theophilus Tanner: Torn from his family and a gentler life in 1896, Doc has been thrown into a future he couldn't have imagined.

Dr. Mildred Wyeth: Her father was killed by the Ku Klux Klan, but her fate is not much lighter. Restored from predark cryogenic suspension, she brings twentieth-century healing skills to a nightmare.

Jak Lauren: A true child of the wastelands, reared on adversity, loss and danger, the albino teenager is a fierce fighter and loyal friend.

Dean Cawdor: Ryan's young son by Sharona accepts the only world he knows, and yet he is the seedling bearing the promise of tomorrow.

In a world where all was lost, they are humanity's last hope....

Chapter One

As muted thunder rolled across the grassy field, a group of people burst from the bushes, running for their lives.

Many carried bundles of possessions, but most had already thrown away the packs for greater speed. Death was coming fast, and every second counted. Their convoy had been ambushed at a water hole, and most of the mercies hired to guard them from coldhearts were aced already. Now there was nothing else to do but run.

"The Devils are here!" a burly man shouted, pulling a rusty blaster from within his ragged shirt and thumbing back the hammer. "Head for the trees!"

Some of the fleeing people did as ordered. Others ran mindlessly across the open ground. A few fell weeping to the ground in surrender. Only two others pulled weapons and turned to face the onrushing enemy. The man held a homemade scattergun, the woman a crude crossbow built from car parts. As the man cocked back both of the hammers on the shotgun, the woman pulled a razor-tipped arrow from the quiver on her back and nocked it.

"Aim for the front," the first man commanded, licking dry lips. "With luck the rest will be close behind and they'll crash into the one we ace."

"We ain't gonna ace nobody," the woman growled. "Nothing can stop the Devils."

Constantly wiping his sweaty hands on his trousers, the man with the shotgun said nothing and tried to control his breathing.

High above the screaming people, sheet lightning crashed among the purple and orange clouds, while black velocity streamers sliced through the sky like the slashes of a knife. Suddenly from out of nowhere, an arc of fire streaked across the polluted atmosphere as another predark satellite descended too low and was caught by the gravity to be disintegrated in a fiery reentry.

On the ground, a wave of black-and-silver motorcycles bounded into view from over a groundswell, the riders carrying nets and clubs to take their prey alive. Each rider had a human skull, painted red, attached to the yoke of the handlebars. Some had a tuft of hair still in place, but most were missing teeth, or entire jaws, the grisly remains of their victims saved as trophies to adorn their machines. The Blue Devils, coldhearts of the Panhandle.

"Ace 'em!" the leader of the convoy shouted, then fired his blaster twice at the oncoming motorcycles.

A spray of sparks leaped from the handlebars of the lead Harley as a slug ricocheted off the chromed steel. The bikers paid no attention to the incoming lead and spread out after the sprinting people.

Tracking her target, the woman released the arrow, which hit a bald biker in the leg. The man cursed as his machine swerved, then the rest of the gang were among the defenders, the heavy nets filling the air.

A spread of net caught a woman, dragging her to the ground, and as she tried to rise another rider slammed her with his club, knocking her unconscious. Rising from the thick grass, an older man shoved a wooden spear into the spokes of a passing Harley, but missed completely. However, the attack was noticed and the lead coldheart sharply changed direction and revved the bike's big engine. The front of the vehicle raised off the ground to then slam down on the attacker, crushing his chest with the horrible sound of splintering bones.

More nets flew through the air and people fell

tangled in the ropes, tiny hooks woven into the mesh catching skin and clothing alike. The leader of the convoy fired his blaster at a nearby biker, but there was only a spray of sparks from a misfire. Jouncing over the irregular field, a fat biker covered with tattoos swung the barrel of a scattergun toward the leader's skull. But the man ducked just in time and pulled the trigger again, this time a roar sounding from the blaster. Blood sprayed from the biker's arm, and he swung the scattergun about to pull both triggers. The double explosion caught the leader full in the face, blowing off his head in a frothy eruption of bone, brains and blood.

More lightning flashed across the sky as the big engines roared, the bikers circling their prey, driving them closer together while they pulled more nets from bulging saddle bags. The woman let fly an arrow from her crossbow again, hitting nothing, and then was hit from behind by a net. She dropped squirming to the ground, then pulled a knife and buried it into her chest, bright blood gushing from the mortal wound.

Dropping the empty scattergun, the older man raised his hands in surrender. A Devil biker slammed into him from behind, spinning the whitehair, who crashed to the ground in a tangle of limbs. Soon, the roar of the engines mixed with the cries of the trapped people. Another blaster discharged, and a biker smashed a young man across the back with a thrown club, sending him sprawling to the ground.

With the blasters empty, the battle was over in minutes and the captives were freed from the nets. Hands tied behind their backs, the prisoners were kicked and shoved into a line before their grinning captors.

This close, the old man could see that the biker gang was dressed in rags draped over their thick leather jackets to hide their wealth, but were armed to the teeth with more blasters than any two villes worth of sec men. The machines they rode were old and patched, draped with saddlebags bulging with supplies and a few precious cans of slick, grain alcohol cut with traces of gasoline to fuel the big Harley engines. Every member of the pack was armed with some kind of a blaster, mostly scatterguns, yet only three of the bikes had an intact headlight, and only one had a windshield. The machines were battered, but still powerful, able to go places that no heavily armored war wag could ever reach.

"What's the total?" Cranston asked, the lead biker leaning over the handlebars of his purring machine.

The man was a craggy giant with closely cropped

blond hair. His nose was flat and wide, but whether that was a natural mutation or a very old injury was impossible to discern. The handle of a knife jutted from each boot, a big bore handcannon rode on his right hip and a longblaster wrapped in dirty rags was strapped across his back. The stock was deeply carved, and feathers dangled from below the muzzle of the weapon. The old man knew what that was for. To test the direction of the wind when he was placing a long shot.

"Ten people, four corpses," Krury announced, running a hand across his bald head. "A pretty fair haul."

"Not bad." Cranston grinned, killing the engine on the bike, then using the edge of his boot to force down the stand. Stepping off the Harley, he walked over to the line of prisoners. Ignoring the men, he checked the women, separating the very old and the one pregnant girl from the rest.

"You boys can fuck these," he said. "But no broken bones. We want them fresh for the market. Start a fire going and jerk the corpses to smoke the meat.

"Cannies!" the old man gasped. "You're not slavers, but nuking cannies!"

In a blur of speed, Cranston slapped the man across the face, driving him to the ground. The prisoner looked up with open hatred in his face, blood trickling from a split lip.

"Don't back talk me, wrinklie!" the biker snarled. "We don't eat people, but we know folks who do, and they pay us in plenty of slick for our wheels in exchange for the long-pig meat. So it's the mines or the stew pot, take your choice."

Slowly, the prisoner stood in a surprising display of strength for a man with so much gray hair. "How about a third choice?" he said, hawking to spit the blood from his mouth. "Bet that I can chill any one of you cannie coldhearts with my bare hands."

At that, the bikers roared with laughter.

"Black dust, but the wrinklie's got balls!" Cranston smiled, then his eyes went as hard as broken glass. "Well, we got enough to spare one for some entertainment. Okay, slave, if you win, you take the place of the stud ya chill. Never have enough men with real guts."

"And if I lose?" the old man asked, standing straighter.

The rest of the prisoners stayed motionless and silent. Their doom was sealed; this madness had nothing to do with them.

Hooking both thumbs into his leather gun belt, Krury sneered. "Then we deliver ya to the cannies alive," he said in an edged voice. "They got a ceremony called the Blood Dance. Starts with taking off your skin and feeding it back to ya. Something about sweetening their food."

"Then they get creative," another biker added, rubbing his crotch. "And guess what ya eat next?"

The old man swallowed with difficulty, but said nothing.

"Still game, old man?" Cranston demanded, resting a hand on his blaster.

A stiff breeze from the stormy clouds overhead ruffled the prisoner's gray hair as he nervously flexed both hands.

"The name's Denver Joe," he said softly. "Denver Joe Sinclair, although I'm really from Indy." For some reason this seemed to be important to the old man, a source of pride.

"Be smart, old-timer!" Another biker laughed. The man had long dirty red hair tied off in a ponytail that reached his waist. "Choose the mines and live. Anything's better than being a toy for the cannies."

One of the women prisoners burst into tears at that, and the others merely trembled. A man on the end of the line looked as if he were about to be sick.

"Yeah, I should work in the mines," Denver Joe

shot back. "But then a gutless feeb like you would suck scabbies in a gaudy house to stay alive. I'll go down fighting, ya mutie lover!"

Vastly amused by the unexpected display of rebellion, the bikers laughed even louder this time. With a snarl, the redheaded rider started forward, drawing a hatchet from his belt, but Cranston stopped the man with a stiff arm across the chest. The two stood there for a moment, like a breed master holding back his prize bloodhound.

"Whatcha think, Larry?" Cranston said, glancing at the skinny old man and then the muscular biker. "You missed twice with your net and killed a slut we could have ridden tonight. I think you owe the pack some entertainment."

"Anytime," the biker snarled.

"Winner take all?" Denver Joe added as insultingly as possible. "My life against your place in the gang?"

"Done!" Larry growled, starting to strip off his leather jacket and spare weapons. Kneeling as if in prayer, the old man took some dirt and rubbed it into his palms.

Cranston narrowed his eyes at that. Dirt in the palms was a fighter's trick from the arena of a baron. A person did that so the sweat wouldn't make him drop his knife. But the wrinklie didn't have a blade. Was this some sort of trick, or worse, a trap? It almost seemed as if the whitehair was trying to goad the biker into a fight right then and there. But that made no sense. Larry was twice the old man's size, and there wasn't a chance in hell the outlander could win. Gut instincts learned in a hundred battles told the chief biker there was something very wrong here, but he couldn't figure out where the danger was. No sense taking chances, though.

"Not here," Cranston announced loudly. "We'll drive to the mesa near Death River, and you two can fight after we eat tonight."

"Gonna chill him now!" Larry snarled, his face contorted with hatred, and he charged at the helpless old man.

With surprising agility, Denver Joe dodged out of the way of the lumbering biker, then held his bound wrists toward Krury. Face-to-face, the two men stood for a long moment, then the biker pulled a blade and slashed the ropes around the old man's hands. Now free, Denver Joe brutally kicked the biker in the balls and grabbed the knife from his limp hands just in time to block another slash from Larry. The two men circled each other, looking for an opening to end the fight fast. The oily knives gleaming evilly in the setting sunlight, the fighters darted in slashing, then moved apart again, while the watching bikers cheered and laughed. Mute as forgotten stones, the helpless slaves said nothing under the watchful blasters of the remaining cold-hearts.

Diving forward, Denver Joe stabbed at the biker's face, driving him backward. But Larry shifted to the side and speared his knife into the older man's thigh. Blood welled from the wound, and Denver Joe cursed loudly as he grabbed the wound, trying to staunch the blood flow. One inch more inward, and the blade would have cut the big artery in his leg. He had to move faster and end this quick.

The bikers cheered as Larry danced in closer and stabbed Denver Joe again in the leg, and then the side, the smaller blade of the oldster only cutting air as he tried again and again for a death blow to the throat.

But the blood loss was starting to slow his hand, his breathing becoming more labored. Backing away from the younger fighter, Denver Joe headed for some weeds and was soon splashing in ankle-deep water. Then he dramatically slipped and fell into the shallow creek. Grinning in triumph, Larry charged in for the kill and Denver Joe threw a fist-ful of mud at the biker's face. Larry easily side-stepped the gob and went straight into a tangle of weeds. Tricked! As he tripped, the biker threw himself forward to avoid going down, and Denver Joe rose to rake his knife deep along the exposed neck of the fumbling man. Now the cheers and laughter of the biker gang stopped completely.

Blood spurted from the severed artery, and the hapless biker dropped his knife to grab the ghastly wound in both hands. But tiny squirts of red continued to pump from between his dirty fingers. Denver Joe shifted about in the muddy water, seeking another opening as his adversary mouthed curses and removed a hand from his gore-streaked throat to pull a small blaster hidden inside his shirt.

"Here's something for ya, wrinklie!" he stormed, thumbing back the hammer.

Moving fast, Denver Joe threw the stolen knife as hard as he could and it slammed deep into the biker's wrist, pinning his hand to his chest. Fingers convulsing, Larry accidentally triggered the blaster and the rear of his shirt ballooned as the .22 slug blew out his side.

Cranston inhaled sharply at that, and started to draw his own weapon, then paused. Larry could still win this. It was only a flash wound, nothing more, and Denver Joe was defenseless. Just pull out the knife and shoot him dead. Do it, boy!

Blood was swirling in the muddy water, as a pale Larry pulled the hand free and fired twice at the older man, missing each time. Diving into the mud, Denver Joe rolled closer to the biker and incredibly came up with the earlier dropped knife to ram it to the hilt in Larry's crotch. A geyser of blood pumped from the hideous wound, and the biker screeched as his adversary slowly stood, using the strength of his legs and arms to force the blade upward through balls and stomach. As Larry started to convulse, Denver Joe grabbed a fistful of hair to yank back the dying man's head and then cut the exposed throat open from ear to ear.

Gurgling horribly, Larry fell face forward into the filth of the creek to weakly shudder before going completely still, only a few small bubbles of escaping air rising from his buried face.

Breathing hard, Denver Joe waded to the shore of the water hole and tossed the crimson-splattered blade on the ground before the stunned bikers. Dead silence reigned for an impossibly long time before somebody spoke.

"Black dust, ya did it," a burly biker snarled in amusement. "Cut Larry open like a hog."

Rubbing an old scar, Krury added, "Never seen that done to a man before."

"He was a punk," Denver Joe wheezed, his

clothing trickling red from the minor wounds. He was still at the mercy of the coldhearts, and lived or died at their whim. Killing Larry hadn't been enough. He had needed to do the chilling with style and win their respect, too. But if he'd gone too far and earned their fear, he would be gunned down before taking another step. When you were captured by the Blue Devils, you joined by blood trial, or were taken as cargo.

"Well?" Denver Joe asked impatiently. "Somebody going to give a man a hand out of the fucking mud?"

"Do it yourself," Cranston ordered brusquely, releasing his grip on the handcannon at his belt. "The Devils don't ask for help from nobody. Remember that."

So he would live. Forcing his trembling legs to work, Denver Joe clambered through the weeds and back onto solid ground.

"Which one is mine now?" he said, trying not to weave while standing. He felt ill, but any sign of weakness could send him back to the chains.

Spreading his cracked lips in a grin, a bald man covered with crude tattoos jerked a thumb at the empty motorcycle parked amid the dozen bikes. "The bike with the knucklehead engine is yours now," he said. "Own her fair and square."

Stiffly walking to the bike, Denver Joe checked the saddlebags and found some clothing that wasn't too dirty to bandage the small wounds. He was pleased to see some supplies tucked away in the bag, including a plastic jar of honey. Smearing the cuts with honey, he then tied them off with the cloth, grunting as the crude bandages cinched tight.

"What the fuck you doing?" Ballard demanded, puzzled.

"Honey is a natural—" Denver bit back the pre-dark word. "The wounds won't fester and rot."

"By using honey?" The biker chortled. "Nuke me, never heard that shit before. Sure it works?"

"Like a bullet in a blaster," the oldster said confidently.

"How do ya know that?" Krury demanded.

Larry's gun belt was draped over the handlebars, with a big bore blaster tucked into the oiled leather. Near the skull a badly nicked hatchet was jammed into a spring-clamp on the handlebars for fast action, and a double-barrel shotgun jutted from a leather boot alongside the flat-top engine. Drawing the scattergun, Denver Joe checked the load inside and closed the breech with a solid satisfying snap. "I used to know a healer," he said, pulling the blaster to check its ammo. Then he tossed the blaster to Krury who made the catch.

"For the loan of the knife," Denver Joe said gruffly.

Snorting a laugh, Krury slipped the blaster into his belt. "Worth it," he said.

"So what we do about that?" a woman biker asked, indicating the muddy corpse with a motion of her chin. Angelina was fat with a roll of belly resting on her wide belt. Her leather vest laced together showing a wealth of acne-scarred cleavage. She was the chief bitch of the gang, but also the best butcher they had. Meat spoiled fast in the summer, and unless the bodies were cleaned and smoked properly, there was nothing to deliver to the cannies in exchange for the slick.

"Put him with the rest," Cranston said, climbing onto his bike and kicking the engine alive. "Then we leave this place right now. Anybody says different and I ace them. Move!"

Having done this many times before, the bikers got busy tying a corpse across the rear fender of each bike, and lashing the prisoners together. The slaves could either run to keep up with the Devils, or fall and get dragged to their deaths and be added to the meat supply. It really made no difference.

Drinking deeply from a canteen of warm beer, Denver Joe wasn't surprised when Larry was put on his bike, and the small palm blaster given over as part of the loot. It was a .22 derringer with four barrels, and he'd never seen one like it before. Interesting.

Twisting the throttle, Denver Joe gunned the big engine, blue and gray smoke blowing out the twin exhaust pipes. Studying the reactions of the engine, he eased back on the choke until the single-stroke engine was purring with controlled power.

So far, so good. He had specifically joined the caravan traveling in this direction hoping they would be attacked by the Devils so that he might have a chance of joining the gang.

However, leaving the flatlands before dark wasn't to his liking, yet there was nothing he could do without drawing unwanted attention to himself. This wasn't working out exactly as expected, but he would stay the course. Denver Joe had great faith in the plans of the Trader.

Chapter Two

Slowly, the wisps of electronic fog filling the mat-trans unit faded to nothingness and the seven people sprawled on the gateway floor began to stir.

Stomachs heaving from their passage through the predark transporter machine, the companions writhed in agony. It had been a bad jump, but unfortunately there was nothing to do but suffer through the nausea and pain until the aftereffects of the instantaneous journey eventually subsided.

"Anybody hurt?" Ryan Cawdor asked, coughing as he held his sides against the racking pain in his belly. It felt as if fire ants were eating his guts, and his skin seemed to be moving about, shifting positions as if draped loosely over his aching bones.

"I'm a-alive," J. B. Dix whispered, kneeling on the floor. An Uzi machine pistol hung at his side, and a pump-action S&W M-4000 scattergun was strapped across his backpack. A canvas bag lay on the floor alongside him.

Fighting a tremor, J.B. wiped a string of drool from his mouth with the cuff of his leather jacket. "J-just not sure why after that slice of hell."

"I hear ya," Ryan agreed, bracing a scarred hand against the cool armaglass wall and forcing himself to stand. A Steyr SSG-70 rifle was sticking out of his backpack, while a 9 mm SIG-Sauer pistol rode at his hip alongside an eighteen-inch-long panga.

Blinking hard to clear his vision, the one-eyed man could see that outside the mat-trans unit was a hexagonal chamber with cream-colored walls laced with a gold lattice pattern. That scheme was unfamiliar, which meant they had never been to this redoubt before. The walls of each gateway in the network of underground installations was a different color, the purpose of which was, the friends concluded, to let a jumper know immediately where he or she landed.

Leaning against a wall, Dr. Mildred Wyeth pulled a canvas satchel into her lap.

"H-here, t-try this," she muttered, fumbling to open the bag. Inside was an assortment of precious surgical tools. The physician was slowly building a collection of medical supplies—sterile water, plastic baggies filled with sterilized cloth, a jar of sulfur dust for wounds, and such. Hardly little more than supermarket curatives back in her day, but enough to save a life in the shockscape known as the Deathlands.

Extracting a canteen, Mildred screwed off the cap and took a healthy swig before passing it to a boy almost in his teenage years. Physician heal thyself, she thought, waiting for the throbbing headache to ease.

Sitting on his butt, an arm propped against the floor to keep himself upright, Dean Cawdor accepted the container and took a long drink, sloshing the fluid about in his mouth to try to cut the taste of bile before finally swallowing.

"Tastes awful," Dean said, making a face and handing the canteen away to a nearby woman with impossibly red hair.

Sitting with her legs folded, the woman was almost completely hidden by the shaggy bearskin coat. She threw back her head, revealing a face of inordinate beauty and eyes as green as the troubled sea. Her slim hand shook slightly as she raised the container and took several very small sips from the battered canteen.

"It's not supposed to be delicious," Mildred retorted, brushing away the beaded plaits from her own face. "Just calm your stomach enough so we don't puke out our guts from jump sickness."

"Need it for this one, that's for damn sure," Krysty Wroth said, passing the canteen to a pale teenager, crouched on his hands and knees.

Snow-white hair cascading past his pale face, Jak Lauren shook his head, ruby red eyes narrowed to mere slits in his pale face as if the stubborn youth were fighting the jump sickness by sheer willpower. Jak always fared poorly after a jump and usually was violently ill. This time was no better.

"What's in this batch?" J.B. asked, accepting the canteen but taking a sniff before he drank. Some of Mildred's brews worked pretty good, but others were totally useless. And one memorable batch actually made them feel sicker afterward.

"It's the last of the aspirins, some vitamins, mint, skag root and a shot of brandy I've been saving for an emergency."

"Fair enough," J.B. said, and took a deep drink.

His churning stomach calmed almost instantly, and the headache cleared in only a few minutes. Feeling much better, he passed Ryan the canteen and reached into his shirt pocket to pull on his pair of wire-rimmed glasses. The wiry Armorer always took them off in case he fell sprawling to the floor and broke the spectacles.

Splashing a few drops into his palm, Ryan wiped down his face before taking a swig, holding the concoction in his mouth for a moment to cut the metallic taste of the bad jump. As he swallowed, he scowled deeply at the mat-trans unit. A sprawled form wearing an antique-style frock coat remained still, an ebony walking stick inches away from an outstretched hand.

"Mildred, something's wrong with Doc!" Ryan snapped.

Grabbing her satchel, Mildred crawled over the floor and awkwardly rolled the silver-haired man onto his back to check the pulse in his neck with a fingertip. But the beat was strong and slow with no sign of arrhythmia. The frilled shirt rose and fell as the old man breathed steadily.

"He's fine," Mildred announced. "Just passed out from the jump. They always hit him hard."

"Because he's from another time, or because he has jumped so much more than us?" Dean asked in concern. "Are the jumps going to get worse for us over the years?"

"Good question. However, I have no idea," Mildred answered honestly. "But let's hope not. Any worse than this one and we'll arrive as corpses."

"Besides," J.B. added, straightening the fedora on his head. "We haven't been..." Here, the Armorer fumbled for the right word, then chose the truth. "Experimented on by the lunatics who built the redoubts, or tortured for years by an insane baron."

"Sometimes I'm surprised that he's sane at all, poor thing," Krysty said softly.

"Indeed, m-madam," Doc Tanner rumbled, slowly raising his head in a saurian manner. "So a-am I, if any are t-truly sane these d-dark days."

"Aw, stuff it, ya old coot," Mildred said, but the words carried no anger. "You'll outlive all of us combined."

"Perhaps I already have," Doc said, "and that is the problem from the start." Then the tall man shook as he violently coughed, but that subsided and he gazed at the others with clear eyes. "Cream and gold, I perceive. We have not been here before, my dear Ryan."

"No, it's a new redoubt," the one-eyed man replied, tossing the canteen.

Across the chamber, Mildred made the catch and shoved the container into Doc's grasp. "Here, drink the last of the jump juice. Do you a world of good."

"Somebody else made it, then, madam, and not you? Excellent news."

"Shaddup drink," Jak growled, slowly standing. The teen weaved slightly, but then the weakness passed and he stood without hindrance.

Draining the last of the brew of meds and roots, Professor Theophilus Algernon Tanner soon felt the universe slip into focus once more and he recapped the canteen, returning it to the physician with a grateful nod.

Smoothing the frilly front of his white shirt, Doc tightened his black string bow tie, then used stiff fingers to try to control his unruly crop of silver-white hair. Although only thirty-eight years old, his forced journeys through time had visibly aged the man, and scrambled his memory until often the past and the present mixed freely.

With careful hands, Doc checked the massive blaster at his side to make sure none of the black powder charges had come loose in the jump. The .44 LeMat was a Civil War revolver carrying nine chambers in the primary cylinder, and a short 12-gauge barrel set under the main barrel. It was slow to load, but hit like a cannon. But even more important, the weapon was from Doc's own time period, a direct physical link to his lost home and the family still waiting for him in the distant past.

Hawking to clear the phlegm from his throat, Ryan spit into the corner of the chamber and fixed the leather patch that covered the puckered ruin of his missing left eye, a gift from his brother Harvey. In grim efficiency, Ryan then did a weapons check, briefly touching his small arsenal of blasters and knives.

Pulling out his SIG-Sauer blaster, Ryan clicked off the safety and then racked the slide to chamber a round for instant use. Everybody was back on their feet, so it was time to recce the rest of the redoubt to see if there was anything useful in the storerooms.

There was something odd about this redoubt. The air coming from the wall vent was warm, instead of cool. Sniffing carefully, Ryan couldn't detect the smell of an electrical fire, or lava. Last year, a jump to a tropical redoubt had the group arriving just as the local volcano erupted. They had barely escaped, with chunks of the molten stone actually arriving with them at the next redoubt. And that was cutting the razor edge of life just too damn close by anybody's standards.

"Get ready, people," Ryan growled, and the rest pulled blasters and checked their loads.

"Ready," Krysty said, closing the cylinder of her .38 S&W revolver.

"I got your back, Dad," Dean added, levelling his Browning Hi-Power. The rest simply nodded, holding their weapons in an easy grip. They had done this a thousand times before, but routine made a person careless, and careless got a person chilled in the Deathlands.

Stationing himself near the door of the chamber, Ryan stood guard alongside J.B. while the man checked the portal for boobies. Traps were unusual, but a few other people knew about the secret of the redoubts, and while most of them were now in the boneyard, some were still sucking air and walking around.

But this time the door was clear, and at J.B.'s signal, Ryan worked the lever to swing it open. The SIG-Sauer leading the way, Ryan took the point into the control room with the others fanning out behind. The room appeared to be deserted, the only motion coming from the comps that operated the military base.

Comp screens lined the walls, and control consoles winked and blinked in silent frenzy as the massive comps went silently about their imponderable functions.

Then Doc whistled softly and gestured with the barrel of his big LeMat. An entire section of the monitors were dark. Ryan didn't remember ever seeing that before. It made him uneasy to see the complex machinery do anything out of the ordinary. That almost always meant trouble. Mildred went to the front of a monitor and flipped down the tiny control panel to check the contrast and power.

"Live and functioning," she reported after a minute. "These are dead because they're not receiving any data."

"Leave," Jak said with a scowl. "Busted here, means busted elsewhere."

Listening to the rest of the comps humming softly, Ryan gave the matter some serious thought. A malfunk could mean the rest of the base was frozen solid with ice, or flooded, or airless as the moon. Opening the door to the hallway could bring instant death. The comps did everything here, and if they were broken, then anything was possible. Damn things might have even cycled open the blast door to the outside world and let in anything, stickies, runts, hell hounds or a host of various muties. Automatically, Ryan checked the implo gren in a coat pocket. Need a lot of space to use the gren, but it could stop just about anything. The trick was to make sure the person throwing the implo didn't get aced along with the target.

"No, we aren't leaving yet," Ryan decided, rubbing his unshaven jaw. "I want to check the hallway before deciding to make tracks. J.B. and Mildred, stay by the door to the mat-trans chamber.

But if we come running back, slam it tight behind us.''

"Got ya covered,'' J.B. said, and the man and woman went back through the other doorway and into the chamber.

This time, Krysty and Jak stood guard, while Ryan placed a palm against the corridor to check for heat. It was warm, but not hot, so he listened for a moment for any sounds coming from the other side, then worked the handle and opened the door a crack.

The corridor was empty. The overhead lights were working, but the bright glow of the fluorescent tubes had been reduced to a dim bluish sheen from the passage of the years. The air vents were still blowing warm air instead of cool, but Ryan was starting to wonder if that was deliberate. Maybe the redoubt was at the North Pole, or inside a glacier, and it needed to be kept this warm. Anything was possible. The predark government had hidden the subterranean bases in the oddest places.

Placing fingers in his mouth, Ryan whistled sharply twice, and J.B. and Mildred rejoined the group. With practiced ease, the group spread out in groups of two and checked the offices lining the corridor, one person staying at the door while the other went inside. Then the pair switched and did the next room. As usual, Doc served as the anchorman, the colossal .44 LeMat held as reserve firepower.

As he kept track of the others as they moved from room to room, just for a split second the scholar thought he heard a metallic noise and almost called out a warning. But when it didn't occur again, he grudgingly relaxed.

After a few minutes, the companions regrouped at the end of the corridor near the elevator and the door to the stairwell.

"This place is clean as a glass lake," Krysty stated, sliding off her heavy coat and tying the arms around her waist. The heat was starting to bother her slightly.

"Found a humidor with two cigars," Mildred announced, patting a pocket. "But since J.B. is trying to quit, I'll just add them to the trade goods."

"Thanks a heap," J.B. muttered

"No ammo, no booze," Jak added. "Lots bottles, all dry."

"Couple of pencils," Dean said, reaching into a pocket. "And a lighter. Anybody need a replacement?"

Tough and resilient, butane lighters were the gold of the new world. Even after a hundred years they still sparked a flame and worked for months with careful hoarding. Nearly worthless in the pre-dark society, now the plastic cartridges were a month of eating, or a week of pleasure in a ville's gaudy house.

"Mine's almost dead," Mildred said.

Without a comment Dean passed it over. The woman flicked the lighter to make sure it worked, then tucked it away. "Thanks. Nothing like them for cauterizing a wound."

"No prob," the boy answered, feeling a touch of pride at finding something useful.

Suddenly snapping her head to the left, Krysty frowned at the empty corridor.

"Something?" Ryan demanded softly, glancing about with his good eye. The hallway was clear, not even dust moving on the floor.

The woman started to speak, then shook her head. "Nothing, I guess. Must have just been the air vents."

Doc frowned at the comment. "Indeed, madam. I also thought there had been a noise before," he rumbled. "But dismissed it as superfluous clatter."

Holstering his 9 mm blaster, Ryan eased the butt of the Steyr SSG-70 out of his backpack and worked the bolt. First it was too hot in the redoubt, now mysterious noises.

"Okay, get hard, people," Ryan ordered. "Jak,

Dean, watch the elevator. Anything that comes out, blast it. Doc and Mildred, guard the stairs. The rest of us will walk down to the reactor on the bottom level. Then come back up before searching the upper levels. This way we can know nothing is coming from behind.''

Cradling his Uzi, J.B. added, ''Any trouble, fire a round. If nobody comes back in ten, then come running.''

''I shall serve as Horatius,'' Doc rumbled, taking position near the corner of the hallway. This offered a clear field of fire in two directions and possible cover in case of incoming rounds.

''Horatius had two companions with him on that bridge,'' Mildred muttered, joining the scholar, ''and they both died.''

Leaning against the wall, Doc smiled widely, displaying his oddly perfect teeth. ''Which is exactly why,'' he said politely, ''I was very careful to state that I alone was Horatius, and not you.''

Glowering at the man, Mildred said something in Latin that made his eyebrows rise in shock while Ryan eased open the door to the stairwell. As he did, a sound was clearly heard echoing down from the levels above. Something metallic and moving. Then came a horrible scream.

Chapter Three

"Air vent, my ass," Ryan cursed as the scream echoed away.

He started forward, then paused, and for a tense moment sharply debated leaving. Whatever was happening here probably wasn't their concern. Then again, the redoubts were the lifeline of the companions. If there were people in here, they needed to know how they got inside and what, if anything, they knew about the mat-trans system.

"Dad?" Dean asked anxiously, his knuckles white from the tight grip on his blaster.

"That could have been a child," Krysty said, remembering a particularly gruesome event at a redoubt where the companions had arrived only seconds too late to save a young girl who was starving to death from taking her own life.

Anxiously, Doc added, "Knowledge is power, my dear Ryan."

Yeah, the Trader used to say that, too. "Okay, we move as a group," Ryan decided, almost against his better judgment. "I'm on point, one yard apart, two on two formation. Let's go!"

"Just a sec," J.B. countered, walking to the elevator and hitting the call button. The indicator lights in the lintel chimed in response as the cage started to descend from the upper levels.

Ryan nodded in approval at the distraction; every little bit helped. Doc and Mildred quickly joined the others in the stairwell and, moving fast, the companions quietly started up the ancient stairs of the redoubt, blasters leading the way.

At each level they paused, straining to hear anything, but there was only dusty silence. The dining hall, barracks, communications, medical, storage, each section was as still as a empty tomb. At the top level, the companions paused before the last door and were rewarded by some sort of humming noise.

"Dark night, but that's familiar," J.B. said, setting his fedora farther back on his head as a prelude to a fight. "Just can't recall what the nuke it is, though."

"I don't like this," Krysty whispered, her hair coiling tightly in response to the tension.

"Got something?" Jak asked, flexing his left hand. A knife slipped from the sleeve of his leather jacket into his palm at the gesture.

"No," the redhead said slowly, as if unsure. "I'm not reading anything. This just feels wrong, a gut instinct."

"Same here," Mildred added, chewing at her lip.

With a worried expression on his young face, Dean grunted in agreement.

There was no light coming from under the jamb, so working the latch carefully, Ryan opened the door slightly, and held out a hand toward Doc. The scholar passed over his ebony stick and, easing it through the crack, Ryan reached toward the nearby light switch, flicked it on with a loud click and threw open the door.

This top level was the garage of the redoubt, tool benches and storage rooms to the left, the exit corridor to the distant right. The rest of the cavernous room was filled with vehicles, mostly civilian wags—compact cars and station wagons, some falling apart from body rust, others in decent condition.

However, a few of the larger machines were military wags, 4×4s, some Hummers and even an APC. The armored personnel carrier was lacking wheels, the axles resting on the stained concrete floor above a dark grease pit, but the chassis seemed intact.

"Hot pipe, over there!" Dean cried and started to fire his blaster.

Ryan turned fast and triggered his longblaster
without conscious thought. Across the garage was
a three-foot-wide crack in the nukeproof wall. That
was unusual, but not startling. They had found
damaged redoubts before. Some of the weapons
used in skydark had been fantastically powerful.
But standing directly in front of the crack was
something potentially more dangerous than any
nuke.

At first glance it resembled a chrome-plated hu-
manoid, stooped over slightly like a hunchbacked
ape. Its domed head was fronted with large crystalline eyes, the body composed of chrome rods,
two elongated arms, one armed with a pneumatic
hammer, the other sporting a set of tarnished blades
that spun at blinding speed. That was the source of
the humming noise.

Even as he fired the Steyr, Ryan narrowed his
eye. A sec hunter droid! The companions had pre-
viously encountered the mech guardians of the redoubts. Once a hunter got your "scent," it could
track a person through a crowd of a thousand other
people and across ten thousand miles, locked on to
the target's genetic code. The droid couldn't be
turned off, diverted from the chase, and never
stopped until the allocated target was aced.

With a grinding noise of rusted gears, the machine turned away from the crack and started for them, the hammer thumping loudly as the spinning blades thrust forward.

"Double line!" Ryan shouted, and the companions hit the droid with everything they had, knowing only seconds remained before it would reach them, and in the cramped confines of the stairwell they would be chilled.

Dropping to their knees, Jak and Doc threw thunder at the hunter with their big bore blasters, while the others fired over their heads. Lead and steel hit everywhere on the machine in a deafening cacophony of firepower, but the droid seemed undamaged. Then the impossible happened—one of the chrome rods dented, then another and a third broke apart. Encouraged, the companions concentrated on the opening in the droid's armored body. Wires snapped, and something crackled with electricity inside the machine. When only yards away, smoke began to pour from the battered torso, then the spinning blades jammed motionless almost tearing off the arm. The droid slowed its advance, but the companions continued to fire, expending ammo at a frightful rate. Suddenly, the pneumatic hammer stopped, the lights dimmed in the crystal eyes, fat blue sparks crackled over the machine and it tipped over from the incoming barrage to crash onto the floor, sparking and oozing hydraulic fluid. Its limbs twitched for a few seconds, then the machine went still with a ratcheting noise.

The companions stopped shooting and for a few moments could only stare at the smashed war machine in amazement.

"Nuke me," Ryan growled, levering in another round purely out of habit. "We took out a sec hunter. That never happened before, not this easy. Damn droid must have been held together by little more than its wiring and paint job."

"It appears that immutable time has done the job for us," Doc stated, waving the thick acrid fumes away from the muzzle of his blaster.

"Best stay sharp," J.B. warned, removing the spent clip from his Uzi and easing in a fresh one. "There could be another."

True enough. The companions once found five of the droids in a redoubt and barely escaped alive. At a gesture from Ryan, Jak and Doc started doing a recce sweep of the garage, moving through the amassed collection of civilian and military vehicles searching for other droids in hiding. While the rest of the companions carefully watched the men, Krysty walked past the pile of mechanical debris on the floor and held out her fingers testing the air.

"Feel that?" she said. "This crack is where the

hot air is coming from. Might reach all the way to the outside.''

Fireblast, she might be right, Ryan realized, and quickly checked the rad counter clipped to his lapel to see the device was registering only standard background activity. It was just heat, not radiation from a nuke crater in the vicinity.

"Think it's another volcano?" Krysty asked, sniffing.

Inhaling deeply, J.B. held the breath, then exhaled and shrugged. "Don't smell any sulfur, but that doesn't mean the area is clear."

"What about that scream we heard?" Dean asked, kneeling to look underneath the parked wags nearby. "Think it was somebody trying to get in and the droid aced 'em?"

"Sure as hell might be," Mildred said, frowning. Reaching into her satchel, the physician unearthed a flashlight and pumped the small handle attached to the survivalist tool several times to charge the batteries inside. She pressed the button, and the flashlight gave off a weak yellowish light. The bulb was old and the batteries were gradually dying from sheer age, but it was a lot better than the candles and torches the companions carried in their backpacks.

Playing the pale beam around inside the crack,

she could see the jagged opening only reached a few yards into the thick wall and appeared to make a sharp angle to the right.

"Looks like a dead end," Mildred said hesitantly, then a scraping noise caught her attention, and the woman pulled back just in time as a wriggling creature charged into view. In the feeble beam of the flashlight all she could see were fangs and wild hair.

"Muties!" she screamed, scrambling backward and firing her blaster.

The creature screamed like a human child, and the companions paused for a moment, unsure of their target until the thing reached the edge of the crack and reared into the light. Even in the fluorescent lights, at first it appeared to be some kind of a fuzzy worm, or a big caterpillar, its belly coated with thousands of tiny legs endlessly moving. But the head possessed no eyes or ears, only a wide segmented mouth and a set of fanged pinchers that closed to overlap each other like scythes.

"Millipedes!" Krysty cursed, shooting steadily. So that was what the droid had been doing, trying to keep out the mutant insect.

"Aim for the head!" Ryan yelled, stepping around the redhead to get a clear view. Fireblast, the thing had pinchers on both ends! So which was the head, or was the brain somewhere in the middle?

Firing a short burst from the Uzi, J.B. cursed as the rapidfire jammed on a bad cartridge. Dropping the weapon, he pulled the S&W M-4000 shotgun out of his backpack, jacked the slide with a jerk and cut loose with a hellstorm of fléchettes. The millipede exploded into gobbets of pulsating flesh, tiny legs flying everywhere, as the fusillade of steel slivers cut the writhing mutie in two, both ends pumping geysers of pink blood. But incredibly, both ends continued to move and attack.

"Not the head, aim for the heart!" Mildred cursed, dancing out of the way of the sharp pinchers. The fanged mandibles closed on a piece of the droid, denting the metal. Even as the companions peppered the creature with lead, it savaged the broken droid for a few seconds before turning back toward them.

What the hell? Ah, the damn bug was probably attracted to the intense magnetic fields of droids, and the huge power plant in the bottom level of the redoubt. Mildred remembered hearing about how nuclear power plants back in her day had endless problems with invading cockroaches and such. Great, then the area around the redoubt could be infested with dozens, maybe hundreds of these monstrosities!

Climbing onto the buckled hood of a car, Jak held the Colt Python in both hands and aimed downward at the snapping mutie. ''Where heart!'' he shouted, cocking back the hammer.

''The thick red band in the middle!''

''Which one? There are two bands, madam!'' Doc shouted, ducking sideways as he triggered the thunderous LeMat once more. A fist-size chunk of flesh was ripped off the mutie, blood hosing from the gaping wound in one of the red bands around its body. But the thing never slowed nor stopped.

''Hit 'em both!'' Ryan commanded, blowing flame at the furry horror.

Moving behind the creature, Dean crouched and discharged his Browning directly into the segmented face of the bleeding millipede. But the end of the bug only rippled from the impact, as if he were shooting into a pool of water.

''Use the grens?'' the boy shouted, emptying his blaster at point-blank range, but only succeeded in cracking a pincher. The broken stub oozed blood, but the bug seemed only enraged, not mortally wounded from the damage.

''We're too close!'' his father growled in reply. ''Gotta take it out this way!''

As it surged for him, Dean jumped out of the way of the mutie and the fuzzy creature went underneath the APC. "Look out, it's behind us!" he warned, yanking the spent clip and reloading. Down to one more loaded clip, then he would have to use his knife.

Dropping onto his belly, Dean spotted the piece of bug circling around the axle to come back for him. Jak appeared from the other side of the chassis, and they both pumped hot lead into the mutie. Guts flew everywhere, spraying the belly armor of the APC with stringy goop, and the bug curled into a ball as it pumped out sticky blood and died.

"Got one!" Dean cried, standing and looking for another target.

But the last section of the millipede was already reduced to ragged pieces, the companions crunching the segmented body flat under their heavy combat boots.

"Anybody hurt?" Ryan asked, yanking out a spent magazine from the Steyr and inserting a new one. When there was no answer, he continued. "Okay, let's find something to block that bastard hole!"

Going to the nearest wag, Krysty grabbed the rusty door of a smashed station wagon and tried to pull it off the frame. With hardly any effort on her part, the door ripped free and hit the floor bursting into pieces, completely eaten by rust. Useless.

Lifting a piece of the droid, Ryan tried to shimmy it into the crack, but there were too many gaps around the chrome metal from the irregular shape of the crevice. He left it there as a start and checked the droid for anything else, but all of the other parts were either too large, or much too small.

"My kingdom for a bag of nails," Doc muttered. Then he spied the workbench and headed that way.

"Mebbe we can use busted glass from the windshields," J.B. suggested, thumbing fresh cartridges into the shotgun. "Used to work keeping out the rats back in Colorado."

"Sounds good," Ryan grunted, turning away from the droid.

Spent brass falling to the floor in a musical rain, Mildred reloaded her target pistol and snapped the cylinder shut. Tucking the blaster away, she yanked a hubcap off a civilian wag to hold it at arm's length inside a civilian vehicle.

Still on its hood, Jak smashed the windshield with the butt of his Colt and the glass shattered into a million pieces, overfilling the hubcap. In disgust, Mildred stared at the pile of tiny, sparkling green cubes.

"Safety glass," she snorted, pouring out the

hubcap. "Couldn't cut yourself on the stuff if you tried."

"Use headlights," Jak suggested, then frowned. "No, not enough. What else use?"

"Hell, I don't know!"

Checking the gauges at a fuel pump, J.B. turned and shook his head at the others. The reservoir was completely dry, only a faint exhalation of escaping gas came from the nozzle.

"Went dry over the century," he told them, returning the nozzle to its indented rack. So much for a firewall to stop the bugs.

Taking the keys from the ignition, Dean opened the trunk of the car and carried over a spare tire, sliding it into the crack on top of the piece of the droid, then he rushed away to rummage for another. Busting open a dusty soda machine, Krysty started throwing in glass pop bottles, the glass shattering at the rear of the crack. But there were only a few, the rest made of plastic or aluminum cans.

Carrying over a corroded bumper from a Cadillac, Ryan added it to the pile, shoving the chrome-plated metal as far back as he could. Not much, but a start.

Leaving the workbench, Doc went to a nearby closet and yanked open the door. "By the Three Kennedys!" he cried, hauling a twenty-gallon container into view. "Gasoline! Hundreds of containers!"

But Ryan could see the military identification number on the side of the cans and knew what the man had found was a lot more valuable than gas, or shine—it was condensed fuel. Unlike other flammable liquids, the stuff simply didn't evaporate worth a damn, yet worked equally well in civilian engines and military diesels. What the hell it was made of he had no fragging idea, not even Mildred could take a guess, but the stuff did the job and that was all that really mattered.

"This is what the droid was set to guard," Ryan grunted, as he hurried closer. "Juice enough for a fleet of wags! Okay, start hauling them out. We can block the crack with a fire bowl, use a hubcap as a basin and some rope as wick. Two or three should do the job."

"Nothing like fire," Jak said, then grimly added, "Except stickies."

"Then mebbe we can get one of these wags working and leave," J.B. added. "The farther we get from this hellhole, the better!"

"I'll find some rope," Dean said, running to the workbench on the far wall.

"Check the Hummers," Ryan suggested. "They always carry spare tackle."

"On it!"

"I'll find more bottles for Molotovs," Krysty said. "Maybe there's some of those foam coffee cups in the kitchen."

"Jak, go with her," Ryan ordered brusquely. "Nobody goes anywhere alone until we are far from these tripcursed things!"

The albino teenager grunted in agreement and joined the woman at the stairs to disappear into the bowels of the redoubt.

Meanwhile, the remaining companions started for the closet to assist in clearing out the fuel cans. Four of the containers were already in a line on the garage floor, and as Doc turned back for another load, he spit a curse in Latin and pulled out his LeMat to shoot from the hip. Something screamed like a child inside the closet and blood sprayed onto the floor.

"There's another crack!" Doc shouted, backing away from the room of volatile fuel. He was holding the trigger down on his single-action weapon, a raised palm hovering above the hammer to fan the black-powder cannon into action, but he withheld shooting. The bugs were crawling over the cans of fuel! One ricochet and that entire area of the redoubt could be engulfed in a firestorm of burning fuel.

As a millipede dropped off the last row of cans and started out of the supply closet, Doc shot it twice at both ends, blowing off its pinchers. Already moving, Ryan and J.B. charged forward to hit the door with their full weight. It slammed shut, cutting the insect in two. Pumping blood, the mutie wailed in agony and Doc soundly kicked it away, the dying bug hitting the wall with a splat and leaving a gruesome stain.

"That's where the first crack leads to," Mildred cursed, her ZKR trained on the door. "The damn fuel storage closet!"

"Droid couldn't stop them there without chancing the whole damn base would blow," J.B. added. "And neither can we!"

"How many bugs you think there are?" Dean demanded, quickly thumbing fresh rounds into the spent clip of the Browning. He shoved it into a pocket and started on another. Not too many loose rounds were left, so he'd have to make every shot count.

Even as the door shuddered from an impact on the other side, Ryan caught saw a flurry of motion in the crack.

"Too many!" Ryan snarled, pumping lead into the darkness. The muzzle-flash of the weapon lit the crevice in a wild strobe just enough to show a swarm of millipedes crawling along the sides and top of the opening past the makeshift barricade.

"Back to the mat-trans!" Ryan ordered, firing the Steyr. There was a gush of blood and a childlike scream, but another mutie crawled over the twitching corpse to reach the edge of the crack and snap at the companions.

Riding the Uzi in short controlled bursts, J.B. laid down some suppressive fire with his blaster, while the others retreated for the stairs. From there they covered the man until he joined them.

"What the hell is going on?" Krysty demanded from the next level below, her arms loaded with foam coffee cups.

"We're leaving!" Mildred grunted, leaning against the stairwell door to try to keep it closed. "Anybody know a way to lock this thing in place?"

Whistling sharply, Jak tossed a knife upward and Ryan caught it by the handle, then rammed the thick blade under the doorjamb. Hesitantly, the others released the door and it held, but clearly not for long.

Nobody needed any encouragement to start racing down the stairs. As they reached the middle level, there was a slam from above and a rustling sound that grew in volume. The companions charged through the flickering control room. Jak tried to stab another knife under the jamb, but it wouldn't hold. Abandoning the effort, the group moved into the antechamber, closed the vanadium-steel door and locked it tight.

"Safe at last," Doc exhaled in relief, mopping his brow of a handkerchief.

Seconds later, there was a thump against the metal, followed by a scratching noise as something raked across the dense material.

"Bugs are fast," J.B. said, removing his glasses and tucking them into a shirt pocket.

"Mildred, any more jump juice?" Ryan asked, heading across the chamber.

"Not a drop," she said, shaking the empty canteen.

"Too bad for us, then. Everybody in!" Ryan ordered, striding to the chamber.

As the companions crowded into the unit, the heavy thumping increased against the steel portal to the chamber, then a soft electronic mist started to gather at the ceiling and floor. A tingle filled their bones, but even as the companions felt themselves drop through the floor into the infinity of the subelectronic void they noticed a change, a subtle shifting from the usual procedure, and they instantly knew that something was terribly wrong.

Chapter Four

"We'll camp here," Cranston shouted over the engines, and eased the big Harley off the dried riverbed and over a bumpy culvert to head toward a gigantic rock mesa.

The jagged column of stone rose from the sun-baked red ground to dominate the countryside for miles. Several tiny creatures with wings circled the top of the mesa, but the details and even their cries were lost in the distance. The sheer sides of the mesa were vertical walls of grayish rock, impossible to climb. No plants grew from the sides of the mesa, not even vines of scrub brush. It was as bare as a dead man's bones.

Riding along the swells of ground, the coldhearts circled around the mesa until reaching the shadows of the eastern face. Now masked by the darkness of the setting sun, they drove into a deep arroyo that cut into the mesa like a wild lightning bolt, a zigzagging path of culverts, dead ends, caves and cutoffs. Slowing to a crawl, the bikes went single file, endlessly making turns until they were deep within the stony maze. Flexing his hands to keep a grip on the handlebars, Denver Joe had to appreciate the location. Anybody not knowing the correct path would soon become lost and easy prey for any snipers hidden in the rocky face soaring high above the pebble-strewn floor of the canyon.

Open space suddenly exploded around them as the Devils rolled into a box canyon. The ground here was smooth and flat. Several huts lined the far side of the canyon, with sandbag nests on top for guards. There was a shaded corral for the bikes, a pit edged with barbed wire for the slaves and a still surrounded by rusty barrels.

Riding through the middle of the canyon, the gang passed a low stone pillar with a rusty I-beam laying across the top. The beam was dripping with chains, while the pillar was decorated with grinning human skulls, the stone darkly stained. A shiver took Denver Joe as he spotted a few black scorpions crawling about picking at the sun-dried bits of blood and flesh still attached to the old bones. So that was the Learning Tree the others had been talking about on the ride here, a grisly monument where slaves were whipped, bikers beaten for disobedience and enemies slowly tortured until they begged for death. It was where outlanders and muties learned the wisdom of pain.

Entering the shadows again on the western side, it felt good just to be out of the direct rays of the sun, but Denver Joe felt there was a definite coolness in the air, and as he parked his bike near a hut, he saw a tiny waterfall splashing out of the side of the mesa into a small pool. There were green plants growing alongside, some corn and marijuana, the broad splayed leaves unmistakable.

"Hell of a find," Denver Joe stated, climbing stiffly off the motorcycle. "This our ville?"

"One of 'em." Krury laughed, kicking a leg over the bike to stand. "We never stay in one spot very long, and nobody can find ya. Wheels mean freedom, man."

"Loads my blaster," Denver Joe said in agreement, trying not to groan aloud. He felt sore in every muscle, his back a knotted lump of cramps. The predark paved roads in the area were in poor shape with potholes everywhere, and the drive across open ground was even worse. The nukescaping was pretty bad here, although the others said it was even worse to the south, toward the Texas Badlands. Been a hell of a rough trip.

Then the man felt like a feeb for thinking that, as he glanced at the bedraggled slaves, heaving for breath, their bound hands held in front of them as if they were still running to keep up with the bikers. Most had bleeding feet, and two of the older folks had fallen and been dragged to their deaths before the Devils stopped to gather the corpses. Only the pregnant girl had been allowed to ride on a Harley. But then, if she gave birth to a healthy norm baby, she would be worth more in ammo and fuel than a hundred slaves. More than one baron would pay big jack for a healthy child.

After the slaves had been shoved into the pit for safekeeping and the bikes given some maintenance, it was time to dress the corpses. As the newbie of the group, Denver had to assist. Attaching chains around the ankles of the dead people, the bikers hauled them into the air from the crossbar of the Learning Tree and cut away what remained of their clothing. Then it was purely a matter of skinning and scraping the bodies, much the same as butchering a fat hog. When the last of the organs had been removed, the Devils built a smoldering fire under the gutted figures and let them dangle in the thick smoke to cure.

Darkness came with sunset, and a bonfire was built of rubbish and some wood taken from ruins along the dried river. Dinner was canned beans and some freshly killed dog. Good food, but Denver Joe had to force down his share to not appear weak from the horrid butchery. He had washed his hands four times in the runoff of the little pool, but could still detect the coppery reek of human blood and entrails.

As several of the bikers lit up joints and passed around a bottle of triple-brewed shine, Denver claimed he was still too tired from the earlier knife fight to join in the gang rape of the female prisoners. The man he replaced on watch was delighted to swap, and Denver Joe was given a Winchester longblaster to watch the opening of the arroyo, more for snakes and wolves than any possible human invaders.

Putting the Learning Tree at his back, he fed wood chips into the campfire and tried not to listen to the screams from the slave pits. Then when he was fairly sure nobody was watching, the old man reached into his boot and removed a flat plastic box. The casing had been slightly cracked from the fight at the creek, but there didn't appear to be any water damage. Unfortunately, he didn't know of any way to test the damn thing. The transmitter either worked, or it didn't. As surreptitiously as possible, he laid the predark device near the campfire and watched as it hopefully was accumulating electrical energy from the heat of the campfire. Something about a thermocouple, but exactly what the old tech talk meant was far beyond him.

As the silver crescent of the moon rose over the mesa walls and filled the canyon with silver light, Denver Joe added a branch to the campfire and knocked the device into the crackling flames. The transmitter caught fire and burned very quickly from the oily rags stuffed inside to protect it from moisture, and soon there wasn't a trace remaining that it had existed. Soon his replacement guard sauntered over, naked except for his boots and blaster, smoking a handrolled marijuana stogie. Denver Joe listened to the biker boast about the sex in the pit for a while, then passed over the Winchester and stumbled off to bed for some much needed sleep.

Masked by the deep shadows of the sandbag nest on top of the largest hut, Cranston smoked a cig laced with jolt and wondered what in hell the newbie had been doing at the campfire. Unfortunately, the Learning Tree had been in the way and the chief biker never got a clear view. Mebbe he was just trying not to be sick in front of the others. Made sense. Lots of men vomited their guts out cleaning a deader for the first time. But the secretive actions made him mighty uneasy, and Cranston spent a long night thinking hard on the matter.

AS THE ELECTRONIC FOG faded from the mat-trans, Ryan cursed in recognition at the cream-colored walls with their golden lattice pattern. They were in the exact same redoubt!

Glancing about, Jak frowned. "Went nowhere!"

"Damn LD button must have shorted, or something," J.B. growled, sliding on his glasses and peering at the control panel. There was no obvious damage to the array of buttons, but who could really tell with the predark machinery?

Shifting the Steyr rifle on his shoulder to a more comfortable position, Ryan rubbed his good eye, debating the possibility of trying one more time to jump out of the infested redoubt. But his gut feeling was that the machine was broken, and that they had been riding luck from the first moment they arrived.

"Should we try again?" Dean asked, hitching the straps of his backpack.

"Can't take the risk," his father said grimly. "A malfunk in the mat-trans could send our atoms to the middle of nowhere."

"Think the entire network is down?" Krysty asked in concern, looking around as if she could see inside the armaglass walls.

"Only one way to find out," Mildred said, scowling at the sole door of the chamber.

Just then the lights in the chamber flickered, and a scream erupted in the control room.

"Fireblast, the muties are eating the comps!" Ryan cursed, pulling a weapon and striding forward. "That's why we can't leave!" To the bugs, the intense EM fields of the comps had to be like jolt to an addict.

Rushing to the door, the companions prepared their blasters and threw open the portal. In the control room, a dozen of the hairy millipedes were crawling over the control banks, several of them partially inside the delicate machinery.

Aiming the SIG-Sauer, Ryan paused in frustration. Nukeshit, they were caught again! If they missed a bug, the blasterfire might destroy the controls. A bug hissed at their arrival and started forward with surprising speed.

"Blades only," Ryan ordered, holstering his 9 mm blaster and pulling his panga.

"No, wait," Krysty countered, dropping her pack and rummaging inside. "I have a better idea. Just keep these things off me for a minute."

Jak jerked his arm and the handle of a knife appeared in the forehead of the onrushing mutie. It reared in pain, and Doc slashed out with his sword, ending its life. But the noise attracted other millipedes, and now several headed their way, crawling along the floors and walls.

Standing in triumph, Krysty yanked the cap off a road flare, and scraped the top of the waxy tube. As the flare sputtered into life, she thrust it at a nearby millipede and the furry body caught on fire. Keening in agony, the insect hastily backed away from the sizzling, popping flare.

Sporting a grin, J.B. unearthed another flare from his munitions bag as did the rest of the companions. In a concentrated effort, they herded the cringing insects into the far corner where they stomped the muties flat, gore splattering the walls and consoles. A few of the muties scurried out the open doorway, the sec controls no longer functioning, but that was okay. Once the control room was clear, Dean manually shut the door, and Jak rammed another knife into the jamb to hold it shut. Then Ryan grabbed a chair and stuck it underneath the handle.

"That won't last long," Krysty warned, as her flare sputtered and died. The air reeked from the fumes of the road flares, yellow drops of the excess burned material crusting the dirty floor.

"We only need a little time," Ryan said, tossing away his flare as it went out. "Watch the air vents!"

"Think we can fix the controls to do a jump?" Mildred asked. "Hit the reboot switch, maybe?"

Before the question could be answered, there was a rustling noise in the ceiling, and the companions turned to fire at the exact same moment. Shot to pieces, the ceiling panels burst apart and a bleeding millipede dropped to the floor. Putting the tip of his blaster to its featureless face, Ryan fired the SIG-Sauer once, the slug blowing out its other end and the mutie went completely still. Good, they were learning how to efficiently chill the triple-damned things, but at a tremendous expenditure of priceless ammo.

"Mebbe fix self," Jak said hopefully, going to the main console in the control room.

"Should have done that already," Ryan noted, checking the hole in the ceiling for any further movements. No more muties were in sight, but he was taking nothing for granted.

"Looks like we have to get out the front door," Dean said slowly, "past all of the muties upstairs."

"The muties don't seem to like fire, so we can make torches," Ryan added gruffly. "But that means searching the darkness for something to use as a staff. Broom handles, mops, table legs, anything like that would do."

"Check. We can cut up our spare clothing for

the swaddle, or get some sheets from the base laundry. But we don't have anything to grease the rags.''

''Grease in garage,'' Jak reminded. ''Bugs too.''

''Cooking grease will do,'' Mildred suggested. ''Or machine lubricant from the reactor in the basement.''

''Easier to scrape some off the elevator cables,'' Ryan said, thoughtfully scratching the scar on his face with the tip of his blaster. ''Sounds good. We can do this.''

Suddenly, there was a series of loud clicks and the emergency lights crashed on, filling the control room with a harsh white light.

''Son of a bitch,'' J.B. whispered with a growing smile.

''Farewell the necessity of crude torches,'' Doc rumbled pleasantly, then frowned as the light noticeably lessened. ''By gadfrey, they are weakening already. We must be swift to play Prometheus and light the darkness!''

Just then, the door shook as something hit it from the other side. The companions trained their weapons in that direction, but withheld firing.

''We better hit the kitchen first,'' Krysty said. ''Find some water glasses or jars to put our candles in so the flames don't blow out if we have to move fast.''

''Any idea how long will the air hold out?'' Dean asked, fighting to keep a touch of nervousness from his voice.

Standing in the closest, Mildred placed a reassuring hand on his shoulder. Even though a veteran of the Deathlands, he was still only twelve years old. ''About two days,'' she said calmly.

''After that?''

''Well, we'll start getting headaches from the accumulation of carbon monoxide, unable to sleep but always be tired, then we fall asleep and never wake up.''

''We sleep,'' Jak stated as a fact. ''Bugs eat.''

With a grimace, Doc rumbled, ''Indubitably, my succinct friend.''

''Bad way to go,'' J.B. added grimly, a bead of sweat trickling down his face. ''Although, there ain't really a good way, either.''

''We'll use the implo grens if it comes to that,'' Ryan stated. ''Take the dirty little muties to hell with us. But we can always open the blast doors in the garage to bring in fresh air.''

''But without power...'' Dean stopped himself, remembering that the bases were designed to operate after a nuke war and were built to open without hard current. There were stored power cells inside the walls, and even jacks for the nuke batteries of wags to get wired up to power the hydraulic system that opened the main exit. Worst case, there was a hand crank, but that was harder than pushing a tank uphill with your bare hands. Hopefully the wall units still worked.

"Sure wish the APC was intact," the boy added wistfully, changing hands holding the lighter. "Be nice to just climb in and blast our way out."

With a start, Ryan perked up at the mention of the armored personnel carrier. Yeah, that might just work. As dangerous as kicking a nuke, but then what wasn't these days?

"I know that look," J.B. said to his friend. "Okay, what's the plan?"

"Yeah, I got one, but you aren't going to like it." As he explained, the faces of the companions grew tense, then hopeful.

"Hell of a gamble," Krysty said, as the door shook once more, and something raced overhead across the ceiling. "But I think it might work."

"Okay, forget the kitchen, we hit the offices first," J.B. ordered, opening his munitions bag and pulling out the lone stick of dynamite. It was old and wrapped in sticky electrical tape to retard sweating pure nitro, but it was the only explosive they had aside from the grens, and they were just too damn powerful.

"Better switch to candles. Can't be swapping grips when these lighters get too hot."

Following the sage advice, the companions were soon ready. Kicking the chair away from the door, Ryan took the lead into the heart of the infested redoubt, one hand holding a candle, the other his blaster. The hallway was clear, but every open doorway was passed as if it were the muzzle of a loaded cannon.

Reaching the stairs, the companions went past the deactivated elevator and went carefully up the stairs. Millipedes were found scurrying along the walls or sitting on the ceiling. To conserve ammo, the muties weren't harmed unless they attacked first. But each fight seemed to attract more of the creatures, constantly slowing their progress. To reach the office of the commanding officer of the base, the companions passed close to the armory and briefly paused, trying to decide if they should look inside, but the emergency lights were starting to seriously dim by that time and they had to move onward. Seconds counted now, before they were fighting in the darkness at the mercy of the deadly insects.

"READY, GO!" Ryan shouted, awkwardly opening the sagging door to the garage.

Cutting loose, the companions opened fire on the scurrying millipedes, blasting a tight path through the living carpet. Reaching the wrecked vehicles, the friends hastily climbed on top and jumped from hood to hood so the insects couldn't bite them from underneath the wags. However, the noise from the millipedes quickly grew in volume as more and more of them poured into the garage at the arrival of the companions.

Placing his shots carefully, Ryan felt his heart pound at the sight, even though it was exactly what they wanted. Attracted by the mag fields of the base, once inside the things found virtually nothing to eat and were slowly concentrating their attention on the only food available. The humans.

Situated high in the corners, the emergency lights were beginning to turn yellow at this point, and as the companions jumped to the roof of the APC a bulb started to flicker. It was horribly obvious that the lights were dying faster than expected.

"Left side!" Ryan snarled, and the companions concentrated their blasters there to clear a section of the floor free of bugs.

Jumping down, Dean placed a coffee can on the floor, a tiny nubbin of prima cord sizzling on top as a fuse. Kicking a bug off his boot, the boy grabbed the hands of his friends and climbed hastily back up out of reach of the chittering muties.

"Okay, right side!" Ryan shouted, shooting a millipede off the bare concrete ceiling above them.

Now Krysty did the same thing, while Jak used a broom to shove the third charge underneath the armored vehicle. As they scrambled back on top of the war wag, Mildred put the last charge on a flat section of the armored roof, the burning fuse less than an inch long.

"Get inside!" Ryan growled, chilling two more smaller bugs charging across the rooftops of a nearby Hummer. "Move!"

Firing from the hip, J.B. used the shotgun to clear off the rear hatch, and the companions jumped to the floor and threw open the double doors with their blasters firing. The single small millipede sitting on the floor was torn to pieces and the companions piled inside the steel box, kicking out the twitching body before slamming the hatch shut and locking it tight.

"Seal the rest!" Ryan ordered, checking the gunners hatch in the ceiling and finding it already bolted tight.

"Hot pipe, there's no lock on this one!" Dean yelled as the driver's hatch trembled slightly and a millipede appeared at the crack, snapping its pinchers.

Twisting the head of his ebony swordstick, Doc withdrew a thin sword of Spanish steel and plunged it through the face of the bug. It screamed in agony and withdrew.

Yanking off his belt, Dean looped it through the handle of the hatch and pulled the hatch tight. Removing her gun belt, Mildred fed it through Dean's and managed to stretch the leather just far enough to reach a stanchion and anchor it securely. The makeshift pulley would hold, but not against a lot of the determined bugs, or for very long.

Krysty already had two candles lit and placed on empty machine-gun mounts to fill the gutted war wag with vital illumination. From outside the APC, she could see that the flickering of the emergency lights was getting worse, then one array suddenly began to strobe wildly and died outright, casting the section of the garage into darkness. Gaia, they were cutting this close.

"We're secure!" J.B. announced, tightening the latch on the belly hatch.

"Okay, start cutting!" Ryan growled, holstering his blaster and drawing the panga.

Whipping out their knives, everybody played a candle flame over the blade for a precious second, then nicked a finger and started smearing blood around the louvered air vents and small blaster ports of the vehicle. Even though they knew it was risking a finger to stick it outside, they spread the blood about as far as possible. But at the first imagined touch of a mutie, they yanked the endangered hand back and dabbed the blood merely around the ports.

The chittering soon became a muted roar, and the APC actually shook slightly from the arrival of countless dozens of the muties. The smell of blood was driving the millipedes crazy, and within moments every air vent and blaster port was alive with pinchers and slimy tongues reaching for the food.

"Wait for it," Ryan commanded, as the tapping of the pinchers grew until it sounded like rain on a tin roof. Watching the second hand move on his wrist chron, the one-eyed man waited until the sixty-second mark and shouted, "Now!"

Covering their ears, the companions opened their mouths to equalize the pressure and try to save their hearing when the entire world seemed to erupt. The APC rocked violently from side to side from the concussions of the explosions as the dynamite charges in the coffee cans detonated slightly out of sequence.

The blasts punched through the air vents like invisible fists knocking the companions about, Ryan slamming into a hatch and crumpling to the floor. Outside, the chittering of the muties swelled into screams for a split second and then was gone as the reverberations of the trip-hammer explosions and stilettos of flame stabbed through the air vents and blaster ports, and a monstrous crunching sound filled the garage. Screeching as it scraped along the concrete floor, the wheelless APC was shoved sideways and brutally slammed into another vehicle, then flipped over sideways, tumbling the companions together into a heap and extinguishing the candles.

In the smoky blackness of the APC nothing moved, aside from the slow drip of blood.

Chapter Five

With the coming of the dawn, the Devils rolled out of the box canyon and headed north along the dried riverbed to finally reach a scraggly plain of scrub brush that slowly changed into a grasslands and finally to forest.

After the heat of the desert, it was a very welcome change for the bikers. The line of chained slaves didn't seem to notice the difference, their every thought concentrated on placing one foot ahead of the other.

Passing a copse of trees, a group of stickies charged at the biker gang, hooting and waving their arms like the mad things they were. The Devils hit the muties with firebombs made from glass bottles, rags and shine. Several of the muties were engulfed by the chem flames, but still chased after the escaping food, until they simply toppled over dead, their brains literally cooked through.

"Black dust, those are hard to chill," Denver Joe said, returning a Molotov into his saddlebag. "Is it much farther to this cannie ville?"

"Another day's ride," Cranston growled, glancing sideways at the newbie. "You'll know it when we get there."

That sounded rather ominous to Denver Joe, but he made no reply as the miles steadily rolled underneath the purring bikes, and the frantically running slaves.

High above, the purple and orange clouds crackled with sheet lightning, warning of a coming storm, mebbe even a twister. But there was no smell of acid rain, so the bikers kept their leisurely pace along the forest trail. Dead slaves were of no use to anybody, so every couple of hours the bikers would slow and let the people walk a few miles to catch their breath. For the hungry slaves, food would come at the end of the day, but the Devils ate while they drove, tearing off greasy chunks of dried dog wrapped in oily cloth, and drinking warm water cut with juniper-berry juice from battered aluminum canteens.

The trees were becoming thick in the heart of the forest, and soon the gang was rolling along a narrow trail through the tall evergreens and oaks, the ground covered with a thick carpet of pine needles that sweetly scented the air. Without warning, there was a loud crunching noise to one side and a thick tree snapped off at the base to come crashing down across the path, blocking it completely.

"Razor up," Cranston ordered, drawing his longblaster and thumbing off the safety.

The bikes eased to a halt and the point men instantly slipped longblasters off their shoulders, while the women pulled levers to draw their crossbows and nocked iron arrows into place.

Resting both legs on the uneven dirt road, Cranston throttled down his bike's big engine and listened to the silence of the forest.

"Whatcha think?" Ballard asked, his good eye sweeping across the trees.

Paying no attention to the man, Cranston leaned over the handlebars to inspect the soil. The ground here was moist, but not swampy, and there was no sign of rot on any of the other trees in the area. There was no reason for a tree to just fall over like that.

Krury scowled into the shadows under the dense canopy of evergreens. "Could have been from the rumble of our bikes," the bald biker said slowly, almost as if he were trying to convince himself of the idea.

"Tatters, check the base of the tree," Cranston commanded, pulling a pump-action shotgun from a leather holster strapped to his back.

Holding tight on to the pump, he racked the weapon with one hand by simply jerking it up and down. The solid mechanical sound of the receiver taking a fat 12-gauge cartridge was reassuring to the biker. The first cartridge was predark, in prime condition. The rest were handloads of questionable power. Oh, they would fire all right; he just wasn't sure how far they could throw the combo of lead and razor blades.

Turning off his bike, the skinny Devil kicked out the stand and rested the machine carefully, watching the trees as much as he did the Harley. As the youngest member of the Blue Devils, Tatters always got the shit jobs.

Engines purring softly, the members of the biker gang stayed on their vehicles, the patched exhaust pipes steadily puffing blue-gray clouds of exhaust, as they closely watched the teen go over the base of the big tree and check the exposed roots. Nobody spoke. There was a palatable tension in the air, as thick as a rad fog above a glass lake.

"Looks rotten to me," Tatters called out, prying back a rubbery root with the tip of his long knife. The weapon was actually a cavalry saber taken from a predark museum, but the blacksmith sharpening the blade had been careless and ground a good foot off the steel before being stopped. The short saber worked fine, and the sheath bore the same tattoo that had once been on the arm of the clumsy blacksmith.

"No greasy smells, or acid smell of plas?" Cranston demanded, the blue-steel of the pump-action shining oily smooth in the dim of the hidden sun.

Craning his neck, Tatters breathed in deep, then smiled. "Nah, it's just a dead tree. Krury must be right. It fell over from the vibes of the bikes."

"Mebbe, mebbe not," Cranston stated, easing his grip on the shotgun. "Everybody stay sharp. Shoot anything that moves. David, Shelly, Denver—stay here and cover us. This looks clean but I got a tingle in my bones like when those swampies tried to jump us outside Alamo."

A chorus of grunts signaled agreement, and the group split into two unequal parts. Revving the big engines, the coldhearts eased in their clutches and rolled off the road onto the wild grass and weeds lining the trail. Twigs snapped under the studded tires, as the motorcycles drove past the leafy crown of the dead tree and safely reached the other side of the road.

Easing his stance, Cranston sheathed the shotgun and sharply whistled at the other bikers. A lot of crap about nothing. If this had been some sort of trap, nobody in their right mind would have let half of the group just leave.

Revving their engines, the guards rolled around the tree and joined the pack again.

"Wasn't nothing but a tree," Dee said, her greasy shirt tied under her massive breasts to give them some support. The woman jiggled outrageously with every bounce, but no male in the gang ever complained about the sight.

"Seems so," Cranston muttered nervously, working the throttle as the bike started to stall from overheating. The damn carb was sticking again, he thought. Have to clean that tonight.

Then the chief Devil added, "But I still got me a tingle. Let's waste a few gallons and rocket this road. There's something wrong here, I can fucking well feel it."

Krury nodded assent. Denver Joe just grunted and shrugged. Whatever they decided was fine by him.

But before the bikers could travel another yard, a loon called from the deep shadows under the evergreen. Instantly, Denver Joe dived off his bike and rolled into the bushes as if he were on fire. The unattended machine toppled over, and the engine died with a sputtering cough.

"What the fuck are you doing?" Cranston

stormed, then stopped as there was a sudden movement among the trees, and he had only a split second to react before a massive log suspended from thick ropes slammed into his chest with the force of a cannonball. Blowing guts out his mouth, the dead man was thrown off the bike and arched through the air to land sprawling in the pine needles as boneless as a bag of shit. Then rusty bear traps snapped shut with bone crushing force, the zigzag blades slicing off his hands and removing most of his thigh.

"We've been suckered!" Krury cried, firing his blaster blindly into the trees.

That was the cue for all of the bikers to cut loose with their weapons. In response, six more logs came swinging from the leafy tops, two missing the bikers completely, but the others smashing men and women from their saddles, the lifeless corpses hitting tree trunks with the sound of wet clothing.

Rising from behind a bush, Denver Joe sprayed the Devils with his blaster, blowing hot lead and flame at the coldheart holding the chain of the slaves. As the man stumbled backward pumping blood, the lead slave grabbed the keys off his belt and started fiddling with the locking mechanism.

"Son of a bitch!" Ballard cursed, firing at Denver Joe and then at the slaves. The first prisoner caught a round in the belly and doubled over, but the second snatched the keys before they touched the dirt and started on the lock again.

"Retreat!" Krury shouted, walking his bike around in a circle, but then another tree fell over, blocking the way again, and then a third, sealing them tightly into a killing box.

With the gang cut into two groups, panic took the Devils and they wildly wasted more lead as incoming rounds started slapping into the bikers, the sniper fire cutting them down like helpless old wrinklies. Both groups pulled their bikes into circles and took refuge behind the machines, trying to get a glimpse of the attackers. But the shadows were too thick, and the only signs were brief flashes of muzzle-fire, stabbing from the darkness in a hundred different locations.

"Nuking hell, how many of them are there?" a biker demanded, reloading frantically. Bullets hummed past the man, but he continued to shove fresh rounds into his longblaster with shaking hands. He knew that being scared didn't chill a person, but freezing motionless in fear sure as hell did.

Flinching as a round scored her cheek, Dee shot back and growled, "What's with this sniping shit? Why didn't they just nuke us with more trees?"

"How the hell do I know? Mebbe they want our

hogs!'' Tatters cursed, grabbing Cranston's fallen scattergun. Briefly, he checked the weapon, then triggered the 12-gauge at the hidden snipers as fast as he could.

Mostly just leaves went flying, then a man cried out and fell into view, his leg pumping blood. The bikers cheered, but then two of the Devils broke ranks and tried to make a run past the fallen trees. As they climbed on top, a machine gun opened fire, cutting them down. Just then a biker shouted in warning, and Krury turned to see the slaves escaping into the trees, Denver Joe waving them on to safety. Son of a bitch was a spy! If he ever got his hands on the mutiefucker, it'd take him a year to die on the Learning Tree!

Using a knife to slash open a saddlebag, Krury grabbed spare ammo from the tumble of supplies, then froze as he felt a tremor shake the ground. Underfoot, the pine needles began to dance about, the vibration slowly increasing until he heard a crashing noise and a huge armored wag rolled into view from down the path. Then another appeared in the opposite direction, the two transports covered with machine-gun ports and stubby cannons spitting flame.

''War wags! Use the Molotovs!'' Krury shouted,

then flipped backward as a burst from the hidden machine gun blew open his skull.

''Throw 'em now!'' Tatters ordered, lighting a rag fuse and heaving the glass bottle over the fallen trees. Fireballs whoofed into existence from the Molotovs, and the gang heaved the firebombs in every direction until it seemed as if the forest was on fire.

Grabbing a bag of ammo from a dead friend, Tatters lead a charge into the billowing clouds of smoke, firing at anything in his way, trees, bushes, and chilling a startled slave. Crashing through the underbrush, the teen led the gang through a thicket, the thorns ripping every inch of exposed skin, only the thick leather sleeves on their raised arms protecting faces.

Something streaked through the trees to violently detonate in the leafy greenery, a tree blowing apart and sending out a lethal spray of flaming splinters. A biker dropped, the entire left side of his body riddled with burning debris. The Devil alongside the dying man grabbed his fallen blaster and took off running, leaving the mortally wounded man to gasp out his breath last alone in the bushes. Another biker tried to fire over a shoulder and ran face first into a tree, the crunch of bone was loud as a pistol shot. The limp manner she slumped to the ground was more than enough to indicate that the woman had just chilled herself.

Scrambling over a rock, Tatters paused to catch his breath as a familiar sound caught his attention. That was waves lapping on a shore. They had to be near the Nasay River!

Endless crashing sounded behind the gang, as the war wags tried to force their lumbering way through the thick growth of trees. Machine guns hammered steadily, tracer rounds stitching through the air over the racing bikers as they took off on an angle following the sound of the water.

Then the bushes abruptly stopped at the edge of a crest and there was the Nasay! A wide span of clear blue dotted with tiny islands. Knowing the heavy war wags could never follow them into the muddy river, the coldhearts threw themselves down the sloping bank, tripping over exposed rocks and roots, a few losing their footing. Splashing into the shallows, the bikers hastily waded for the deep water, the current tugging at their limbs constantly trying to drag them down.

As they reached the midspan, harsh illumination crashed across the river from a sandbar upstream and the Devils cursed to see two predark Hummers sitting on the hard-packed sand, brilliant halogen headlights fanning across the water.

"Get those lights!" Tatters cried, shooting his blaster. Then the handcannon jammed on a bad round and he bent to afford as small a target as possible while he struggled to clear the breech. Bastard reloaded bullet had blown, and the split brass had flowered in the ejector. Damn blaster was useless now.

Casting it aside, the teen abandoned the rest of his gang and dived into the water, trying to swim away while submerged. The chaos above became only flashes of light and muffled thumps. Hitting his head on a rock, the teen almost passed out and fought to stay underwater, trying to get around the obstruction, until his aching lungs forced him to surface. Gulping in a breath, Tatters saw a group of Devils cut to ribbons as the M-60 machine guns mounted on the Hummers cut loose, the heavy-duty combat rounds chewing a path of destruction across the river until reaching the men. Red blood spurted from a dozen wounds, and one man flipped over backward, hit by multiple slugs.

Now the shrubbery along the riverbank was smashed flat as a massive war wag parked on the slope, bright headlights crisscrossing the water, its forward machine guns swiveling about for fresh targets. Then a box on the roof opened wide exposing a bank of rockets inside.

Rockets? Tatters couldn't believe his sight. It was like the old war stories the wrinklies told about. Who the bloody hell was after the gang?

The last handful of the Devils scattered at the sight, each going in a different direction. Machine-gun rounds chewed the river in sweeping patterns over and over again, as if supplied with unlimited ammo.

Diving under the water once more, Tatters tried to get across the swift current in the middle of the river, digging his fingers into the mud to crawl underwater until the teen thought his burning lungs would burst from the need for air. Then he felt weeds mixed with the mud and rocks and knew he had made it across. The sounds of battle were a distant murmur as the biker briefly raised his head to suck in a breath and continued desperately crawling into the reeds of the bank.

A broken slab of predark concrete jutted from the water, and the biker put that between himself and the war wags. Go slow, stay low, and he might just live another day. Squirming on his belly through the black mud, Tatters startled a frog before collapsing upon a dry path of dirt.

"Made it," he wheezed softly, the sound broken by a strained laugh. "Nuke me, fucking made it out alive!"

"Not quite, feeb," a woman's voice said, followed by the racking of a scattergun.

Looking in that direction, the biker saw a tall woman in clean clothing, holding the biggest shotgun he had ever seen. His blaster jammed, knife lost in the current, and too weak to try to ace the bitch, the biker knew he was trapped.

"Don't shoot!" Tatters begged, weakly raising both hands. "I—I'm an e-escaped slave!"

"Bullshit," she growled, walking closer until the cold metal of the weapon touched his flushed face.

"I k-know where the Devils store their slick," he said hastily, cringing from the outlander. "Blasters, ammo, all ya can want. All ya can carry! It's yours, just don't ace me and it's all yours!"

The tall woman curled a lip in disgust. "I don't make deals with dead men," she said, pulling the trigger. The barrage of double-aught buckshot blew off the top of his head in a horrid spray of bones and brains and blood. Mouth still working to plead for life, the corpse dropped into the mud, fingers wiggling and feet kicking in a pantomime of life. Racking the weapon, she aimed at his neck and fired again, finishing the job.

Wading across the river, the woman joined the people on the bank as they sorted through the corpses of the bikers, knives slashing every throat in ruthless efficiency. Splashing behind her, a Hummer fought over a tangle of broken tree branches and dead men, catching for a moment with its rear wheels spinning as it fought to finally get loose from the mud and surge onto dry land.

"Glad to see you're alive, Kate," a big man said as she joined him, his left arm tucked into his belt to keep it motionless. There was a bloody stain at the shoulder, but the red wasn't spreading. It was just a flesh wound, one of many over a long life of fighting.

"I see you caught one, Roberto," she said, pulling fresh shells from a looped bandolier of cartridges across her chest and shoving them into the scattergun.

"Bastards threw enough lead at us. Somebody had to get lucky," Roberto said calmly, then added, "Or unlucky, depending on how you look at who got shot."

"Well, don't die on me yet," Kate said, slinging the shotgun over a shoulder. "We got a long ways to go before this is over and done."

He grinned. "With you all the way, Chief."

Just then, the crowd of armed men and women on the shore parted and Denver Joe limped over, escorting a skinny man dressed in rags. Obviously one of the freed slaves from the condition of his feet.

Running stiff fingers through her wealth of golden blond hair, Kate greeted Denver Joe with a nod, which he returned. Tracking the signal of his transmitter had only brought the convoy to a mesa, but after that it had been no great trick to guess where the bikers would be heading next and cut them off in the forest.

"Nice to see you on this side of the grass, D.J.," she said amiably. "Do we have a problem here?"

Denver Joe jerked a thumb at the man standing alongside. "Wants a favor," he said.

"With your permission, Baron," the man said with a bow.

Kate frowned. "Ain't no barons here," she drawled. "Whatcha need?"

The man glanced nervously toward the imposing war wag sitting high on the riverbank, its arsenal of blasters radiating visible waves of heat as they continued looking for targets.

"May I speak with him?" the man asked reverently.

"The boss took lead saving your ass," she lied. "So he's about to go under the knife. No visitors."

"My prayers will be with him," the man said,

making some sort of symbol in the air with his hand.

Behind the thick tinted plastic of the dome, a figure sat tightly in a chair, dimly seen others moving around him. But the person in the chair didn't seem to move at all.

"Yeah, well, it takes more than some coldheart lead to chill the Trader," the woman said, then hawked and spit blood on the bedraggled corpse of a Devil.

Accepting the rebuff, the man was lead away to a Hummer where a man was passing out predark sneakers and MRE packs.

"And so the legend grows," Roberto said softly.

"That's what keeps us in biz," Kate said, cracking a smile. "The more folks fear him, the less we're attacked."

With bloody water lapping at his combat boots, the man nodded. "True enough, I guess."

"So what was the breakage?" Kate asked brusquely, starting up the bank toward War Wag One. The side hatch was open and an armed man was standing guard, watching their approach with an M-16/M-203 assault combo cradled in his hands. An ammo pouch on his belt was heavy with spare clips.

"Two of the bikes got shot up pretty bad, the

rest are fine, Chief,'' Roberto reported, then cursed as he slipped in the mud. Kate started to offer a hand, but held back as the man scowled darkly and righted himself.

"No casualties on our side," he continued, as they reached the crest and got onto level ground. "But we lost a lot of the prisoners."

"Damn," Kate growled. "Okay, keep the broken bike for spare parts, then strip the dead. We'll split the blasters and ammo with the surviving prisoners. They can have any of the Devil clothing they want, except the leather jackets. Those we keep. Then we'll escort them back to that ville by the waterfall."

"That's two days out of our way," he reminded her. "And we're low as hell on fuel."

She shrugged. "Can't be helped. These poor bastards couldn't hold off a one-legged chicken right now. We turn them loose here, and that is the same as acing them ourselves."

"I'll find room for them in the Hummers," Roberto stated. "Wasting a lot of time, though."

"Time we got," Kate said, stepping through the open hatch of War Wag One. "But we needed those bikes to get control of that waterhole so we can cross the Great Salt."

Yeah, it was always the same old battle, the man

thought to himself, weight versus fuel. Hauling more water meant using additional fuel, which meant more fuel to carry so there was less room for water. And so on, and so on. It wasn't the Core, or the muties, or the rad storms that kept them out of north Texas, it was the Great Salt, a flat featureless desert made of pure salt. He'd heard tell there was something similar way up north near Utah called the Great Salt Lake, but this was no body of salty water. Just salt, compressed hard as rock and stretching for more long miles under the blazing white sun than he liked to think about.

As the man and woman maneuvered through the ammo bins and humming comps filling the front of the big transport, the crew at the control boards and machine-gun blisters hailed them in passing. Vid screens showed views from all around the vehicle, and the radio crackled with the conversations of the guards on foot patrol. With all the nukeshit in the atmosphere, a radio couldn't work for more than a few miles, but that was more than enough to give the convoy a fighting edge nobody else had in the Deathlands—communications.

Safe behind a tinted Plexiglas blister, Kate watched the busy crew at their tasks and said nothing.

"Okay, Jake, let's get moving," she ordered,

slumping into a chair and draping a leg over the metal arm. "We got a lot of traveling before we can finally end this triple-cursed war permanently."

"About time," the redheaded driver growled, starting the big diesel engines of the armored transport. "That damn Scorpion God has needed chilling for a bastard long time."

SLUGGISHLY, RYAN came awake clawing for his blaster. Then recalling what had happened, he released the weapon. Groaning loudly, he raised himself off the wall and sat with his shoulder against the roof. The interior of the sideways APC was dully illuminated by a reddish glow coming from through the starboard vents and blaster ports. He could see the others laying crumpled nearby, slowly showing signs of life.

Rummaging for a candle on the wall, Ryan found one and carefully used his hands to squeeze the squashed wax back into shape before using a butane lighter to ignite the wick. As weak as the flame was, it brightened the interior considerably.

"Okay, we survived," Ryan said quietly, wincing as the word sent daggers through his head. "Did they?"

"Damned if I know," J.B. groaned, straightening his glasses. His beloved fedora was partially showing from underneath Mildred, but he made no effort to reclaim the hat. ''Dark night, it feels like we did a bad jump and landed in a cement mixer that exploded.''

''Any damage, John?'' Mildred asked, panting from the exertion of sitting upright.

''Nah, just bruised everywhere but my teeth.''

Extending a hand, Ryan help Doc to extract himself from a tangle of canvas webbing. ''You okay, Doc?''

''I only injured my pride,'' the scholar rumbled, straightening his rumpled clothing. ''Running from a pack of overgrown bedbugs is hardly conducive to vainglorious edification. *Gloria brevis!*''

That was old talk, from before even skydark. Ryan rubbed his chin. ''Which means what?''

''All glory is fleeting.''

''Yeah, but getting aced is forever,'' the one-eyed man added grimly.

From the nose of the APC, Jak groaned. ''My arm…''

Hurrying closer, Mildred checked over the albino teen. ''It's not broken, just dislocated,'' she said. ''You know what that means.''

''Fix,'' he growled through clenched teeth.

Placing her boot in the youth's armpit, Mildred took his limp arm by the wrist, gently turning it ever so slightly, then in one fast move pulled with both arms while shoving with her leg. There was a hard smacking noise and Jak bared his teeth from the intense pain, then relaxed to exhale deeply, gingerly flexing his fingers, then elbow.

"Th-thanks," he gasped. "Better."

"No charge," Mildred said, probing the shoulder with her fingertips. There was no deep tissue damage; it had been a clean separation. "How about you can do me next time?"

"Deal."

"Hot pipe, I can't see anything out there," Dean said, squinting through an air vent. "There's a lot of smoke."

"That'll take a while to clear with no ventilation system working anymore," Krysty stated. "Unless something is on fire. Mother Gaia, what about the fuel dump!"

"If it had caught fire, we'd be ashes already," Ryan stated firmly. "But we better go see, just in case."

Forcing himself to walk to the rear doors, he released the handle and the hatch swung down to loudly slam against the hull. The noise painfully stabbed through his forehead, and this time Ryan touched the sore spot to find his hand coming away

smeared with dried blood. Fireblast, just how long
had they been unconscious?

While J.B. and Dean had moved close beside the
man, their blasters out and ready to give cover if
needed, Ryan stepped through the hatchway and
carefully stood.

The garage was in ruins, the predark wags
smashed against the walls, even the Hummers had
been flipped over, one of them dribbling oil from
a cracked engine block. Ryan relaxed a bit when
he realized it was the puddle of oil that was burning
and causing the dense smoke. A thick plume rose
from the blaze, spreading across the ceiling in a
roiling blanket of fumes. Thankfully, the fuel storage closet seemed undamaged from here.

What little remained of the mutant bugs was
scattered absolutely everywhere in a grisly display
of pinkish organs and black legs. Several pieces of
millipede were lying in the puddle of motor oil,
spitting grease as they cooked from the heat. The
horrendous stench hit them now, and the companions were forced to tie cloth over their faces to keep
from retching.

"An emperor worm by any other name," Doc
muttered from behind a handkerchief.

"Stop mixing your Shakespeare," Mildred replied haughtily, holding a sleeve across her face. "Even though I agree with the sentiment."

Standing near each other, Ryan and Krysty shared a private look and briefly touched hands. They had taken a hell of a gamble, but it worked and they were still alive.

J.B. had cut the single stick of dynamite in his possession into four smaller charges and stuck them into coffee cans filled with office staples. When the dynamite exploded, the entire garage had been filled with a brief hellstorm of flying shrapnel. More than enough to kill every bug in the room.

"Unfortunately, the blast also got the wags," J.B. commented dryly, waving his crumpled hat to fan the air. "The ones that weren't wrecks before, sure as hell are now."

"Better them than us," Jak said, coughing slightly.

Ryan started to reply, then cursed instead. There was a clear puddle of fluid in front of the supply closet. The source was trickling fuel from a score of punctured containers. The spill was only yards away from the oil fire and extending fast.

"If that goes, we're dead!" Dean cried, pulling off his jacket. Advancing to the fire, he started to beat the flames. "We've got to get this out!"

"There was an extinguisher near the workbench,'' Doc told him, heading that way through the maze of twisted military vehicles.

''No time! Quick, give me a hand,'' Krysty said, climbing onto the side of the APC. Standing on tiptoes, the woman lit a butane lighter and thrust it at the thick smoke, but was still too far away. Joining her on top of the transport, Ryan grabbed the woman around the waist and lifted her as high as he could until she was lost inside the layer of smoke, able to play the tiny flame against a sprinkler set into the ceiling. At first nothing happened, and Krysty started to cough from breathing the oily fumes, but refused to quit. But then after a few moments, every sprinkler in the garage released, gushing out volumes of an orange fluid that soon doused the fire and washed the floor clear of the potentially deadly fuel spill.

''That's not water,'' Mildred said, tasting a drop by licking it off her palm. She made a face and quickly spit it back out. ''Some sort of chemical composition. Must be designed for oil fire, since this is the garage.''

''Makes sense,'' Ryan stated, watching the excess flowing into hidden drains set along the walls.

The stink was soon cut from the atmosphere, and the companions went back inside the APC to get out of the downpour. But after only a few more minutes, the sprinklers began to sputter, the rain of fire-retardant chem foam slowing to a mere dribble, and then stopping completely.

"No electricity means no pumps to maintain pressure," J.B. said, wiping his glasses clean. "Good thing this wasn't a major blaze."

Just then, a millipede crawled into view from the cracked ventilation shaft in the closet, snapping its pinchers at the orange residue of the retardant covering the fuel containers. Pulling a knife with his right hand, Jak passed it to his left and threw. The blade hit the mutie in the mouth and it recoiled, snapping as blood gushed from the wound.

"The blast didn't get all of them," Krysty said grimly, lowering her own knife and tucking it away. "Stay sharp. There may be others."

"However, the bugs really don't like this stuff," Ryan said, brushing back his hair to tie a handkerchief around his forehead. "And that gives us an edge again." The chems were making the cut on his forehead throb with pain. Hopefully, the cloth would help. He knew that Mildred could stitch the gash shut, but there was no time right now. They had only a few candles and lots to do.

"Okay, there's lot of wreckage now to block both of those cracks, so let's get moving," Ryan ordered, kicking a foam-drenched mutie carcass out of his way. "We'll start with the big crack, then do the closet."

"Haul out fuel cans, then push busted car against door," Jak suggested, massaging his shoulder. "Not get past."

"And in case they do, we can use the flame retardant as bug repellent," Mildred said, scooping a handful off the dented hood of a luxury car and smearing it over the legs of her Army fatigue pants. "That should keep them off us, for a while anyway."

"Going to need more light than these damn candles," J.B. added, scrunching his face in thought. "Mebbe I can rig a nuke battery to some headlights. Worth a try."

"Some of these trunks don't appear in too bad a shape," Krysty commented. "With some luck we might get something running and drive out here, before another swarm of those damn things arrive."

"What if they're outside, too?" Dean asked, sounding worried.

Ryan glanced around the wreckage filling the level. "No sweat, son. Anything we get moving should easily outrun the bugs."

That was, Ryan added privately, as long as there was open ground outside. If they were on the side of a mountain or buried under the debris of a collapsed predark city, it was going to be the last train west for all of them.

"Besides," Doc said, flicking a dead millipede head out of the way with the pointed tip of his sword, "there is no place else for us to go, but out."

Chapter Six

Working by the flickering glow of tallow candles, the companions emptied the closet of the fuel cans and then completely jammed it with wreckage, next pushing the corroded hulk of a Cadillac against the door to hold it closed. Then the wall crack received the same treatment. A millipede caught inside the crevice almost got Dean's hand, but missed and only sank its pinchers into the sleeve of his jacket. Instantly, the boy ducked out of the way and his father cored the bug with a handball round from the SIG-Sauer.

"Tough bastards," Dean muttered, using his knife to hack up the face of the millipede until prying off the pinchers.

Meanwhile, J.B. had extracted a couple of nuke batteries from the military vehicles and was trying to wire a headlight from a Hummer using a starter solenoid to control the current flow. Each time he flipped the switch, the bulb would burst from the surge of raw power. Yet the man was determined that he could fix the technical problem.

As Ryan stepped away from the fortified crack to pound the solid barrier with fist, there was a dazzling wash of light, the huge makeshift flashlight filling the garage with brilliant illumination.

"Well done, John." Mildred smiled, clicking off her pocket flashlight. "Now we can... Shit, over there by the GMC!"

Two millipedes hidden under a tipped over GMC 6×6 wag scurried for the darkness. But the bugs moved much too slow. The companions converged on the area and quickly dispatched the insects with makeshift clubs.

"A messy job, indeed," Doc muttered, snapping his sword to the side to whip off the blood of the millipedes. Briefly, the fluid filled the words etched along the length of Spanish steel and then was gone.

Testing the balance on his tire iron, Jak flipped it into the air and caught it effortlessly. "Saves ammo," he stated, prowling through the broken vehicles for more prey.

A thorough search revealed that the garage level of the redoubt was clean of the deadly bugs. Checking their blasters while J.B. assembled two more of the nuke battery–headlights combinations, the companions proceeded into the redoubt and a full sweep of the dark interior. The air tasted bad, sour with dust, and the emergency lights set in wall niches were dead or dying everywhere, but the nukelamps more than made up for that. Checking in lockers and underneath desks, the friends did not find another sec hunter droid, and only a few millipedes. Disoriented by the searing beams, they were easily aced.

The kitchen yielded only a few cans of self-heat soup, some rice and beans. Everything else in the fridge and freezer was inedible. Added to their jerky, the staples would last them for a good week.

Yanking out some of the dried venison, Jak chewed on the tough stuff until his jaws ached. But it eased the pain in his belly for the moment. Breakfast had been a million years ago, or so it seemed, and he had no idea when dinner would be coming around. Best to eat anything and stay sharp. This was sure as hell not the place for a prolonged meal, and nobody knew what was waiting for them outside.

"Trade ya," Dean said, offering a stick of chewing gum from a MRE military ration pack.

After a moment, Jak nodded and the items were exchanged. Chewing steadily, the two youths patrolled the darkness, their hands full of loaded steel.

The supply room was empty, only a few yellow transfer papers in military code strewed about.

However, in the armory the companions discovered
an entire pallet of U.S. Army ammo boxes, filled
with cardboard cartons of .22 cartridges still sealed
in plastic. The ammo looked good, but unfortunately, none of the companions used that caliber in
their blasters. But lead was lead, and gunpowder
could be transferred, so they each took several cartons and stuffed them into their backpacks. The
ammo would also make a good trade item. If they
found a ville outside, between the cigars, fuel and
these boxes of cartridges, the companions could
barter for weeks of hot food and clean beds. It was
quite a find.

Going through the barracks, Ryan lead the way
as they group checked the footlockers set before
each bed. Often they found small luxury items the
soldiers had left behind by accident, but such
wasn't the case this time. Every footlocker was
empty; not even a scrap of paper had been left behind.

"Mebbe no troops ever here?" Jak asked, nudging a neatly folded blanket with the tire iron. The
material collapsed at the touch, raising a small
cloud of dust to cover the yellow sheets.

"Could be," Ryan agreed. The barracks seemed
to be more than merely empty, it felt totally deserted, as if no troops had ever been stationed there.

But then, where had the tons of supplies gone? Or had they also never been delivered? Perhaps this was only a partially built redoubt, caught unfinished by the war. The idea made a lot of sense and explained everything they had seen so far.

Making an inarticulate noise of displeasure, Krysty angrily pulled at the orange-soaked top of her jumpsuit. "This dried foam is becoming sticky," she complained. "Our blasters are going to jam if we don't get this crap off of us soon."

"Showers should be over here," J.B. said, leading the way with his nukelamp.

Bypassing the small private showers in the officers' quarters, the companions instead chose one of the big shower rooms for the troops. Without working pumps, they knew that the water pressure would last only for a very brief time, so they would have to clean off quickly and all together.

Leaving the nukelamps safely outside the shower, the group gathered in the middle of the tiled room and turned on the faucets full force. There was a hiss of escaping air for a moment from the ancient pipes, then they were hit by a stinging spray still pleasantly warm. Frantically, they scrubbed the orange residue of the foam off their clothes and out of their hair and barely finished in time before the warm water turned cool, then cold and finally sputtered to a halt.

"Son of a bitch, that feels good." Mildred sighed, shaking her beaded hair to dispel the excess water. With that action, there came a loud crack of glass and one of the nukelamps winked out.

Rushing over to the doorway, J.B. inspected the destruction without touching anything with his wet hands. "The bulb shattered when the water hit it," he said in annoyance.

"Oh, John, I'm so sorry," she stated.

"My fault," he replied, cutting her off. "I should have realized that was going to happen and set these farther back. Damn, what a waste."

"Still three," Jak said, squeezing water from his long snowy hair. "Better than candles."

"Well, that's for damn sure. But nobody goes near the lamps until they stop dripping."

"Wish we had some towels," Dean added.

"Help yourself," Ryan said, gesturing at a stack of thick military towels on a shelf. The fabric was coated with cobwebs.

The boy eyes the neatly folded pile of dust and mold dubiously. "You first," he muttered.

"That reminds me of something an old acquaintance used to say about wishing," J.B. said, reclaiming his glasses from a steel ledge designed to hold soap. "Put a wish in one hand, take a crap in the other and see which gets filled first."

The dripping wet companions shared a laugh at that.

"By gadfry, sir, pragmatic vulgarity," Doc said, ringing his frock coat in both hands with surprising strength. "I think you may have created an entirely new form of philosophy there, my friend."

"Okay, enough jawing," Ryan said, squishing his boots on the tiled floor as he headed for the doorway. "We'll dry faster walking than standing in these bastard puddles."

Staying well clear of the hot lamps, the companions splashed from the shower and once in the locker room of the barracks took the opportunity to carefully check over their blasters. Washing off the foam had helped a great deal, but they disassembled the weapons on the hard benches to clean every part.

Rummaging about in his backpack, Jak unearthed a small plastic squeeze bottle of homogenized gun oil he had looted from the armory of Nova ville so many months ago. The precious lubricant was passed around and used liberally until every blaster was in smooth working condition once more.

Off by himself, Doc retrieved his LeMat from a

shelf inside a locker where he had placed the
blaster before entering the shower room. Although
the weapon wouldn't have been harmed from the
water, the black-powder charges in the revolving
chamber would have washed out, drastically reduc-
ing his precious reserve of ammo and shot. Removing a damp handkerchief from his sodden
pocket, Doc vigorously rubbed the sticky residue
off the huge handcannon until it seemed to be thoroughly clean. But he made a mental note to properly cleanse the weapon in a pot of boiling water
at the first chance.

"Good as ever," Ryan stated, checking the play
on his SIG-Sauer before returning the clip into the
grip with a satisfying click. "Now let's see about
getting the hell out of this bastard tomb."

Rolling up their damp sleeves, Ryan, J.B. and
Krysty each took a nukelamp and led the way back
to the garage level. Setting down the lamps in a
triangular pattern for maximum coverage, the companions got to work searching through the assorted
vehicles for something that could be repaired.

The civilian cars had been garbage to begin with
and had been too close to the dynamite charges and
were even worse now. Going to the military wags,
the companions found another APC, but it was
also stripped to the walls, the 25 mm cannon, ma-

chine guns, seats, radios, and even the engine gone. The war wag was just an armored box with a sagging door.

Ryan had hoped for the Hummers, brute tough wags that could nearly go anywhere. But they had been left running and the engines were burned out, the bearings fused solid from the overheating when the oil ran out. Even the nuke batteries were dead after a century of being left turned on.

"Starting to look like we'll be walking this time," Ryan said, going to the row of big GMC 6×6 M-35 wags marked with the logo of the U.S. Marine Corps. Odd that they often found different services from the predark days all mixed together in the redoubts. It was as if the government had simply grabbed hold of whatever they could and jammed the troops into the nearest redoubt to be sorted out later. Only that time never came.

The first wag had its engine missing, the second lacked tires, but the third seemed in decent shape. The metal and wood framework arching over the rear section was still in good condition, solid and strong, although the canvas covering was lacking. Never installed, lost, or eaten by the bugs, there was no way of knowing. But the first wag had good canvas.

"We do a mix and match here," Mildred said,

sliding off her backpack. "Use parts from one to fix another."

"I'll find some wrenches," Dean offered, rushing over to the musty workbenches to shift through the assortment of parts and greasy cans to locate a few tools. A sturdy toolkit yielded a wealth of socket wrenches and pliers.

Checking under the front seat of the first GMC wag for a jack, Ryan unearthed a plastic box full of road flares. Two of the waxy cylinders crumbled at his touch, but the rest were still firm. He tucked one into a jacket pocket and passed the rest to J.B., who added them to the scant few materials in his munitions bag.

The Armorer was grateful for the flares. Aside from the implo grens, the satchel was the lightest it had been in a long time. Some untrustworthy timing pencils, the spare boxes of ammo, the implo grens, a butane light, and that was about the lot. Good thing the droid had been in such bad condition. Using an implo inside a redoubt was as tricky as firing a shotgun inside a predark phone booth. It didn't matter which direction you were aiming at, some of it was coming right back in your face.

Krysty lifted up the hood of the biggest wag and started to inspect the big diesel power plant, testing the hoses and wires and belts with her bare hands.

She normally left such things to J.B., but this was a major job and all of them would have to help.

"Looks good so far," she announced, bent far over the engine. "Somebody want to check the axles?"

"Hold it. Before we go any further, maybe I should go outside and see where we are," J.B. offered. "Could be daylight out there. Could be a ville only a few miles away and we don't need to rebuild a wag. Just walk there."

Going through the glovebox for a map, Ryan found nothing but transport papers in military code and slammed it shut.

"Nuke that shit. We all go outside together," he growled. "Open that blast door, and there could be a hundred millipedes waiting to rush in. Best to be mobile when we leave in case of trouble."

The mental image of a nest of the muties made the Armorer grimace in spite of himself, and he recognized the wisdom of the caution. Rabbits ran fast, but they always ended up in the stew because they were stupid. Smart and slow was how you kept your head, as the Trader always used to say. True words.

As the companions worked on rebuilding the wag, a millipede scurried past the open doorway of the stairwell.

"Little bastards must be hidden somewhere we haven't looked," Dean growled, starting to reach for his blaster. But the insect was already gone, chased away from the nukelamps. He couldn't imagine why J.B. had never tried making one of those before. They worked great.

"Fuck 'em," Ryan decided, wiping off his hands before taking another bite of the venison jerky. He chewed for a while before continuing. "They can have the base. We'll be leaving soon enough."

In short order, a jack was found and the big wag was given the best of the assortment of tires from the other wrecks. Hoses were exchanged, wires replaced, wiper blades, everything they could replace with the simple tools available. Plus, a box full of spare parts, fuses and such. Just in case.

Slowly the hours ticked by and the air in the redoubt was becoming noticeably ripe from the dead bugs and sweating humans. More than once Ryan thought about opening the blast door to the outside, but decided against taking the chance. There was a small breeze of hot air coming from under the closet door. That would have to suffice until they were ready to roll. Might only get one chance at this, so be it better be good.

"Well, the nuke battery is in place," Krysty said, stepping away from the engine of the wag and wiping off her hands. "We have plenty of power, and the tires are good. Just no juice left in the gas tank."

"That we have to spare," Ryan said, tightening the last of the fourteen lug nuts on the rear tire. "Fill the tank, and let's take twenty additional cans, fifteen for us, five for bartering."

"Why not take all of the cans we can fit?" Dean asked, then paused. "Because we have to leave room for us and supplies. Right. Never mind."

"Trade juice?" Jak asked, starting to lug over the heavy fuel containers. "Ammo best. Few folks got wags, but all barons got blasters."

"Fuel is better," Mildred countered, removing the cap to the fuel tank. There was a sigh of escaping fumes as dry as a Baltimore martini. God, how she missed those. "Also, fuel is less deadly if it comes our way again."

"Never heard of a Molotov?" J.B. asked, lashing the exhaust pipe tighter into place with a twisted length of stiff wire.

Then crawling from underneath the chassis, the man said, "Damn but that's a good idea. Make some Molotovs in case of more millipedes. We got the juice to spare, and there was a bar full of empty liquor bottles in the officers' mess. And Krysty found those foam cups before."

"There was some liquid soap in the laundry, too," Dean added, lugging over a can of fuel.

"Soap is good, but foam is better," Ryan said, using his panga to scrape some corrosion off a set of electrical contacts. "But we're also going to need additional water. The hot air that was coming from the cracked vent could mean we're in a desert."

In exaggerated care, Jak set down the cans with a sloshing thump. "From pipes in pump room. Might be okay."

"Sounds good. But I want to test anything before we drink it," Mildred warned, putting down the empty canister. "Clear doesn't always mean clean."

"Okay. Both go," the lanky teenager told her.

Taking one of the nukelamps, the pair descended into the stairwell, and soon the glow from their light dimmed with distance. Over at the workbench, J.B. had lined up the soda bottles found earlier and started to hack the coffee cups to pieces and making neat little piles.

As Dean brought over another can of fuel, Doc joined him at the task, and Krysty took over pouring the juice into the tank.

"How much fuel and water we should take is the real problem," Ryan said, thinking aloud.

Cleaning the panga on a sleeve, he sheathed the blade and reconnected the electrical contacts. There was no way of checking the diesel until they started it up, so he was done for the moment.

"What do you mean?" Doc asked, setting down the cans and rubbing his palms for a moment.

Sitting on a wheel rim, Ryan pulled out a piece of jerky and chewed off a mouthful. "We don't even know how far it is to the nearest ville, much less the next redoubt," he stated, glancing at the dark tunnel that led to the blast doors. He had been trying very hard to think about what would happen if they couldn't open the exit. Trapped inside with the millipedes until starvation drove them mad. Better to eat a blaster than go down that road.

"If we don't know for sure, let's take an equal balance," Krysty said, pouring more fuel into the tank. There was a gurgling noise as some trapped air fought to reach the surface, and she waited a moment until the turbulence was settled. "That way we're prepared for anything."

"Works for me," Ryan said, standing again, his break over.

Light brightened the stairwell, and the companions stepped behind the wrecked cars with hands on weapons until there was a sharp whistle announcing that everything was okay, and they relaxed. Seconds later, Mildred and Jak appeared in the doorway.

"Found water," Jak said happily, pulling a hand truck up the last of the steps. The teenager then clumsily wheeled it around to then push a large steel drum into the garage.

"The pipes were empty from our shower," Mildred said, carrying the nukelamp in one hand, her blaster in the other, "but we managed to find this drum and fill it with fifty-five gallons of water. It's drainage from the reactor, all we could drain from an access pump."

"Nuke water?" Doc demanded arching both snowy eyebrows. "By the Three Kennedys, madam, I have never been that thirsty! Are you quite sure it is safe?"

"See for yourself," Mildred suggested, holstering her piece, as Jak lowered the hand truck with a bang, the drum sloshing loudly.

Removing the lid, J.B. unclipped the rad counter from his lapel and held it close to the clear fluid. The needle moved slightly.

"Low rads, seems safe enough to drink," he said reluctantly.

"Of course," Mildred stated, then added, "As long as we don't do it too often." The physician had no intention of trying to explain to the others that this was technically not water, but actually deutronium enriched water, heavy-water shielding for the fusion reactor. However, it was nonlethal and potable, and that was all that mattered.

Warily, Ryan checked his own rad counter and got a similar reading. "It's clean, all right. Okay, we use this as our backup supply," he stated. "And the radiator gets it before us."

"No prob," Dean said, rubbing his mouth with the back of a hand. Nuke water. Hot pipe, he'd rather drink mutie pee than touch a drop of that, no matter what Mildred said.

"Done," Krysty stated, screwing the cap back onto the fuel tank. "That's every drop it can hold."

"Put the rest in the back, and let's try the engine," Ryan said, swinging open the door and climbing behind the wheel. "Hopefully all this work wasn't for shit."

Pumping the gas pedal, he set the choke and pressed the starter. The engine sluggishly turned over with a sad groaning noise that slowly started to build in speed and volume. Pumping the gas harder, Ryan adjusted the choke to make the mixture to the carburetor richer and the engine sputtered briefly, then caught with a roar, banging and clanging.

Reaching under the hood, J.B. used a screwdriver

to adjust something Ryan couldn't see because of the angle, and the big diesel suddenly settled down to a low roar of controlled power.

"That'll do it," J.B. said with satisfaction, tucking the screwdriver into his munitions bag. "Better let her run until we're ready to leave. That'll give the seals a chance to absorb some oil before we put them under real pressure."

Playing with the choke, Ryan got the engine lowered to a gentle rumble, the sputters coming with less and less frequency. They needed to run the engine to break it in before leaving, but with the ventilation system gone, the exhaust fumes mixed with the previous oil smoke and the mounting stink of the aced millipedes into a noxious reek that was getting worse by the minute.

"Okay, load her up," Ryan said, resting an arm on the window. "Toss in anything you think we might need. With the power gone, once we're outside, we're not getting back in, so this is a one-way trip. Strip the place to the walls."

The companions moved with a purpose, eager to leave the dying redoubt. Since there were no seats in the rear of the wag, they added a couple of the better mattresses from the officers' quarters, and packed spare blankets, a shovel, spare rope, some chains, the box full of Molotovs, spare pieces of canvas from the other GMC trunks to use as patches, and all of the fuel containers they could comfortably fit. It took everybody, including Ryan, to hoist the water drum into the rear of the trunk, and they lashed it firmly in place in the middle of the fuel cans. Just a bit of extra insurance.

"That's everything," J.B. said, fighting a cough from the thickening atmosphere. "Let's move out!" Slamming shut the gate and locking it into position with steel pins on both sides, he went to the front cab and climbed into the passenger seat alongside Ryan, laying the S&W shotgun between them where it couldn't be seen from the ground.

"Expecting trouble, John Barrymore?" Doc rasped through the tiny slit of the rear window. There was a sliding panel to separate the cab from the cargo space, but it was open at the moment. The man was trying not to show it, but the filthy air was obviously hurting his throat.

"Just get ready for it," the Armorer said tightly, checking the action on his Uzi machine gun.

"Hang on, this is going to be rough!" Ryan shouted to the people in the rear, his voice breaking for a moment. Fireblast, the air was almost thick enough to chew! His forehead was still hurting from the earlier slam, and this crap was making his entire head throb.

Shifting into a low gear, he threw the switch engaging the independent drive system and started to climb over the smashed cars until reaching the floor again. Now going to uniform drive, Ryan fed the big diesel some power and the front steel grate slammed into another wag knocking it aside. The jolt shook the entire group, and the people in the back had to hang on tight and drop their nuke-lamps.

"Put the pedal to the metal!" Mildred shouted, then paid for that by getting a lungful of the billowing smog and almost passing out.

Saving his breath, Ryan didn't reply but did as she suggested and soon a clear area led the wag to another impasse blocked by wreckage. Using the independent drive again, he tried to keep the lumbering wag level as its weight noisily crumpled the hoods of luxury government cars and smaller vehicles.

"Running hot," Ryan growled, shifting gears and pumping gas. "Don't like that!"

"Ignore it. It'll be fine," J.B. answered, watching a millipede dart into the shadows away from the glaring headlights of the moving wag.

With a hard jounce, the wag hit the concrete floor again, and now there was nothing barring their way to the exit tunnel. Designed for much larger vehicles, the GMC 6×6 had plenty of room to traverse the zigzagging path of the antiradiation maze.

A dozen small cracks in the tunnel wall were brightly lit by the headlights of the vehicle, but none appeared deeper than a yard or so, and there was no sensation of a warm breeze. Actually, at this point, they would have welcomed it. Everybody was breathing hard as their lungs labored to draw in enough oxygen, and Krysty looked as if she were going to be ill at any moment.

Reaching the end of the access tunnel, spanning the wall before the 6×6 was a colossal black door large enough for a predark Army tank to roll through without hindrance. The two-and-one-half ton wag was a toy in comparison. Carefully, they looked it over for any warping or discolorization that would indicate a close nuke hit, but the dense metal was as smooth as satin without a mark.

Ryan braked to a halt, the companions staying alert while he slid out of the driver's seat and J.B. went behind the wheel, covering him with the Uzi. Walking to the wall on an angle so that the headlights would illuminate his way, Ryan found an armored keypad set into the frame and tried the exit code, but nothing happened. Expecting that, he pried open a service hatch under the keypad and grabbed hold of the wheel. It took all of the man's strength to get the mechanism working.

The wheel began to turn, gradually becoming looser, and the speed increased until there was a solid clunk. Releasing the wheel, Ryan pulled hard on the lever alongside and there was low rumble as the thick alloy door began to rise. A wave of heat washed into the redoubt, bringing a wealth of hot clean air. The companions breathed in deep, savoring the lack of smells even as wind blown sand hit the windshield of the wag with stinging force.

As Ryan took the passenger's seat, J.B. hit the gas and drove toward the opening. Even as the vehicle reached the blast door, the opening rising door was noticeably slowing, the charge built by rotating the wheel barely enough to move the megatons of armored steel. As the wag drove through the opening, the blast door began to close and there was a screech of metal on metal as it caught the rear gate of the wag. The trapped vehicle was slowly being crushed. J.B. shifted gears and hit the gas, banking the steering wheel hard to angle the aft end free from the grasp of titanic blast door before any serious damage was done.

With a painful screech, the gate was torn free and the door slammed shut, crushing the piece of military steel flat against the jamb of the redoubt as if it were no more than cardboard.

In the silence of the warm night, fresh air washed over the companions and they drank it in gratefully. Lifting a nukelamp out the window, Ryan angled it about, but the powerful ray vanished into the distance of a featureless desert.

"What the...this is salt, not sand," Krysty said, spitting and wiping her mouth. She strained to hear any sound of waves on the beach, but there was only the soft whisper of the hot wind and nothing else. It was as if they were on another planet.

"Damn, it *is* salt. Maybe we're in Utah again," Mildred guessed, taking a drink from her canteen. "Or maybe the Nevada salt flats."

Still panning the brilliant beam about, Ryan narrowed his eye at that comment. Nevada, eh? There was a couple of redoubts there they might reach. Along with some old enemies.

"Could be anywhere," J.B. said, slowing the wag while trying to decide in which direction to travel. His pocket compass said they were heading west, but without knowing where they were that meant less than nothing. And he couldn't use the sextant until the sun rose or stars became visible.

"Keep going straight," Ryan said, turning off the beam and placing the heavy device on the floorboards between his boots. "Often the front door of a redoubt points toward a predark city. Probably another of their safety features."

"Is that why we come out of a redoubt and often find villes and ruins and such directly ahead of us?" Dean asked, his voice already sounding more normal. "Hot pipe, and I thought it was just luck or something."

As the wag bumped through a low depression, his father paused before answering, "No such thing as luck," Ryan replied grimly, the wind from the window ruffling his long hair. "Only brains and guts. Folks earn what comes their way."

Nodding in agreement, J.B. fed more power to the wag and the companions rolled into the Stygian night of the salt desert.

As THE WAG disappeared into the darkness, the ground before the redoubt churned and a swarm of millipedes rose to the surface, snapping their pinchers and running about in circles. The bugs seemed confused that their prey had gotten away, chittering in rage.

Then one millipede paused, its featureless face twitching as it tested the air, searching, tasting. With a high-pitched cry, it surged to the west in hungry pursuit of the metal and heat. The rest of the millipedes soon followed, flowing across the salt like a black cloud in the stormy sky above, instincts telling them that where there was a mag field, there was always living food to be found.

Chapter Seven

The ocean breeze blew steadily over the solitary guard on the stone tower as the cannie watched the bobbing headlights of the motorcycle pack crawl along the cliff road toward the oceanfront ville, the moonlight gleaming off the polished skulls on their handlebars.

Far below the base of the cliff, whitecaps were breaking on the smooth stones of the beach with the sound of distant thunder. There was no access to Hellsgate ville from that direction, which was why the elders had chosen to build here. The cliff was sheer, with no path or trail to facilitate passage. And the Mex Gulf was a death trap, the water filled for miles with bits and pieces of predark wreckage, mostly the rusted remains of warships, but also some scattered chunks of buildings and roads. No ship could land without being smashed to pieces. Not to mention the sea muties that pulled down ships and sometimes wandered onto the shore looking for food. Bad things, as big as houses with tentacles and glowing eyes.

Shifting the longblaster slung over his shoulder, the man fumbled in a pocket of his loose clothing and found a flat box. Pressing the release, the box snapped open on squeaky hinges and he looked through the predark opera glasses to sweep the landscape and find the oncoming bikes. Under the magnification, he easily recognized the big Harley of the Blue Devils and smiled. Excellent! The bikers always had plenty of slaves to trade for slick, and afterward there would be a feast for those in good favor with the elders. The guard smacked his lips at the thought, displaying sharpened teeth. It had been too long since he had last eaten fresh meat. The hated Trader had chilled several convoys carrying food to the ville, and the cannies had been reduced to eating fish caught in nets for their daily meals. Disgusting. Only muties and slaves consumed animals. The warriors of Hellsgate ate man flesh to make them strong! Anything else was offal to feed to pigs.

The elders had a long-standing feud with the Trader. They wanted him chilled, but couldn't find the bastard. He wanted them aced, but didn't care to attack, not with the blasters of Hellsgate commanding the landscape. Nothing on wheels could challenge the ville's monster blasters.

Placing the opera glasses back into their box, the

guard walked past a crackling torch and over to a rope. He tugged hard, and down on the ground a bell rang slow and steady, announcing that outlanders were coming, but that there was no danger.

Releasing the rope, the cannie went to the edge of the tower to see a group of guards holding lanterns gathered in the yard looking up at him expectantly.

"The Devils are coming!" he shouted through cupped hands. "Along the cliff road! Ten bikes! Five miles away!"

A big man dressed in a patchwork cloak waved in response and turned to the others standing nearby.

"So they're finally here," Elder Thomas said in a low growl. He wasn't sure to be glad the long wait was finally over, or nervous that the long-awaited battle was about to begin.

"The day of the Devils," an old woman announced, her six-fingered hands shaking with excitement. "These are not the men you know. Impostors from your great enemy."

The slave wore no chains to bind her hands or feet, and she was dressed well in canvas moccasins and a thick woolen dress to keep her old bones warm. But her weathered face was grotesque, her eyes empty holes ringed by layers of scars where white-hot knives had removed the orbs.

"Yes, I have seen it all happen in my mind," she said, cackling. "Death comes here today." What the wrinklie didn't add, was that she saw the destruction of the ville come in the form of a ray of sunshine. What that could possibly mean was beyond her understanding, so she wisely kept quiet, knowing that she risked death by withholding information, but also at displeasing the chief elder.

"So you say, witch," Thomas growled, fingering the barbed whip coiled at his hip. "You'd best to right this time, or we'll see if you do a better job without your hands!"

She bowed at that, gushing affirmations until he ordered her silent. Damn talky bitch was more trouble than he liked to tolerate, but the wrinklie was a doomie, a mutie with the gift to see the future. A former elder of the Hellsgate had heard that sight weakened the powers of a doomie, and so he had her eyes removed to increase her value to the ville. Only thing wrong with her predictions was that once she told what was going to happen, that changed the course of events, sometimes drastically. The witch was correct more often than not, and thus couldn't be harmed. But the pretense of listening to advice from lowly food was repugnant to the elder, and he eagerly looked forward for any excuse to gut the woman and toss her into the stew pot.

The sea breeze whipped over the tall walls of the ville, bending the torches in different directions, making a few of the men flinch as the flames got too close to their faces.

"The question is, do we take the chance?" Elder Getty asked gruffly, leaning heavily on a yellow cane carved from human thigh bones. His long beard knotted into two strands to resemble the forked tongues of a snake, and he tugged on the end of one thoughtfully. "If we chill the wrong people, we could anger the storm gods and rain destruction upon Hellsgate!"

"Praise be the sky gods," Elder Thomas muttered, pulling a shiny blue .38 Colt from within his shirt and tucking it into his belt with the handle turned out for a fast draw.

Privately, Thomas didn't believe in any unseen gods that ruled the air. The man had traveled far in his youth, and everywhere he went the sky was a boiling mass of rads and chems. Although, Thomas had to admit, why the acid rains never fell upon Hellsgate was something for which there was no explanation. Some said it was because they were the chosen people, or because they ate man flesh to please the gods, and once a demented slave said it was merely because of wind currents from the ocean. That sacrilege sent the slave to the table of the Blood Feast, and his wails lasted long into the night. Oh, yes, Thomas remembered it fondly. The slave had been a very satisfying meal.

"Four miles!" the guard in the tower shouted, silhouetted by the moonlight.

Elder Getty ceased tugging on his beard. "The choice must be yours," he ordered, pointing at the younger man with a skeleton thin hand.

"Accepted." Thomas sneered, pulling his blaster. "Master of the guards, call out your men! Let's get the shields in place before the Devils arrive."

A sec man blew a single clear note on a ram's horn, and guards rapidly spread across the courtyard of the stone ville, shouting orders. The armory was opened wide, weapons passed out to eager hands, along with sealed jars of ammo and even a few grens.

Then handlers appeared from the holding pits, their shaved heads gleaming with oil from the yellow light of the fish oil lanterns as the eunuchs whipped a line of women toward the front gate. Dressed in dirty rags, the slaves were all young, but looked almost as old as the witch, from their poor diet and the daily beatings.

Teams of slaves pushed at the wooden beam holding the front gate closed, the massive slab of wood sliding along a greased notch until out of the way. Now armed sec men pushed the gate open and spread out in a defensive pattern, while the handlers lashed their charges outside the ville. For most of the females, it was the very first time they had seen the other side of the thick stone walls of Hellsgate since they had arrived so very long ago.

Arching in a semicircle around the ville, the wall stood twenty feet tall and was nearly as thick, built entirely of slabs of concrete and pieces of broken warships from the beach. Many times coldhearts and muties had attacked Hellsgate, once even rival slavers from Old Mex, and they always failed to get through the imposing palisade. Even the front gate itself was composed of a framework made of railroad ties, overlaid with slabs of sidewalk concrete. It took twenty strong men to move the gate, and nothing could blast through.

It was a formidable barrier made impregnable by the titanic cannons removed from the Navy ships in the sea, six breechloaders more than twenty feet long with a foot-wide barrel. There had been a larger undamaged cannon in the wreckage down the coast a mile or so, but it was simply too enormous to move by hand and machine. But the six were enough, more than any other ville had in the known world. The cannons weren't movable, resting in beds of crushed stone and timber. But the elders of the time had been very careful to aim the blasters in different directions to cover the entire arch of the great wall around Hellsgate. The few times the cannons had been used against invaders, there had been no survivors and few body parts remaining to scrape off the cliff to feed the pigs.

"Okay, strip!" the chief eunuch ordered, lashing out with a bullwhip. The knotted end cracked in the air like blasterfire, making the girls flinch. "Remove every stitch! And be quick about it!" Relaying the command, other handlers also cracked their whips, urging the confused slaves on to greater speed.

Hesitantly at first, the women began to remove their simple clothing, many weeping as they obeyed. Watching from the shadows outside the circle of light, the cannie guards leered at the display of flesh, and some reached out to cup the tender breasts of the women and brutally squeeze until tears of pain replaced those of shame. The eunuchs tried not to scowl in disapproval at the lustful actions, but few succeeded.

Soon the rags were piled on the rocky ground, and the twenty women stood shivering in the cool sea breeze.

"Chain them up!" the chief eunuch ordered, trying to keep a watch on the slaves as well as on the road near the cliff. The muted noise of the motorcycle engines could be faintly heard now, getting steadily louder. Time was short. "And be quick about it!"

Now the eunuchs pushed the sec men aside and got busy shackling the naked girls to iron rings set into the main gate. Some of the smaller women couldn't reach the ground with their feet, and hung painfully from their wrists, fighting to hold on to the stout chains with their hands or else their own weight could painfully dislocate a shoulder.

Surrounded by armed guards atop the wall, Thomas watched the procedure below and scowled unhappily at the terrible waste. These were farming folks, not gaudy sluts, prime meat for the Blood Feast. But now their only value was that of living armor, their lives protection against the enemies rumbling toward the ville.

When the task was done, the sec men and eunuchs fled back inside Hellsgate and the gate was ponderously closed, the massive locking bar noisily sliding back into position.

"One mile!" the guard shouted, the words carried away by the ever present breeze. "They're past Liar's Point!"

In spite of himself, Thomas had to admit the disguise was well done. He never could have told it wasn't the real Blue Devils without the assistance of the doomie. The gang always had a few new faces among them, and the smoked bodies draped across the rear fenders looked real enough to make him hungry.

Partially covered by the moon shadow of the eastern gun, a girl hanging naked from the cold gate wearily raised her head to see the headlights of the motorcycles turn off the road and head for the ville. Desperately, she mouthed words at the distant machines producing no sounds, and as the bikers charged ever closer, raw hatred filled her bruised body with strength and she finally screamed.

"Please!" she managed to shout, her voice raspy from years of torture. "Kill us!"

As if in response, the bikers braked to a halt along the edge of the cliff and started conferring among themselves, the headlights pulsing to the throb of the big Harley engines.

"They've seen the shields, Elder," a guard said, twisting his hands nervously on an M-16 remake. "What should we do if the witch is wrong? Should we load the eastern cannon? Hate to lose all that food.''

Thomas started to answer the man when something caught his attention. In the glow of the brake lights behind the bikers, he could see the feet of the chained slaves. Shoes. The nuking slaves were wearing shoes! Bullshit. So the doomie was right as usual, and this is a trap of some kind. Probably poison in the bodies. There could be more to this than could be seen. The first elder often said one clever trick from an enemy usually meant two or three more were coming.

''Load the second and third cannons,'' Thomas ordered, working the bolt action on his longblaster and sliding in the single round. ''And load number four, too, just in case this is a diversion for an attack on the other side.''

''Yes, Elder!'' the man said with a salute, and hurried while carrying his torch high, sparks flying on the wind.

Standing alone in the busy courtyard, the doomie turned her wizened head toward the dimly remembered glory of the stars, a worried expression playing across her gnarled features. She felt dizzy, almost sick, her mind a whirlwind of events, the actions of the present too chaotic for her to see what would come to be. Then dimly amid the blood and the madness, she caught a glimpse of a beautiful woman with yellow hair the color of the sun. Golden hair. It was she! A wave of cold took the mutie, and there was no doubt that she had just looked upon the face of death incarnate.

Lifting a box from inside his leather jacket, one of the bikers seemed to be talking to it. After a few minutes, he tucked it away and the Devils began revving their engines, making enough noise to drown out the crashing of the waves on the beach.

"What are they doing?" a sec man muttered, switching the selector lever on the M-16 remake from single shot to full-auto. This was his only clip of ammo for the rapidfire, but this day was why they had been hoarding the lead. All available black powder was reserved for the big guns. The sec man hadn't personally fired his weapon in a year. There was rarely need. Only muties were insane enough to challenge the big guns.

"Dying," Thomas growled, wrapping the sling of the huge longblaster around his arm to steady his aim. Aiming for the fuel tank of the big Harley, he then shifted the crosshairs and zeroed on the rider. As he caressed the trigger, the Remington blaster blew flame, and Thomas saw the Devil fall off the machine and roll straight over the cliff and out of sight. If there was a scream before he hit the rocks below, the winds carried it away. Pity.

In response, the rest of the bikers drew rapidfires, while the slaves threw off their chains and cut loose the dressed bodies, pulling out blasters hidden underneath. Crouching low, they started raking the top of the wall with small-arms fire, flattened slugs ricocheting off the metal and concrete. The ville guards returned fire, but their weapons didn't have the reach.

Then the bikers turned off their headlights and darkness covered the landscape, with only the flashes of their blasterfire showing where the Devils were located.

"Ready the second cannon!" Thomas ordered, working the bolt of the Remington and chambering a fresh predark cartridge. "Blow them off the cliff!"

With the gun crew shouting directions, bald eunuchs lashed a team of slaves to move faster, loading the predark monster with black powder and broken lengths of chain. At this range, the shotgun blast of junk would chew the outlanders into small chunks of flesh, leveling anything along that entire section of the cliff. There was no escaping the guns of Hellsgate.

INSIDE THE DIMLY illuminated interior of War Wag One, the dashboard and control panels cast a rainbow of colors across the tense crew. Then the ceiling speaker crackled alive once more. "Repeat, Trader One, they just aced Denver Joe and have the gate covered with slaves. Main guns are being armed. Repeat, their cannons are being loaded. Do we charge the gate, or run?"

The men and women in the room exchanged tense looks, their hands tight on grips of the machine guns inside the blisters jutting from both sides of the armored transport. Nervously, the seasoned killers chewed gum to stop from fidgeting as smoking was forbidden inside the vehicle because it could damage the delicate comps operating the coms and main L-gun.

"Your call, Chief," Roberto said, glancing backward from the main weapons panel. His wounded arm now hung in a clean sling, but the man could still use both hands to steer the big rig.

Hunched forward in a chair bolted to the floor, Kate clenched and unclenched her fists on the handles of the periscope and watched the events happening just over the hill. Black dust, how had everything fallen apart so fast? The plan had been for the bikers to mine the gate and blow it open so the war wags could roll into Hellsgate and level the place. The gate, that damn gate! It was the only access into the ville, and even then they had to outmaneuver those sixteen-inch cannons. War Wag One had missiles, but not enough to chew a hole through that bastard wall. The armor plating from the ancient warships was proof to almost any weapon. The gate was the only way in, and now it was covered with living slaves as protection.

With their diesels engines idling, two more armored wags also sat behind the hill, their lights off, exhaust puffing into the salty breeze. The additional four cargo wags were far away from the war wags in case of trouble, but well-armed with small-caliber rapidfires and a single precious flame-thrower.

They were ready to give cover fire and help protect the rear from a night creep, but the brunt of any chilling would be done by War Wag One and its heavy weaponry.

Once again, Kate pressed her face against the cracked cushion lining the ob slit of the periscope. Switching from infrared to Starlite, the front of the ville grew into daylight clarity and she could see the naked women dangling from the chains, shouting. Probably begging for death. Her heart pounded as Kate remembered doing the same in the past, and the old scars on both wrists suddenly itched as her mind heard the whip crack of a herder's lash across her back and felt the leather cut into virgin flesh.

This was all the fault of that damn pet doomie the elders had! She had to have screwed the deal, and now the whole plan was a mess. All that time spent tracking the Devils to steal their bikes wasted. Lives lost for nothing. They were stopped again by those damn cannons, with the cannies laughing in victory behind the thick wall. Mebbe the cooks already started the stoves for a special meal this night, the slaves soiling themselves in terror as the eunuchs appeared at the top of the holding pits with chains and knives, laughing at the wails of terror from the people below....

Sounding like nukefall, a cannon of the ville discharged, splitting the night, a lance of flame stretching yards ahead of it. A whistling barrage of shrapnel blew across the ground with the bikes catching a couple of minor pieces. Quickly, the bikers moved their vehicles into the path of the cannon, knowing that they would be safe from another salvo for a few minutes until the weapon was reloaded. However, they also knew the dodge wouldn't work a second time. Because the next volley would be both of the eastern cannons, and from that combined spread there would be no escape.

"Retreat or charge?" The ceiling speaker crackled. "You better answer us right, or we're leaving!"

"Chief?" Roberto demanded. "We need a decision right now."

Releasing the periscope, Kate drew in a deep breath and let it out very slowly. There was no other choice.

"Tell the bikers to pull back and follow in our wake. Try to reach the walls and take out the gun crews. We're going in," she said, yanking the clip from the Ingram SMG slung over a shoulder. "Straight through the gate."

The tension faded from the room, and the gunners flicked off safeties. Roberto fed power to the tandem engines, and the war wag started rumbling around the hill.

"About damn time," he growled softly, then hit a switch. "Eric, prime the L-gun. We're going to Hell!"

FIRING AGAIN at the unseen biker gang, Thomas levered in a fresh round when something trailing fire streaked across the sky and hit the stone guard tower like a blinding thunderclap. The top was blown completely off the structure, stones flying

everywhere to rain upon the ville, crushing sec men
and slaves alike.

"First elder protect us," a guard on the wall
cried, dropping his blaster. "He's here. The Trader
is here!"

Thomas spun in the direction the startled cannie
was looking just in time to see a huge war wag
crest the northern hills, the armored hull bristling
with blasters spitting flames. The elder forced himself to raise the longblaster and shoot at the oncoming machine even though he knew it could do no
good. The thing was enormous and bristled with
machine-gun blisters, missile pods and stubby barrels of 40 mm gren launchers.

A double flash erupted from both sides of the
juggernaut, fiery contrails extending directly for the
chained women at the gate, then unexpectedly arching up and over the wall at the very last moment
to sharply dive inside the ville. The world seemed
to explode as harsh light blossomed and the concussion almost shoved Thomas off the wall. As he
collected himself a few second later, the elder could
see a gaping crater in the center of the ville, with
most of the barracks gone, along with the meeting
hall and the gaudy house. The keep in the center
of the ville seemed undamaged, but the entire glass
side of the greenhouse was gone, sparkling pieces

flying through the moonlight. Even as he watched, two running eunuchs were caught under the downpour and diced to pieces, the glistening shards slicing them to ribbons. Horribly alive, the men shrieked insanely as internal organs spilled onto the ground between their clutching fingers.

Ignoring the dead men, Thomas gasped in horror when he saw the plants inside the shattered greenhouse were chopped into mulch, the entire crop destroyed in a split second.

Shaking in fear and adrenaline, Thomas could barely believe the amount of destruction caused by the rockets. It was incredible! But even with weapons like that, the big guns could ace them in a heartbeat.

''Fire!'' the cannie leader shouted at the top of his lungs. ''Chill them all!''

But only a few blasters on the wall responded to the command, and the big guns did nothing. Turning to scream at the gun crew, Thomas saw the area strewed with bodies, the few slaves still alive strangling the eunuchs with their own chains, one slave setting a sec man on fire with a stolen torch.

A slave revolt! By the first elder, they would pay for that with ten days in the iron cage, slowly cooked alive while being drowned at the same time.

The stormy sky rumbled ominously as two more

rockets cut through the air from the oncoming war
wag, and this time hit the main gate with trip hammer force. The cries of the living shields were instantly cut off, the gate ripped from its row of
hinges, the locking bar snapping apart. In a screech
of dying steel, the portal sagged forward and collapsed to the rocky ground, catching the witch underneath as she frantically tried to get clear. But the
old doomie was too slow, and she was crushed flat
under the tonnage of burning timbers, only a sprinkle of blood hitting the paving stones of the central
court yard.

Exactly like a mouse when you stomped on it
with a boot, Thomas thought in confusion. Almost
exactly the same effect, wasn't that odd.

"They did it," a guard gasped, fumbling to reload his longblaster in the darkness. "They aced
the shields. But you and the other elders told us
nobody would ever do that!"

The cry brought the elder out of shock and back
to reality. "Silence fool, and keep shooting!"
Thomas snarled, backhanding the man across the
face.

The much bigger cannie barely reacted to the
blow, then turned to stare at the elder with eyes
filled with hatred. His hands twitched for a second
on the stock of his blaster. For a moment, Thomas

thought the guard was going to attack, but then the sec man nodded in obedience and turned to shoot at the oncoming wags.

Dark clouds of dust were thrown into the air behind the thundering war machine, then two more appeared from behind the northern dunes, their studded rows of tires chewing paths of destruction through the sandy land. The Blue Devils scattered at the approach of the war wag and reformed to the rear of the machine to snipe from behind its protective bulk.

Then a door was thrown open in the courtyard, admitting a wealth of bright golden light. Scrambling from the armory, a swarm of sec men rushed to the fallen gate and started firing big bore longblasters, the heavy rounds ricocheting off the side of the lumbering war wags to no effect. In return, machine guns rattled from every side of the three enemy vehicles, the heavy rounds hammering the outside of the wall and doing no real damage, but cutting down the men in the gateway.

Mebbe that was it, Thomas thought in delight, shooting at the big machines. The Trader had only those few missiles. The gate may be open, but the elders could win this fight yet!

"Man the cannons!" he shouted through cupped

hands, clouds of blastersmoke drifting over the ville. ''Fire them instantly!''

''Move or you'll feel the lash!'' another elder added, two sec men holding a woman by the arms to keep her standing. Her right leg was gone, the stump tied off with a belt and some rope. ''Kill them all and cut out their beating hearts!''

A rallying cry rose from the sec men and they moved with a will, racing toward the cannons along the eastern wall and hauling moaning bodies of cannies and slaves out of the way to reach the breech. At the third cannon, the sec men had to gun down the slaves as one tried to thrust a burning torch into a barrel of black powder. The man fell, but crawled onward still striving to reach the powder until his dangling chains caught on some wreckage and he was trapped, only feet away from his goal. As the guards converged on him with their knifes, he threw the crackling firebrand, but it missed the open wooden barrel of powder and fell uselessly over the edge of the wall and into the night. The death cries of the slave echoed throughout the chaos of the battle, but only for a moment.

Then a strange, piercing sound rang out from the front war wag and the bikers stopped shooting to cover their faces and turn away. Perplexed by the sight, Thomas saw the rest of the people behind the windows and weapon blisters do the same as the odd horn sounded twice more in warning. Purely on impulse, he copied their posture, daring to peek between the clenched fingers.

Then the outlanders stopped attacking as something cycled up from the roof of the lead transport, a bizarre blaster with cables and thick hoses hissing snowy clouds. As a sharply pitched whine built to painful levels, there was an audible crackle of power. Blue electric sparks flashed between contact points, and the muzzle of the weapon spewed forth a shimmering energy beam of blinding brilliance that swept along the top of the wall setting fire to everything it touched. Bathed in the lethal radiance, the sec men's clothing and hair burst into flames, and they started to scream. Then the beam touched the barrels of black powder and powerful explosions rocked the walls, sending cracks along its entire length.

Thomas could only stare helplessly as the cannons broke free from their shattered moorings and rolled away, crushing more guards and scattering the supplies of powder and shrapnel.

As the beam moved onward, Thomas stood and tried to shoot his longblaster at the energy gun, but his vision was blurred by a moon shadow. Turning, the elder tried to get away, but no matter in which direction he turned his right side was still covered by darkness. It took several moments for him to finally understand he was blind in that eye. By the first elder, that was why the outlanders covered their faces at the sound of the warning horn!

For the first time in his life, cold fear seized the cannie lord and he suddenly had the feeling that they could lose this battle. His mind whirled at the concept. This was Hellsgate, the strongest ville in Texas. Nothing could breach their defenses! Nothing!

But the sizzling beam bathed across the wall again, and Thomas dived behind the palisade, feeling the heat of its passage only feet above. From somewhere came sporadic blasterfire, then the high-pitched cries of people caught in the death ray. Very cautiously, Thomas stole a glance and saw a human torch run blindly by and go right over the wall, the ammo in his gun belt igniting from the heat even as he fell to his death.

They were beaten, Thomas realized, feeling hollow and empty, his courage and strength seeping away like blood from a deep wound. The elders, the cannons, nothing could stop this predark weapon! It was the end of the world. Then the beam winked out, and darkness blew over the ville like a blessing from the storm gods.

Desperately crawling on his belly, Thomas reached a ladder and started down when he noticed a group of elders rush to the burning ruin of the gate armed with four lengths of stovepipe. No wait, it was the bazookas! Yes, that would stop the war machines! Victory, yet!

As the youngest cannies clumsily loaded fat rockets into the rear of the tubes, the oldest men knelt amid the refuse covering the ground and aimed directly for the center of the billowing cloud of smoke filling the hole in their wall. Thomas knew that the moment the lead wag appeared it would be hit with enough explosives to stop a fleet of war wags. The wreckage could block the advance of the other wags, and the fight would be equal once more. With more shields held before them, the cannies could rally behind the bazookas and chase the outlanders into the sea!

Just then, a salvo of rockets stabbed from the smoke and spread wide to hit randomly inside the ville, blowing up the last of the greenhouse and removing the corner of the elders' mansion. The building noisily collapsed as a wave of fire swept through the interior.

Although badly rattled, the elders still fired the bazookas, two of the homemade rockets hitting the remains of the gate, and one arching straight up into

the starry sky. The back blast from that tube ignited
the clothing of a teenager carrying spare rockets.
Wildly shrieking, the lad dropped the ammo seconds before the rockets exploded, blowing him to
pieces. Moments later, the big war wag rolled
through the smoky ruin of the gate, its every
weapon blowing lead and death.

Retreating behind the pile of rubble that had
been the guard tower, the last remaining elders
frantically regrouped and launched the bazookas
once more, bright stilettos of flame stabbing
through the night. The rockets hit the wheeled tank
in a double explosion that deafened Thomas, and
shrapnel sprayed outward from the twin strikes.

Hot pain blossomed in his arm and stomach, but
Thomas didn't duck for cover. Live or die, he just
had to see what was happening. Silence filled the
ville for a heartbeat, as the ever present sea wind
cleared the air. As the smoke thinned, Thomas bit
back a scream as he saw the thick armor of the
mighty war wag barely dented from the impact of
the homemade rockets. If a blister had been hit, the
tide of battle would have changed. But the wags
had rushed too fast, making the elders miss their
one chance and now it was too late.

Belching halos of fire, the gren launchers of the
enemy vehicle started thumping, throwing explo-

sive charges with deadly accuracy. The elders were blown apart, the bazookas smashed into trash. A group of eunuchs struggling to roll a huge barrel of black powder with a sizzling fuse toward the machine were cut to ribbons and the corpses lay there until the charge detonated, blowing them sky-high.

With revving engines, the war wag lurched into motion, moving into the ville and unleashing total destruction. The bikers came next, rolling into doorways with their rapidfires spitting lead, then a second wag entered the ville, but the third parked in the open gateway and aced anybody trying to get out.

Trapped in their own ville like slaves in a pit! The madness threatened to steal his mind, and Thomas scurried for cover behind the fallen barrel of the second cannon as the heavy tires of the war wag rolled close by, cracking the bones of dead guards under their weight. The noise made him sick, and he fought not to vomit.

More rockets from the war wag slammed into the distant guard tower, crumbling the structure like a dried sand castle, and the enemy machine guns never seemed to stop, ruthlessly chilling anybody carrying a blaster. Then from nowhere, a shiny glass bottle arced high in the moonlight to crash onto a war wag, drenching it with sticky fire. Caught near an air vent, a man inside the wag started to scream as he burst into flames and dropped out of the sight behind the window.

The sec men of Hellsgate ville cheered at the death, then instantly stopped as all three of the vehicles shook from a massed volley of missiles and grens. The fiery darts slammed through the predark brick buildings and detonated with nightmarish force, grens falling everywhere. Broken bodies went flying as roiling tongues of orange flame rose from the collapsing structures.

Wiggling deeper into a hole underneath the cannon, Thomas smeared dirt on his face to help hide his presence, pausing as a war wag braked to a halt only yards away. He could feel the heat from the blasters and smell the reek of juice and gunpowder.

Then there came the soft sigh of hydraulics, as a thick door cycled down from the side of the vehicle and a woman strode down the stairs with a large blaster in one hand and a squat box in the other.

Tall and blond, she was pale but well-fed, wearing a battered Stetson hat, a neckerchief around her throat dangling down the front to hide her sweaty cleavage. A tooled gun belt rode snug on her belled hips, a boxy rapidfire was slung over a shoulder and a bandolier of grens was strapped across her chest.

Standing with her back to the hidden man, the blonde holstered the weapon and started to talk into a green box, a shiny silver stick rising from the top reflecting the beams of the headlights.

"Confirmed, the eastern guns are down. Concentrate on the cliff," she said, walking through the destruction, but always keeping her back to the war wag for safety.

From across the courtyard, a group of the motorcycles raced by going in that direction, bounding over the bodies and rubble with frightening speed.

Crouching low in the dirt, Thomas couldn't believe it. They obeyed as if hearing her commands. Obviously the box somehow relayed her voice to the bikers. Could this be their leader? Thomas thought in growing amazement. Was this the legendary Trader? Praise be to the storm gods and the first elder for delivering the enemy into his waiting hands. With her as a hostage, the battle would be over.

Sliding the .38 Colt from his belt, Thomas eased back the hammer, covering it with his other hand to muffle the click until it locked into position. But there had to have been some noise, because the blonde started to turn his way, with a blaster in hand. No time to try for a capture, he would have to chill her on the spot. So be it! Quickly raising the blaster, Thomas aimed for her belly and a booming report sounded.

Gushing blood from the ragged stump of its neck, the headless body of Elder Thomas flopped lifeless to the ground, the Colt discharging a single shot as it tumbled over the paving stones to land near Kate's combat boots. She turned to see Roberto standing in the doorway of War Wag One, a smoking shotgun in his good hand.

"Thanks," Kate said, holstering her piece. "Owe ya."

"Always got your six, Chief," Roberto answered, the double barrels of his sawed-off sweeping the area for any new targets.

"Okay, I want people over at the holding pits to start freeing the slaves," she said into the radio, the command repeated from the loudspeakers set in the hull of War Wag One and echoing across the mounting turmoil of the smashed ville.

"They'll want revenge," Roberto said, breaking open the sawed-off and dropping the spent cartridge to slip in a fresh one. He jerked it upward and the breech closed with a solid snap. "Not only on their former masters, but any of their fellow slaves who worked for the cannies. Could get damn messy.''

Her face a mask of controlled hate, Kate looked over the battleground, the dead and the dying mixed with the rubble and refuse.

"Let them," she said in a voice of icy granite. "What's the status of the laser?"

"We're almost out of fuel for the reaction chamber," Roberto reported. "Plus, a few more minutes of use and the main lens would have cracked. It's just not designed for this kind of fighting.''

"But it did the job. Give Eric my thanks. The man works miracles.''

Just then, a ricochet zinged off the armored prow of the wag only inches from the woman. Instantly, Roberto fired his shotgun at the distant sniper, and Kate dropped the radio to draw the Ingram and hosed a long burst from the rapidfire. Fighting to clear a jam from his bolt action, the coldheart on the rooftop got stitched across the chest by the 9 mm Parabellum rounds and fell away spraying bright blood.

Snapping the sawed-off shut, Roberto grunted at the sight. "Good shot," he said, stepping closer. "Bastard was out of my range.''

"Can't control a rapidfire with one hand," Kate said, bending over to retrieve the radio. "All gunners, secure this courtyard! I want every roof cleaned of sec men, and I mean right fucking now!''

Every gunner inside the three armored transports did as requested and the crisscrossing barrage of .50-caliber rounds from the vented machine guns tore the roofs apart, shattering the red tiles and sending two more snipers to the last train west.

''Roofs are secured,'' a voice reported crisply over the radio.

''Good,'' she answered. ''Jeffers, Daniels, Dink, start a recce of the buildings and watch for boobies. The locals are fond of traps. Be safe and shoot everybody you find.''

''All of them?'' the voice asked, startled.

''Confirmed,'' Kate growled. ''If they ain't in chains, put lead in their head!''

''Will do, Chief!'' The radio crackled, even the short distance affected by the rads in the sea.

''Knives are cheaper,'' Roberto stated, staying close to the woman, the sawed-off held level at his waist with both hands.

She shrugged in reply. ''Fuck it. We got the ammo. Besides, I'll damn well not lose another one of our people cleaning out this viper's nest,'' Kate shot back furiously. ''Ten rounds now will save us a hundred in the future.''

There was a scrambling motion at the base of a second guard tower, and from the gaping doorway stumbled a bloody man in robes with both hands raised. Roberto fired before Kate could even register the fact, and as he fell the cannie elder was then torn apart by crisscrossing blasterfire from a dozen directions.

"Standard divvy among the dead?" Roberto asked, tightening his lips into what could have been a grin as he reloaded again. The 12-gauge sawed-off did a nuking amount of damage, but he was always shoving in shells. Too bad there wasn't such a thing as a clip fed shotgun. Wouldn't that be a pisser?

"Not this time," the woman answered. "We turn the entire contents of the ville over to the slaves. They earned it in ways we don't want to think about. Then we divvy half of our food with them, too. Toss everything found in the kitchens and storehouses into the sea. It's all dirty. Who knows what they used to bake the bread, or fried the fish in."

Mebbe human fat, Roberto comprehended, going queasy. Dark night, he never would have thought about that. "Good call, Chief," he stated, swallowing hard. "I'll see it done personally. But we're still taking shine and fuel, right?"

Removing her hat, Kate fanned away the smoke from the burning buildings, the fumes carried a reek of burning flesh that made her cringe. ''Damn straight, all we can carry,'' the woman added without any trace of humor. ''From here we can finally risk a journey to the north.''

Roberto frowned. By that, she meant across the Great Salt. A hellzone considered by many to be the bleeding ass of the Deathlands with its rad storms, quicksand, tornados, muties and worst of all, the Scorpion God.

Machine-gun fire sounded from somewhere in the ville, ending with a wailing scream, followed by cheers. Sounded like the slaves were free and already equalling some old scores.

''Be a mighty good day when we ace the Scorpion,'' Roberto said grimly. ''A lot of debts to be paid there, too.''

''More than you know,'' Kate muttered, tucking her hat back on her head.

Chapter Eight

Sucking on a dry piece of jerky, Krysty was taking her turn behind the wheel as dawn began to lighten the eastern sky behind the wag. Straight ahead, the bright headlights of the old wag bounced wildly with every irregularity of the ground, and she was forced to slow to a mere crawl to keep from crashing into the occasional hole or rock. She hoped nothing attacked the wag, because at this miserable speed, they couldn't outrun a fat baron.

When Ryan was driving the wag, at first it had seemed they were following a predark road buried beneath the salt. But soon it became obvious that this was merely a wash, the vestigial remains of a dried river that snaked through the desolate landscape. Aside from the shallow depression of the river, the land was flat and featureless without even mountains on the horizon, the largest dune of sandy salt only a few feet in height. It was as if the world had been sandpapered smooth.

No, it was sandblasted smooth, Krysty corrected,

by the bombs of skydark. Whatever had once been here had to have been mighty important in the old days for it to receive such a concentrated bombing. Some sort of military base, or factory town. Had to have been big.

Sitting in the passenger side of the cab, Dean scowled alertly at the endless vista of dried salt with open hostility, J.B.'s scattergun expertly cradled in his hands. The boy carried a harmonica in his shirt pocket, a gift from long ago, and he was slowly getting fairly good on the instrument. But for some reason he felt the music would have been inappropriate. Dean found that he was sometimes a little nervous when it was just him and Krysty, kind of as if he were a small kid being watched over by a parent, instead of a young man of nearly thirteen years standing guard. The weirdly mixed feelings confused the hell out of the boy. Mildred told him it was normal for him to feel that way. He was in transition from childhood to adulthood. Adolescence, it was called. Dean wished it would just pass him by.

Buried under a pile of blankets, the rest of the companions were sleeping in the rear of the vehicle, huddled in a group to share body heat and help fight off the nighttime chill. It had to have been dawn when they arrived at the redoubt, but as they escaped from the installation, the warmth quickly faded from the air and the desert turned deeply cold. Krysty and Dean had the heater under the dashboard to keep them comfortable, but the rest simply had to cope as best they could.

As the sun slowly ascended, it burned away the blanket of polluted clouds and filled the desert with the rosy gleam of predawn, turning everything delicate shades of pinks. Soon the biting chill was no longer whistling into the cab from around the mismatched doors, and the woman turned off the heater to save juice. Once long ago, in an Alaskan redoubt, Krysty had studied a map of the old world. This could be the middle of the Australian desert, literally thousands of miles away from anything. Every drop of fuel needed to be saved until the companions had a better idea of where they were headed.

Slow miles passed as Krysty continued rolling on through the brightening desert. As they jounced through a shallow crack in the riverbed, the land gently rose into a swell and Krysty realized she was no longer in the wash. Maybe the predark river had turned at some point, or went underground, there was no way of telling. But now the wag was rolling across the desert floor, the heavy tires crunching steadily on the crusty salt ground. She debated trying to backtrack and find the wash once more, but decided to stay on course. J.B. had placed his compass on the dashboard, and the needle was still pointing due west.

"Damn, there's nothing in sight for miles," Dean said, leaning out the window. "Mebbe we should stop and take a rest. Let J.B. find out where we are, and such."

"I was thinking the same thing myself," Krysty replied, grinding gears. "Also, the engine has been starting to run hot. Might be something wrong."

"Might be low on water," he suggested, glancing at the gauge.

"Could be," she agreed, easing the speed of the rattling wag to the merest crawl. "But it's best to make sure."

Slowing to an easy halt, Krysty turned off the engine and waited while the machine rattled to a complete stop before setting the parking brake. Warily, the two companions checked the area around them before leaving the cab. Walking across the ground, their combat boots steadily crunched on the crust of dried salt.

"Well, one good thing about this stuff," Dean muttered, shifting his grip on the scattergun. "At least nobody can sneak in close without being heard."

"That's for damn sure," Krysty agreed, a hand on her own blaster. "Unless it was flying, but I don't see anything around for a screamwing, or skeeter, to eat."

The boy nodded in agreement, but kept a closer watch on the open sky for any signs of movement. Aside from the departing toxic clouds, the air was a clear azure blue and thoroughly empty.

Reaching the rear, Dean stood guard with the shotgun while Krysty untied the lacings holding the canvas flaps shut and threw one aside admitting the morning sunlight into the back of the wag. Amid the water barrels, fuel cans and piles of backpacks, there was a lumpy mound of mixed blankets with a few boots sticking out from underneath.

"Good morning!" Krysty called, shaking the nearest boot. "Rise and shine."

The mound of blankets stopped snoring and started to break apart under her urgings.

"Already awake. Been for a while," Ryan said from the shadows in the corner, and the man stepped closer into the light. Mildred had been afraid that his head wound might be serious to make him slip into a coma if he went to sleep too soon, so the one-eyed man reluctantly decided to back her call and stayed up the whole night. Much as he wanted some sack time, Ryan was bastard sure he didn't want it to last forever. Head wounds chilled in a way no other wound did.

"You look like hell, lover," the redhead said to the disheveled man.

He grunted at that and stiffly climbed down from the rear of the wag onto the hard ground. Loose white sand was blowing across the land, and Ryan again tasted salt in the air. This was no desert, but an ocean. Some of the nukes during skydark missed their coastal targets and hit the sea bottoms, throwing up boiling tidal waves of salt water dozens of miles across the mainland, sometimes hundreds of miles. Over the years the salt mud dried into a thick crust over the once living soil, forming hard flat deserts.

"Makes the Washington Hole seem almost like Eden," J.B. said, adjusting his wire-rimmed glasses as the creeping dawn began to fill the rear of the wag, warming it noticeably.

Soft thunder peeled in the shifting clouds, sounding like distant artillery as J.B. slapped his fedora into shape and tucked it on the back of his head. At least they wouldn't have to worry about acid rain for a while. That was something good, at least.

"Broke down?" Jak asked, appearing from under a pile of blankets. The rosy tint of dawn was already fading to become the clear hard light of daytime.

"Nope, but the engine is running a little hot," Krysty replied. "We thought it best to stop, give it a rest."

"And make breakfast," Dean added.

"Better check hoses first," Jak mumbled, holstering the blaster and shuffling forward to jump off the end of the wag. His boots sank inches deep into the salty sand. He hated the desert and longed for a smell of a proper bayou again.

Shoving away the blankets, Doc gave a bone-cracking yawn and ran stiff fingers through his silver hair.

"What a desolate location," he rumbled, exiting the vehicle to blink at the reflected dawn. "We could be in the middle of the Sahara or the Gobi desert for all we know."

"Could be the Painted Desert of New Mexico," Krysty added. "Sure isn't Colorado or Ohio."

Stretching to work off the fog of sleep, Ryan became alert at that remark. Ohio was neutral territory, but there were a bastard lot of folks who wanted their hides in New Mex. That was the very heart of the Deathlands.

"Well, I'll have us fixed in a few minutes," J.B. stated, pulling the minisextant from his jacket pocket and looking through it to sweep the sky until locating the sun.

"I'll make coffee, if somebody starts a fire," Mildred offered, fighting off a yawn. She spent the night spooning with John, but any trace of a romantic interlude had been neutralized by the close presence of the rest of the companions also huddled under the blankets.

"No wood for a fire," Dean said, gesturing around them. "Nothing."

"Damn, you're right," the physician grumbled unhappily. "Guess it'll be an MRE of meat loaf for breakfast, and cold coffee."

"We've had worse," Krysty commented, opening her backpack to pull out a tin mess kit. "Better than boiled boot."

Mildred made a face. That had been a hell of a meal. The closest they had ever come to starving to death.

"Be right back," Ryan announced, drawing his blaster. Stepping behind the largest dune for a few minutes, the man soon returned zipping up his fatigues.

"Got our position yet, J.B.?" he growled.

"Not just yet. Too many clouds in the way," the Armorer answered, squinting through the sextant. As carefully as possible, he centered the unobstructed sun in the lens, balancing the horizon against the half mirror inside the optical device. This gave him the reading and writing down the numbers, he did a few calculations and checked the plastic map from his backpack.

"We're back in Texas," J.B. said, lowering the sextant. "About six hundred miles away from that gateway at the Grandee."

"Good enough," Ryan said, rubbing his unshaven jaw. The gateway wasn't a redoubt, just a stripped down mat-trans chamber, but it would take them to a redoubt. If it still worked.

"Six hundred miles is a mighty long way." Krysty sighed, loosening her collar. "Especially in this heat." Her bearskin coat was hanging from a bolt in the back of the wag, a little extra cover in case the others needed it during the cold night. Now it seemed like she wouldn't be needing it during the day, either. Already she could tell it was going to be a scorcher. Good thing they had a lot of water, even if it was slightly radioactive.

Just then, a trio of tiny red scorpions scurried out from under a rock, closely followed by a much larger black scorpion. The black arachnid grabbed a red one and started tearing it apart on the spot, stuffing the juicy gobbets into his mouth. The other two made good their escape under another rock, while the third was being eaten alive.

A scratching sound seemed to fill the air. The companions pulled their blasters and glanced around. But aside from the scorpions battling each other, there was nothing in sight anywhere.

"Could be the wind," Dean said hesitantly, as if not believing the possibility himself. The wind in the Deathlands often played tricks, making faraway things sound right behind you, sometimes even making sand seem to be splashing pools of water. Back at Nicolas Brody's school, he had heard of people lost in the desert going feeb from the wind and the heat.

"Something is wrong here," Krysty said, her hair flexing and curling. "Do you think we could be standing on a..."

Then the sound came again with a haunting familiarity, and icy-cold adrenaline flooded Dean's body as he saw the surface of the desert moving like a low wave in the water from something underneath the salty crust. Then the crystalline sheath cracked and a featureless head appeared with pinchers snapping.

"Bugs!" Dean shouted, kneeling to fire the shotgun across the swarm, as the compacted salt broke apart and out rushed a carpet of millipedes flowing their way like a river of death.

A dozen millipedes were blown away from the barrage of fléchette rounds, but the rest just kept coming as unstoppable as the dawn around them. The muties had to have been following the wag since it left the redoubt. Either that or the desert was infested with them. Bad news either way.

''Get the wag moving!'' Ryan ordered, squinting against the wash of daylight behind the bugs even while triggering his softly chugging SIG-Sauer. Fireblast, the damn things couldn't have chosen a better time to attack! With the light in their eyes it was triple-hard to aim, and once the insects were among the companions they would be reduced to scraps in a few minutes.

The closest to the cab, Krysty scrambled inside the wag and started to crank the engine. Meanwhile, the rest of the companions threw down a wall of lead, salt dust mixing with black blood as the insects died, but kept on coming nonetheless, as mindless as a storm. Rushing to the back of the wag, Ryan grabbed a Molotov from the wooden box, lit the rag fuse and smashed the bomb directly in front of the bugs, the pool of fire momentarily slowing their advance.

Shoving the Uzi into Mildred's hands, J.B. frantically rummaged in his munitions bag and pulled out an implo gren. Setting the release, he pulled the ring and threw the gren hard toward the bugs clustered around the Molotov puddle. The millipedes scattered momentarily as the sphere hit and bounced a few times to finally land behind the insects.

"Missed!" Jak roared, his Colt blowing fire.

"Like hell I did!" J.B. shouted, grabbing the canvas side of the wag and bracing himself. "Hold on!"

Suddenly, there was a brilliant flash of searing blue light and a muted roar that became a powerful rush of air that almost pulled the companions off their feet in a whirlwind of loose salt as the predark device created a microsecond well of supercondensed gravity. Then the field was gone with only a steaming hole to mark the spot.

The implosion had aced only a handful of the bugs, but dozens more had been pulled backward from the vacuum of the reverse blast, and were scrambling about madly in the smooth glass crater totally confused. Precious time had been bought, with only a few of the muties still coming, pinchers snapping. But more were heading their way again with every tick of the clock.

On the ground, the black scorpion dropped its

partially finished meal and raced away for safety under a rock.

"Use another!" Dean cried, hammering the bugs with his Browning. "Use them all!"

"Too close! Get off the ground!" Ryan ordered, scrambling backward into the rear of the wag, his blaster throwing hot lead. A millipede squealed as a score of legs were ripped off its belly by the 9 mm slug, but it continued to move, bleeding badly but very much alive.

Throwing a couple more Molotovs into the fire of the first one to spread the blaze, Doc and Jak then shoved Mildred into the wag and jumped in after her, with Dean close behind. Taking back the exhausted Uzi from the furious physician, J.B. fed it a fresh magazine from his munitions bag and stitched a line across the foremost wave of bugs. But exactly as before in the redoubt, the wounded kept coming until they died.

The wag vibrated, the exhaust pipe belching smoke as Krysty fought to get the stubborn diesel to turn over. What could be wrong with the thing? Hellfire, it was still warm from before, power read good on the dashboard and she knew there was plenty of fuel. Mebbe the mix was too rich? Pumping the gas pedal and pulling the choke all the way out instead of in, Krysty hit the starter and the engine briefly sputtered, paused as if stalling, then surged into life.

Moments later, the millipedes rushed underneath the wag, biting at the tires, the dead scorpion and the dropped wrapper from an unconsumed MRE pack. Several started to crawl up the sides of the wag, and Krysty used her Smith & Wesson to blow off a twitching head that appeared at the open passenger-side window.

"Come on, get this heap moving!" Ryan bellowed, exchanging clips.

The noise of the bugs was getting deafening loud, and he wasn't sure the woman had heard him when the wag started rolling forward, the bugs cracking like popcorn beneath the wide tires.

But by now the millipedes were swarming over the vehicle, the companions firing in every direction.

Barely reloading in time, Dean fired as a millipede crawled into view around the side of the awning. Headless, the bug stayed on the material, pumping blood from its neck until Mildred kicked the legs loose and it fell away.

"Son of a bitch little bastards!" Mildred cursed in revulsion. God, she hated bugs!

Holding his bare sword in a tight grip, Doc dropped the hammer on the LeMat as he spotted

a shape moving on top of the canvas sheet covering
the rear of the wag. A patch of material the size a
fist was torn away, and the corpse fell away, but
another took its place.

"Haste is our salvation, madam!" the scholar
told her, yanking back the big hammer on his
weapon, searching for a clear target. A movement
on the floor almost made the man shoot, until he
realized it was an implo gren that had fallen out of
J.B.'s munitions bag. The thought of what would
have happened if he had shot the predark bomb
made his blood run cold. That had been a close
call! Too close.

Throwing the engine into high gear, Krysty tried
to build some speed as she gamely fought to maintain control of the shuddering wag across the uneven ground. Every loose item in the vehicle was
shaking and jumping, and as the wag went through
a jagged ravine a fuel can went over the tailgate,
followed by a blanket and a shovel. Holding on for
dear life, the companions tried to keep fighting, but
the gyrations were making it impossible to stay on
their feet, much less hit what they were aiming at.
Unfortunately, the bouncing and crashing seemed
to have no effect on the multilegged bugs.

"Go slower!" J.B. ordered, dropping a magazine
for the Uzi.

The Gold Eagle Reader Service™ — Here's how it works:

Accepting your 2 free books and gift places you under no obligation to buy anything. You may keep the books and gift and return the shipping statement marked "cancel." If you do not cancel, about a month later we'll send you 6 additional books and bill you just $29.94* — that's a saving of 10% off the cover price of all 6 books! And there's no extra charge for shipping! You may cancel at any time, but if you choose to continue, every other month we'll send you 6 more books, which you may either purchase at the discount price or return to us and cancel your subscription.

*Terms and prices subject to change without notice. Sales tax applicable in N.Y. Canadian residents will be charged applicable provincial taxes and GST. Credit or Debit balances in a customer's account(s) may be offset by any other outstanding balance owed by or to the customer.

If offer card is missing write to: Gold Eagle Reader Service, 3010 Walden Ave., P.O. Box 1867, Buffalo NY 14240-1867

NO POSTAGE
NECESSARY
IF MAILED
IN THE
UNITED STATES

BUSINESS REPLY MAIL
FIRST-CLASS MAIL   PERMIT NO. 717-003   BUFFALO, NY

POSTAGE WILL BE PAID BY ADDRESSEE

GOLD EAGLE READER SERVICE
3010 WALDEN AVE
PO BOX 1867
BUFFALO NY 14240-9952

Get FREE BOOKS and a FREE GIFT when you play the...

LAS VEGAS

GAME

Just scratch off the gold box with a coin. Then check below to see the gifts you get!

YES! I have scratched off the gold Box. Please send me my **2 FREE BOOKS** and **gift for which I qualify.** I understand that I am under no obligation to purchase any books as explained on the back of this card.

▲ DETACH AND MAIL CARD TODAY! ▲

366 ADL DRSL

166 ADL DRSK
(MB-03/03)

FIRST NAME

LAST NAME

ADDRESS

APT.#

CITY

STATE / PROV.

ZIP / POSTAL CODE

7	7	7	Worth TWO FREE BOOKS plus a BONUS Mystery Gift!
			Worth TWO FREE BOOKS!
			TRY AGAIN!

Offer limited to one per household and not valid to current Gold Eagle® subscribers. All orders subject to approval.

"Faster!" Dean yelled, over his banging 9 mm Hi-Power.

"Mother Gaia!" Krysty cursed, and the wag slammed down and then brutally up again, tilting so far to the right that it almost flipped over sideways before violently righting itself.

With the jolt, bugs and people went tumbling about. Then with a ripping sound, the ropes holding the big water barrel tore apart and it crashed to the floor. The lid popped off and out gushed the nuke water, washing away ammo clips, MRE packs, spent brass and a couple of dead bugs. One large millipede stubbornly stuck to the corrugated floor until Jak shoved his blaster between the dripping wet pinchers and blew out the rear of its ugly head.

Nearly slipping on the wet metal floor, Ryan couldn't understand where the bugs kept coming from. The main swarm was far behind, which only left... Fireblast! He should have realized that sooner. Had to be dizzy from that earlier knock to the head.

Stumbling across the jumbled supplies, Ryan found the wooden box of Molotovs and stuffed two into his shirt. He wanted more, but that was all he could carry. Holding on to the ribs that supported the awning, he made it to the front of the wag and slashed open the side of the canvas with a stroke of his panga.

"Slow down when I tell you!" Ryan shouted through the passenger-side window.

"I'll be ready!" Krysty replied, both hands white from their death grip on the shaking steering wheel. Her blaster was in its holster even though a millipede clinging to the outside of the driver's-side gave her an unobstructed view of the grinding fangs in its segmented mouth. If she removed a hand from the wheel to shoot it, the wag would crash at its current speed, so she could do nothing but pray that the glass was strong enough for a little while longer.

Holstering his blaster, Ryan held on to the rib while he used a butane lighter to ignite the rag fuse. "Now," he cried, throwing the bottle forward.

Not daring to use the brakes, Krysty took her foot off the gas and downshifted to try to control the deceleration.

Immediately, the wag sped forward and the Molotov hit the hard desert salt to explode into a pool of fire.

Seconds later the slowing wag drove through the middle of the flames, letting them play across the bottom of the chassis. Childlike wails of pain rewarded the tactic, and a rain of burning bugs fell to the ground in their wake.

As Ryan threw the next bottle, Jak passed him another Molotov, and the companions did it again and again until there was only silence from below.

"Should be clear by now," J.B. said, both legs splayed as he rocked to the motion of the lolling wag. At the lower speeds, the Armorer had no trouble staying on his feet.

"We're not quite done," Ryan growled, grabbing hold of the tubular steel frame supporting the sideview mirror, and swinging into the cab to land on the seat near Krysty.

With both hands tight on the wheel, the redhead leaned far back and he fired the SIG-Sauer, the soft chug lost in the explosion of shattered glass as the last millipede was blown away.

"Now it's finished," he said, brushing the ejected brass and glass pebbles off her clothing. "You okay?"

"Been better," Krysty muttered, dropping the speed of the wag even more. The gauges were still reading hot, and she could only hope the engine hadn't been damaged in the firefight.

Tick by tick, the seconds slowly passed until the companions were a mile away from the battle zone, and they started to relax when a strong stink filled the wag.

"It's coming from under the hood," Ryan said with a frown, sniffing the rank cab air. Even with the windows open, it smelled like a roasting boot in here.

"Could be an aced bug frying on the manifold," Krysty replied, furrowing her brow in concern. "Should we stop and check?"

"No," Ryan decided. "Keep going. The farther we get from those bugs, the better."

Steering around a small crater in the salt, Krysty started to agree when the engine went completely silent and every gauge in the dashboard swung their needles high into the red danger zone.

Chapter Nine

Throwing the gearshift into neutral, Krysty quickly killed the ignition and let the wag coast along until braking to a full stop in the lee of a small dune.

"Get sharp, people!" Ryan commanded. "Those things could be hot on our ass." Climbing down from the cab, he checked the clip in his blaster. Four rounds remained, and he had two more loaded clips.

Wearily, the rest of companions climbed off the big vehicle and spread out behind it with their blasters at the ready. However, they knew there were no more Molotovs, and only three implo grens remained. A couple had been lost in the tumultuous fight through the salt flats, and their ammo reserves were low.

If the bugs returned, the implo grens were the first line of defense, then blasters, and after that, they would be reduced to knives and running.

After checking under the chassis for any unwanted passengers, Ryan, Krysty and J.B. went to the front of the wag, and Ryan flipped up the hood with the others covering him in case a bug was waiting inside. But the engine was clean of insects, only some scattered bits of fibrous black material and thick streamers of oily smoke.

"Burned through a fan belt," J.B. said, lifting a piece for inspection, then dropping it and blowing on his singed fingers. "Two of them, in fact. Look down there."

Leaning on the nuke battery, Ryan could see the damage, and agreed it wasn't from the Molotovs. Just old belts that shredded under the strain. "It was running hot before the bugs appeared," he added. "This wag is dead."

"Can we fix it?" Krysty asked, looking between the two men. "Cobble something together with our belts, or rope, or something?"

"Mebbe," Ryan replied sullenly, the lack of sleep wearing on his nerves. He felt constantly angry, and the throbbing of the gash on his forehead was affecting his judgment. "Hell, I don't know. All our boots laces tied together wouldn't take the strain. We could buckle some belts together, but they wouldn't fit. Too wide."

"And what rope we have is too thick," she added. "We could loosen the weave, but that could take a hell of a lot of time."

"And the longer we sit still, the closer they get."

"Well, we're sure as hell not going to walk six hundred miles."

"Might have to."

"And mebbe not. Now it could just be this heat, but I got a crazy idea," J.B. said slowly, tilting back his fedora. "Might work, might not, but I'll need a really sharp blade, the best we got."

"Mildred, bring a scalpel!" Ryan called, motioning the woman over.

"To fix a wag?" the physician replied, coming their way.

"What are you planning to do?"

"J.B. has a plan," Krysty replied, stepping back to give the others some more space to work.

Reaching into her satchel, Mildred pulled out a small canvas bundle. The scalpel was really only an box-cutter blade from a high-school art department, but it was the sharpest, thinnest blade they owned. "Whatever you're planning is going to ruin the edge," Mildred stated, passing over the blade. Even though the blade was segmented, every portion was precious.

"Can't be helped, Millie," J.B. said, starting to loosen a retaining bolt with a big crescent wrench. After a few moments, Mildred could see what he was planning to do, and bent over the engine to lend a hand where she could, her slim fingers reaching deeper into the complex machine than his muscular hands.

"Okay, we're not going anywhere for a while," Ryan stated, moving away so he wouldn't block their light. The dune was throwing a much needed shadow across the hot vehicle, cutting the harsh sunlight to a tolerable level. "We better get hard in case they come back. We're going to need a lookout, and you're the lightest, Dean, so up you go, son."

"Check!" the boy cried resolutely. Grabbing hold of the exposed ribs of the tattered awning, Dean pulled himself onto the roof of the wag. Balanced precariously on the riddled canvas, the boy shaded his face with a hand to try to see into the eastern light if the bugs were still in pursuit.

"No sign of them!" Dean called down.

"Yet," Doc added, removing his sword from its ebony stick and plunging the steel into the salty ground nearby for fast access.

With a breeze spreading his frock coat like dark wings, the scholar expertly purged the spent chambers of his LeMat and started the laborious process of reloading the black-powder weapon. Three chambers were still charged, but Doc never liked to have such a thin defense between himself and the world. Time and time again, the universe had proved it wasn't on his side, and Doc never planned on giving it an even break.

Whistling to get Dean's attention, J.B. tossed up his Navy longeyes and the boy made the catch. Extending the telescope to its full length, Dean scanned the simmering desert.

"Let us know if anything comes this way," Ryan directed, thumbing another round into the clip to finish the reload, then returning it into the grip of the SIG-Sauer.

"Even if it's just a whirlwind or a tumbleweed," he added grimly. "They got the drop on us last time from underground, so stay alert."

"Gotcha," Dean answered, the brass length of the telescope held in both hands for a steady view.

"Use fuel cans," Jak said from the rear of the wag, passing down a container. "Set perimeter. Bugs come, we shoot."

"A firewall," Krysty grunted. "Best we can do, I'm afraid. Here, pass one over."

Holstering their blasters, Krysty and Doc started to help the others haul the cans of fuel into the desert, placing them fifty feet away and about ten feet apart. Hopefully, the cans were far enough apart that shooting one wouldn't start a chain reaction and ace the companions along with the millipedes. But there was no way to test it, so they simply had to depend on a best guess.

"Still clear," Dean asked hesitantly. "Just some dust blowing to the west." Or was it dust? Hmm, the boy wasn't really sure. Could that have been smoke? He trained the longeyes in that direction again, but whatever it had been was gone now, dissipated by the sluggish currents rising off the warming plain of hard salt. Then he caught it again, high in the sky.

"Buzzards," Dean announced. "About a mile to the east."

In the process of checking his backpack for additional loose rounds, Ryan spun at that. "Must be feeding on the dead bugs," he said, holstering the blaster and sliding the Steyr SSG-70 longblaster off his shoulder. "That's a break for us."

"How?" Krysty asked, loosening her shirt. Already she was perspiring badly. Maybe it was the presence of the salt, but this was much worse than any desert she had traveled before. Breathing was becoming difficult.

"We give them something else to eat instead of us," Ryan said, working the bolt on the weapon and adjusting the focus on the scope. Taking careful aim, the man squeezed off a shot, and a second later there was an explosion of feathers in the distance and a buzzard plummeted from the sky.

"One bird won't stop them," Krysty said, mopping the sweat off her brow. "But the blood might attract other scavengers, scorpions, lizards, maybe even a few screamwings."

"Sure hope not," Jak muttered, rubbing an old scar. Damn muties moved faster than arrows and would attack anything with a ferocity unequaled in the animal kingdom.

"And there they are," Ryan said pointing as two more buzzards began to circle the fresh kill. Raising the longblaster, he fired twice more in rapid succession and both of the birds fell dead.

"That'll keep them off our back for a while," Krysty said in grim satisfaction. "But not for very long."

"No," Ryan admitted honestly, "not for long."

Tense minutes passed as the companions stood guard, watching the ground under their boots for any suspicious activity, while Mildred and J.B. worked diligently on the engine. Their muttered curses from the front of the wag gave no clear indication of how well the job was progressing.

Slowly rising high overhead, the blazing sun filled the desert with tangible waves of heat until a thickening haze of reflected illumination formed over the crystalline landscape. Loosening their clothing, and tying handkerchiefs around their necks to save the sweat, the companions kept the conversation to a minimum, and tried to remember to breathe through their nose and save irreplaceable moisture. However, the brutal combination of the rising temperatures and the salted dust seemed to be leeching the fluids from their flesh. But the companions knew survival tactics for this kind of territory. Sucking pebbles helped folks keep their mouths shut and conserved moisture. Plus, Mildred had long ago taught them to take some grease from the wheel bearings and smear it over lips. That stopped chapping and made a person feel less thirsty. The tricks helped a lot, but if the wag couldn't be repaired, then the loss of the water barrel was going to prove a serious problem. Quite possibly, a matter of life and death. Aside from what little remained in the canteens, the companions were out of water and standing in the middle of a salt desert.

They heard the yowl of a big cat, possibly a cougar or mountain lion, and then a screech unlike anything they had heard before.

''The other predators have arrived,'' Krysty commented calmly. ''Too bad the cat didn't pass this way. We could have sliced its skin into rawhide to fix the wag.''

Adjusting his eye patch, Ryan growled, "The problem with rawhide is that it can get too tight, shrinking so much the bearings burn out and junk the engine permanently."

Draping a cut piece of blanket over his head as protection from the direct sunlight, Dean nodded at his father's words as if filing the information away.

"Okay, I think we got it," J.B. announced, closing the hood. "At least for now."

"Here's hoping," Mildred added.

Careful of touching the metal handle on the door with her bare skin, the woman climbed into the cab, set the choke and tried the ignition. Incredibly, the diesel started at once without the slightest hesitation.

"All right, turn it off!" Ryan shouted, turning his back to the sun. "Let's grab those fuel cans and get moving while we still can!"

"What you do?" Jak asked curiously, placing socks on his hands before lifting two of the steel fuel cans.

Shrugging out of his leather jacket, J.B. tossed it into the front of the cab and went to help reclaim the containers. Damn, it was hot! "Did the only thing we could," he said, carefully placing his fingerless leather gloves around the handles of a couple of cans. "I split a fan belt in half lengthwise and used it for both pulleys."

"That going to work?" Dean asked. "Doesn't sound very strong."

"It isn't," Ryan said, grabbing four cans and striding to the back of the wag. "So we have to go bastard slow and be a hell of a lot more careful. But it got us running again."

Placing the cans roughly on the floor, Ryan went for more as Mildred pulled them away from the edge and started lashing them to the ribs with some spare rope.

"Can we do that again with another belt if one of these breaks?" Dean asked, panting from the effort of carrying two cans. They weighed a ton, but the boy was determined to always do his full share of the work.

"Nothing left to split," Ryan stated, slowing his pace so the boy could keep abreast. "If these snap, we start walking."

Once the wag was loaded again, the companions piled into the rear, with Ryan behind the wheel and J.B. riding shotgun in the passenger seat. Ryan gently tried the ignition and the diesel easily started. Slipping the transmission into a low gear, he drove away slowly, babying the overheated engine.

As THE STRUGGLING wag headed for the horizon, swaddled figures rose from the ground like masked ghosts. They watched the vehicle for a brief while, then slipped back down into the earth as nothing truly human could, and were gone from sight.

KEEPING A CAREFUL watch on the dashboard gauges, Ryan drove the wag onward through the stifling heat. With the temperature rising every hour, even shielded by the roof of the vehicle, the companions had to apply more of the grease to their lips. But the heat was becoming oppressive, and the conversations lagged, everybody simply concentrating on breathing and trying not to exert themselves too much. There were a few scattered clouds in the blazing sky, small and darkly colored, but any shade they cast was nowhere near the companions and their tantalizing presence only seemed to make their sweating more unbearable.

Over the long miles, the hard-packed salt became mixed with golden sand, more and more windswept dunes rising as they departed the dead zone and the land became a simple desert. Finding a stand of cactus, Ryan slowed the wag to a mere crawl and Krysty got out of the back to use Doc's sword to safely hack off chunks of the plant, spearing the pieces and bringing them back to the wag. Eagerly, the companions used their knives to cut off the thick barbed thorns and cut the cactus open to munch on the moist pulp inside.

"Kind of bitter," Dean said unhappily, his face smeared with the sticky juice.

"Indeed, yet ambrosia compared to some of the things we have eaten to stay alive, lad," Doc rumbled, chewing each mouthful slowly before forcing a swallow. "Actually, it is rather similar to pickled turnip, albeit a tad more spongy."

"That's from being so close to the salt lands," Mildred said, wiping her mouth, but then added, "Turnip?"

Lowering his pale green slice, Doc smiled, flashing his oddly perfect teeth. "Most assuredly, dear lady. My mother considered it a necessary tonic for good health."

"Ate a lot of it as a kid?"

"Not willing, no."

It was noon when the dropping fuel gauge forced the companions to stop in the delicious shade of a large dune. Ryan took advantage of the break to get out of the broiling vehicle to refuel the wag even though it wasn't his turn to do the job. J.B. did the same, taking on the disagreeable task of pouring a few pints of saved urine into the boiling radiator. As much as the friends would have liked to stop there and sleep through the remainder of the day, the threat of the bugs was too pressing and they had no choice but to keep going.

Driving back into the harsh sunlight, Ryan saw the break didn't really help reduce the temp of the engine and could only assume there had to be something wrong with the thermostat. When he got the chance that night, he would open the cooling system and remove the bloody valve completely. The bastard thing was designed to keep the heat in on cold wintry days and channel it off during a hot summer. But since there was only heat in the desert, they had no need for the other function and it could be safely removed. But not abandoned. While they kept the wag, they would save any spare parts. Only a fool threw away a blaster just because nobody was attacking at the moment.

"Ville!" J.B. said, squinting to the north.

Shifting gears, Ryan headed in that direction and soon there rose from the sands a ville of tan bricks. The high walls weren't straight, but extended to points like a star, forming deep passages between each section. Ryan approved. Those were murder alleys, where the ville sec men could concentrate their blasterfire to cut down invaders. The lower bricks were shiny with pieces of broken glass studding the surface, and along the palisade were firing slots and some rusty metal frames dangling with nests of rope that he instinctively knew was a lift of some sort for bringing folks in and out of the ville without opening the gate. This was a real hard-site, safe from any army of coldhearts. Unless somebody had a functioning tank, or a working plane, which was about as unlikely as drinkable rain falling from the tortured sky in this desolate part of the Deathlands.

As they got closer, Ryan couldn't see a door or a gate in the walls, and drove around the ville in a wide arc until locating first one, then another door, separated by a starpoint wall. The large doors were both wooden and strapped with metal. The one-eyed man was willing to bet a live round of ammo that only one of those actually opened into the ville. The other would be a sham, a thick door placed in front of a solid wall to make attackers waste time and men by dividing their forces to hit a useless target. Smart. The baron here was no fool.

''Dark night,'' J.B. whispered, shoving his hat back on and pulling the arming bolt of the Uzi.

''I see it,'' Ryan growled, grinding the damaged clutch as he brought the wag to a halt in the open sand.

Directly in front of the wag was a low adobe brick wall only about a foot high that seemed to circle the entire ville at about four hundred feet of distance. Old weathered crosses jutted from the ground, and at one point the skeleton of a man was staked spread-eagle near the little wall, iron spikes driven through the empty sockets of both eyes. The message was clear—cross this line and die.

"In a world of illiterates, this is an easily understandable denouncement," Doc rumbled, using a strip of canvas to tie his silvery hair off his neck. "Most elucidating."

"A simple skull and crossbones would have sufficed," Mildred told him, using the barrel of her Czech-made ZKR target pistol to push aside the tattered canvas awning to peek out from the rear of the vehicle.

"Over there," Dean said, jerking a thumb to the left.

His pale skin painfully flushed from the sunlight, Jak took a tiny sip from his canteen, sloshing the water around in his mouth before swallowing, still hoarding the precious fluid even with a ville only minutes away. Mebbe it was empty, or full of muties. Life had taught him that until it was in your pocket, you didn't have anything for sure.

"Must have a lot of coldhearts in the area for them to go to this much bother," Krysty suggested, her hair coiling tightly to her head. She was getting a very bad feeling about this ville, not a sense of direct danger as if a sniper had them in the crosshairs, but more a sensation of betrayal. Then it was gone, the ghostly impression vanished like a dream in the night.

"Or one big enemy," J.B. guessed. "Might be both."

Turning off the engine, Ryan pushed aside the blankets and stepped out of the vehicle, enjoying the sensation of the desert wind blowing over his sweat-damp clothes. When nothing happened after a few minutes, he pulled a small plastic mirror from his shirt pocket and reflected the bright sunlight along the top of the wall. That should get somebody's attention soon enough.

Almost immediately, there was an answering flash, and the huge metal framework loudly creaked as it rotated out over the wall and slowly began to lower something to the sandy ground.

"It's a man," Krysty said, her eyes picking out the details of the lone sec man. "Blaster, no grens in sight."

"Mighty suspicious folks," Dean muttered, drying a hand on his shirt before pulling his Browning. "Wouldn't even open the door for seven people."

"Seven people in a wag," his father corrected.

"Could be a hundred more of us just over the horizon."

As the man touched ground, a dozen more people appeared along the angled walls of the ville, brandishing a wide assortment of longblasters, crossbows and something that could have been either a piece of stovepipe, or a predark antitank weapon. It was hard to tell at this range, which was probably the idea.

As J.B. dug out his Navy scope, Krysty squinted hard.

"Looks real," she said softly.

"It is," J.B. added, lowering the telescope and collapsing it back down. "That's a 70 mm recoilless rifle, sort of a baby bazooka. Packs a hell of a punch. Might not be loaded, but even a homemade rocket could send us into a world of hurt."

"I'm already in sight," Ryan said out of the corner of his mouth.

"No problem," the physician replied, holstering her handblaster.

She took Ryan's Steyr SSG-70 off the front seat and pulled it into the rear of the wag. Back in her day, the black woman had been an Olympic silver medalist for target shooting, and she was the second-best long distance shooter among the companions. Working the bolt, Mildred checked the clip in the breech to make sure it was fully loaded, then eased the barrel through a slit in the awning and started adjusting the focus on the scope to find the sec man on the wall brandishing the 70 mm recoilless. At the first sign of danger, she would put a 7.62 mm round of hardball ammunition directly into his front temporal lobe, instantly turning the sec man into a mindless vegetable. The second round would go into the firing mechanism of the U.S. Army recoilless, rendering it equally harmless before anybody could get off a shot. There was a scorpion design painted on the weapon that made a fine target.

Surreptitiously readying the rest of their weapons, the companions stayed still while the lone man walked to the low wall and stopped on the other side. He was lean to the point of gaunt, his light-colored clothing tied off at the ankles and wrists, probably to help keep out the windblown sand. A double holster gun belt was strapped around his waist, but only one carried a blaster. The original pistol grip was gone, replaced with a dark wood of some kind, polished bright and cut with the pattern of a trippant scorpion.

Squinting his good eye at the ville, Ryan again approved. Why risk losing two blasters when one would do the job?

"Where did you find our wag?" the sec man demanded, a hand resting on his gun belt only inches from the shiny blue steel of the revolver. "Thanks for bringing it back. Now get out and start walking."

"You mean our wag, feeb," Ryan corrected hotly, feeling a rush of fury at the clumsy trick. He pulled out the SIG-Sauer and let the fool look down the barrel. "Now shut the fuck up and bring out the sec boss, we got business to jaw."

The skinny sec man bared a grin, displaying missing teeth. "That's me," he stated, stabbing himself in the chest with a stiff finger. "I'm in charge here."

Swinging open the passenger-side door, J.B. raised the Uzi into sight. "That's a load of crap," he said calmly. "You're the newest sec man the ville has, sent out in case we ace first and talk later."

"Get your boss," Ryan growled dangerously, "and stop wasting our time. You aren't in charge of wiping the baron's ass."

Startled by the insult, the sec man contorted his face into a mask of rage and started for his blaster only to freeze at the sound of several hammers locking back on blasters. A few long seconds passed in silence, then the snarling man eased his hand away from the piece and turned to walk back toward the ville.

"I'll remember you, One-eye," he muttered hatefully.

His black hair ruffling in the dry wind, Ryan made no comment, but kept the 9 mm blaster trained on the man until he was well out of range.

Going to the apex of the ville, the skinny sec man shouted something to the people along the wall. Shortly thereafter in the second murder alley, there came the squeaking of hinges and the big door was ponderously raised. A group of armed men on horses rode through the doorway spreading out so that they wouldn't present a group target in case of a firefight, most of them stopping about fifty feet from the low wall. Only one rider kept going past the boundary until he reined in the animal only yards away from the wag.

The engine was ticking steadily as it cooled, and the dry wind swirled the desert dust around their boots like miniature tornados. A dusty lizard raced by from out of nowhere and headed into the unknown.

"Who's in charge here?" the sec man demanded. He was wide with muscle, not fat, his features oddly flat as if there were a lot of Oriental or American Indian blood in his heritage, or just a touch of mutie. His long black hair was tied off in a ponytail with a ornately decorated length of rawhide, his boots were some kind of lizard skin and a brace of pistols rode protectively behind the buckle of his gun belt, the handles turned out for a fast draw. The blue head of a scorpion tattoo peeked from under his shirt, and he had too many scars to count.

Scorpions again, Ryan noted. Had to be the crest of the local baron. Yeah, this was the sec boss without a doubt. The son of an East Coast baron himself, he could tell the difference between a hired gun and a leader.

"That's me. The name's Ryan Cawdor."

"Alexander Hawk, sec chief here at Rockpoint ville," the big man replied, openly appraising the people in the wag. There was a lot of hardware on display, pointing his way. "Those blasters work?"

"Only one way to know for sure," Ryan stated calmly, crossing both arms across his chest. "But it'll cost you red."

Leaning forward in the saddle, Hawk barked a laugh. "Fair enough." These outlanders didn't rattle worth a damn. Good, mebbe he could hire them on as mercies. Always needed more blasters during the dry season.

Shifting his stance, Hawk addressed Ryan directly, as if the rest of the companions were no longer of any importance. "So what do ya want here?"

"Food and water," Ryan said, indicating the wag. "Got mil fuel to trade. The good stuff."

"Won't buy ya a thing here. We don't have any wags," Hawk said, stroking the neck of the stallion. "Anything else?"

"Ammo," J.B. said, lifting a small box of .22 cartridges and shaking it to make the rounds jingle. "You've got blasters, don't you?"

The metallic sound snapped Hawk's head around fast, and he squinted as if reevaluating the situation. "Full box of fifty?" he asked suspiciously.

"Count them if you want."

"I will," Hawk warned. "Better not be duds loaded with dirt."

Krysty drew her S&W and fired a single round into the sky. The noise echoed along the plain, and in seconds a dozen more armed people were at the ville wall pointing longblasters their way. Hidden behind the canvas sheets, Mildred didn't take the scope off the man with the 70 mm pointing at the GMC wag.

Hawk stared at the redhead for a moment, then cracked his face into a hard smile. "Fair enough.

Food, rooms and water for all of you for a day in exchange for the box.''

"One day for a whole box?" Dean snorted. "That's feeb talk!"

"A week is more like it," Ryan countered, shifting his boots on the hot ground.

"One day," Hawk declared, shaking his head. "This is the only water east of the glass lakes. Next spring is a week's ride away, if you can find the spot. Take it, or leave. Your call.''

Reaching into a pocket, Ryan pulled out another box of .22 cartridges and tossed it to the sec man. "Two boxes, three days.''

Caught by surprise, Hawk gave that emotionless smile again. "Deal," he said, tucking the ammo into his shirt. Then turning the Appaloosa stallion, he started walking the beast back toward the ville.

Climbing back into the cab, it took Ryan two tries to finally get the engine running, the whole vehicle shaking from the effort of the struggling diesel. Sounded like a seal might have broken, but at least the fan belt was still holding.

With the gauges rapidly climbing back into the red zone again, Ryan drove the wag over the boundary marker heading toward the main murder alley of Rockpoint ville and the large open door.

Chapter Ten

The mounted sec men led the way through the murder alley and into the gate. Keeping to a crawl so the horses could stay in front, Ryan drove the rattling trunk through the opening, the heavy gate rumbling shut behind to leave them trapped inside a short tunnel that penetrated the wall. The sides were smooth and plain, without decorations or even blaster ports for defense. On the other hand, the wag was barely able to traverse the passageway, the canvas awning less than a foot from the ceiling with the tall radio antenna loudly scraping along overhead to the obvious annoyance of the sec men. Any vehicle slightly larger than the GMC would never be able to gain entrance, much less make it completely through.

"An ambush by any other name," Krysty muttered, glancing around them on every side.

"Indeed, dear lady," Doc agreed. "I do believe the operative phrase, quote sitting ducks end quote, would be in order here."

Born and raised in a ville protected by a drawbridge, Ryan agreed with that assessment. To any invaders on foot, the tunnel would be a death trap with nowhere to run or hide from the blasters of the ville sec men.

The tunnel was dark with the front gate closed, but there was no need to switch on the headlights as dim sunlight showed at the far end. As the companions drove into a sunny courtyard, the ville spread before them in disorganized rows as if each house had been built wherever the owner felt like it.

"This is a maze," Mildred stated under her breath, and drew a pencil and notebook to start tracing their way along the twisting streets.

Stretched between the adobe brick buildings were sheets of cloth that rippled with the desert breeze, but the material effectively reduced the devastating effects of the noontime sun to a tolerable level.

An adobe brick machine-gun nest stood directly in front of the tunnel, with two more off to the sides to give cross fire. Stout pylons of gray rock jutted from the blue cobblestone street, and the companions recognized them as tank traps, designed to bust the treads on an APC, rendering it immobile.

As the horses turned into a side street, the wag

followed and the milling people stopped whatever they were doing to stare in wonder at the vehicle. The effect was unnerving until Ryan remembered that Hawk said the place had no wags. Just simple curiosity, then. Or was it something more? In spite of the apparent wealth of Rockpoint, there seemed to be a lot of fear in the faces he saw.

The crowds parted before the armed sec men to keep from being trampled by the unshod hooves of their mounts. But they avoided even looking at Hawk. The sec chief rode like a baron through the streets, the iron-clad hooves of his stallion ringing loudly against the cobblestones, announcing his approach.

The people were sensibly dressed in loose clothing of varied stages of cleanliness, the usual mixture of salvaged clothing from predark days and tanned hides. Shoes were ragged and repaired into faded patchwork that resembled the deliberate camou patterns of military fatigues, with children going about bare foot. Nothing that could be a weapon was in sight, and no machines, even nonfunctioning devices.

In the shade of the rippling cloth roof, a legless leather smith was tanning the hide of a mountain lion, while a young assistant stitched a saddle. A dwarfish woman was sharpening knives of a whetstone, and drunken laughter sounded from the second-floor windows of what was obviously a gaudy house. Situated on a corner, an old potter was palming red clay into the shape of a bowl. Behind him were wooden racks filled with drying plates and pitchers. On the top shelf, the better plates carried the detailed design of a scorpion.

"Ugly design," Dean said, frowning. "Who the frag wants to eat off a bug?"

Doc started to speak, and Mildred rested a hand on his arm, shaking her head. He grimaced, then shrugged. The scholar had tried to explain many times that scorpions weren't insects, but an arachnid, an entirely different species like spiders. But nobody seemed to care. If it had more than four legs it was a bug. *Ipso facto.* Case closed.

"Could be the baron's crest," his father answered, shifting gears.

"See those slits in the ville roof?" Krysty said, pointing above the potter. "This deep in the desert, there would be no easy supply of charcoal for a kiln. So everything has to be sundried."

"Lemons and lemonade," Doc commented wryly. "They turned a problem into an asset."

"Nuking hot enough be kiln," Jak said, shaking to the motion of the wag over the uneven cobblestones. "Even with roof."

"Black dust, I don't like this," J.B. muttered, adjusting his glasses. "Not one damn bit."

"What?" Krysty asked. "Something wrong? The ville looks peaceful enough."

"That's the bastard problem," he said, gesturing broadly. "No gallows."

"Yeah, I noticed that, too," Ryan muttered, glancing down cross streets and into alleys. In almost every ville, there was an execution area near the front gate to warn outlanders to behave or else. But not here. No gallows, chopping blocks, cages, or pits. However, there were always people to chill—thieves, traitors, murderers, whatever. So where did they ace people?

Mildred brushed back her beaded hair. "If the job isn't being done in public, then it's being done somewhere hidden. We better make sure none of us get detained by the sec men."

"Just here to buy water," Ryan reminded bluntly, but keeping his voice low so the sec men couldn't hear. "Not interested in local troubles. If the people ain't happy with the present baron, that's their business, not ours."

"'Aren't' happy," Krysty corrected him.

Just then, there came the sound of a whip cracking, closely followed by dull grunts of pain.

"Spoke too soon," Krysty said, a hand instinctively resting on her gun belt.

The noise grew as the sec men and companions entered a small courtyard, where the cloth roof was gone and the sun blazed down in all its fury.

Set apart from every other tan adobe building in the ville, this structure was made of red brick and looked as strong as a bunker. It was two stories tall, yet oddly without windows, and a set of wide granite steps led to a bronze door green with age. Armed guards stood on either side of the door, routinely checking through the clothing of the people waiting in line to enter, and then again as they came out clutching small clay pots that loudly sloshed.

"I see that water is tightly rationed here," Ryan said casually out the window. "That the ville well?"

"Our temple," Hawk replied with a dark scowl. "You won't be seeing inside there."

The whip sounded again as the horses and wag went around the temple bringing into view a skinny man wearing rags, his hands tied to iron rings set into the brick wall, legs covered with rivulets of blood. A shirt hung in filthy strips from his back, and a large sec man was whipping him with a length of smooth leather.

"Nineteen!" the sec man cried and let the whip

fly. The leather cracked as it touched the prisoner's skin, making another section of clothing drop fluttering to the ground.

The prisoner hardily flinched as a red welt rose on his bony shoulders, an old scar splitting open and fresh blood trickling down his trembling torso. While the sec man reclaimed the whip, the prisoner wheezed for breath through his nose, a wad of dark leather held in his mouth.

"Padding to keep from breaking his teeth," Doc scowled, twisting his hand on the silver lion's head of the swordstick. "Barbaric!"

A sec man jerked his head toward the wag at that, and Krysty jabbed the scholar with a hard elbow to the ribs. Scowling darkly, Doc clamped his mouth shut with a clear effort of willpower.

"So what was his crime?" Ryan asked, as the group passed by the sight, the whip rising and falling in the background.

"Water thief," Hawk said gruffly, shaking the reins to keep his horse abreast of the wag. The animal didn't like to be near the noisy wag with its exhaust fumes and kept shying away. "Remember that sight, or else it could be you. Always need more sacrifices for the Scorpion God."

"No blood, no water," a sec man said in a solemn manner, bobbing his head slightly in a small bow. The rest of the sec men repeated the phrase along with every person in the crowd.

Turning his head that way, Ryan meet the gaze of the sec man who had spoken and was surprised to see the guard who had first met them outside the ville. The two exchanged hostile glares for a moment, then the guard rode onward.

"We're going to have trouble with him," Ryan stated under his breath.

"Heads up," Dean said softly, glancing to the side.

Following the direction, Ryan saw a redbrick building rising above the tan adobe structures. Some sort of a keep, a fort within the walled ville. The windows had thick wood shutters and iron bars, blaster slots were everywhere, and a blue flag bearing the golden outline of a scorpion fluttered from a bare metal pole on the roof.

Standing at a corner of the roof with the afternoon sun at his back, was a man, hands clasped behind him, a double rig carrying a blaster under each arm, a thin trail of smoke rising from the slim cigar in his unseen mouth. Yet Ryan had no doubt that was the baron. As if sensing the attention, the baron turned to look down at the vehicle passing the keep, then he turned to walk inside the fortress, a phalanx of bodyguards staying close with weapons in hand.

"That where we're going?" Ryan asked, keeping his voice neutral. "To see the baron?"

"No need," Hawk replied, gesturing with a finger. "You'll be staying a few blocks over that way, at the motel."

"Motel?" Mildred repeated in surprise. That was a word she hadn't heard in a long while.

Hawk slowed his horse to speak to the woman in the rear of the vehicle. His frank disapproval broke her reverie and sent a shiver down her spine that the woman tried to hide. Then Mildred noticed him looking at her satchel, which bore a red cross. Oh, he had something against healers. That explained it. It wasn't the color of her skin, or her sex, but that she was a healer, a scientist. Odd, but some people still harboured that hatred.

"Motel is what we call the inn where outlanders stay there until it's time to go," Hawk said in disdain. "That is, until they cause trouble and go to the temple."

"No blood, no water," Ryan said without inflection, watching the dashboard gauges start to climb once more.

For a moment, Hawk glared at the man, unsure

of how to react to that, then he kicked the flanks of his mount and rode on ahead of the others.

"A genuine, old-fashioned, water monopoly," Doc murmured. "Fascinating. Control the people by controlling the water."

Mildred added, "Rather similar to how the Aztecs maintained population control by pretending to need human hearts to make the sun rise."

"Quite so, dear lady."

Holding on to a rib of the awning, Dean glanced back toward the red brick building. The crowd was carrying away a body, blood dripping off the form to show he was still alive, although just barely.

"Or do you think they got some kind big mutie in there?" the boy asked nervously. "Could be it drinks blood and pisses water, or something like that."

"Some cave bats drink blood and piss ammonia," J.B. said, removing his fedora to wipe the sweatband with a handkerchief. Then he tucked it back on. "And we can cook that into a kind of explos, so who knows?"

"Changing blood into explosives," Doc boomed, shaking his head sadly. "Never have I heard a better paradigm for existing in this wretched land."

Following the mounted guards past a slaughter-

house and a reeking row of public shitters, Ryan
steered the vehicle away from the protected section
of the ville and into a wide open area exposed to
the raw sun. It was like entering an oven. There
was nobody on the streets, not even a dog or lizard,
the adobe buildings spaced far apart so that it was
possible to see the high wall surrounding the ville
a hundred feet away.

Their goal appeared to be a predark motel situated between a roofless adobe ruin, and a garbage
dump buzzing with flies. The original neon sign on
the cinder-block wall was only a stain, the name
long gone and replaced with a poorly drawn car-
toon of a bed and a spoon on a faded wooden plac-
ard. That was necessary these dark days for the
many folks who couldn't read.

"Pretty clever," J.B. muttered. "Having outlanders living without a roof, must cut their stay
short."

"Make buy more water, too," Jak added, rubbing a hand across his dry mouth. The canteen
hung heavy at his side, but he was holding off until
they were some place out of the direct sun.

"Okay, this is the place," Hawk announced,
reining his stallion to a halt and walking it around.
"You can put the wag in the barn over there. We

have no other outlanders staying here, so you won't be bothering any horses."

"Fair enough. Any laws we should know about?" Ryan asked, turning on the heater to keep the heating engine operating. As a wave of hot air rushed from the vents, the temperature gauge needle flickered and began to move away from the red line in a pulsating motion.

"Yeah, there are. You can leave Rockpoint anytime you want during the day, but not at night," Hawk said, leaning forward in the saddle, both hands crossed over the pommel. "Disobey a sec man, ten lashes. Steal water, thirty lashes. Hurt a horse, a hundred lashes. Go anywhere near the temple, death. Say anything treasonous against the baron, you get into the temple. Permanently. You leave at dawn in three days."

With that done, the big man shook the bridle to start the stallion trotting away. The rest of the sec men rode around the sputtering wag with hands on blasters once in a patent display of firepower, then followed their chief back into the coolness of the covered ville.

"Mother Gaia, I wonder why they let us come inside," Krysty said. "They sure as hell don't seem to want any visitors."

"Only way to get any news about what's hap-

pening outside the walls,'' Ryan explained, turning
the wheel to head for the adobe barn. ''New
plagues, new muties, and such. If they stay too iso-
lated, something big could come their way and they
wouldn't be ready to fight, or run.''

''Simple self-preservation,'' Mildred said in
agreement. ''Nothing more. Walls this thick were
built to keep something out.''

''Or in,'' Doc added cryptically.

Rolling the wag into the barn, Ryan made a wide
arc and managed to turn it around to park facing
the exit. It would be ready to charge and smash
through the door in case they had to leave in a
hurry. Ryan turned off the engine, and he and J.B.
both stayed in the vehicle, listening carefully as it
sputtered and backfired to finally go still.

''Intake is clogged with salt dust,'' J.B. said with
a frown. ''Tricky to fix that.''

Setting the handbrake, Ryan added, ''And we got
to remove that thermostat.''

''Damn straight we do. My legs are feeling like
they've been dipped in acid rain.''

''At least we got the spare juice to flush the manifold,'' Ryan told him, reaching under the dashboard and pulling a handful of fuses. ''But that's
for tomorrow, after we rest and eat.''

"Good," Jak said eagerly, lowering the canteen and smacking his lips. "Starving."

, Tucking the fuses into a pocket, Ryan climbed down from the cab and walked to the rear of the wag to claim his backpack. A slanted shadow cut across the interior of the barn from the setting sun, but if there was a difference in temperature it wasn't readily noticeable. Why anybody would build a ville here in the first place was a puzzle. Then again, maybe it was started by folks fleeing across the salty desert and they found water.

"Dean takes first watch," Ryan directed, checking his wrist chron. "Doc next, then Jak, J.B. and me. We switch every two hours."

"No prob," the boy said, lifting a nukelamp and checking to make sure the device still worked. Even in the daylight, the brilliant beam was clearly visible. Turning it off, he placed the lamp on the ground in the far corner where the beam could shine in the open doorway. Hidden in the shadows behind the light, he would be a hard target to shoot.

Gathering their backpacks, Mildred and Krysty said nothing about being left out of the rotation schedule. They knew that a woman standing guard alone at night would only be an open invitation for serious trouble. They'd do a turn during the day, or by a campfire once the group was far from the ville.

Lifting the hood, J.B. pulled an ignition wire and coiled it into a bundle before tucking it into his munitions bag. Too many folks seemed to know how to jump a fuse these days, so he decided to take some extra insurance. Unless a hijacker had exactly the correct replacement for the same make and model wag, the vehicle wasn't going to move an inch. The rope, shovels and other small items they could safely leave behind. There was only the single entrance, and Dean was a good shot.

"Don't lose that, John," Mildred joked, slinging her own backpack onto a shoulder. "We really don't want to stay here for any longer than necessary."

"Got that right," the Armorer replied, as he slipped the S&W M-4000 off his back and offered it to Dean.

"How about some company?"

"Thanks," Dean replied, accepting the shotgun and resting it on a shoulder. "You hear this, you better come running."

"Or sound the horn," Ryan instructed, checking over the arrangement inside the barn with approval. The site was tight. "See you in two hours."

"No problem," the boy said, racking the weapon.

As the rest of the companions walked from the barn, Dean followed them to the doorway. Watching them head for the ramshackle motel, he noticed a young girl across the street just standing there, her slim arms holding a clay water jug. She was about his own age, just starting to fill her raggedy dress with the shape of a woman. She was so beautiful it was like something from a predark vid, and on impulse he gave a brief wave. Shyly, the girl smiled and that was when he noticed her topaz eyes, bluer than the sky after a storm. Dean started forward, but then stopped, knowing that he couldn't leave the wag unattended. Frantically, he tried to think of something to call out to her, but nothing came to mind. After waiting a minute, the girl shrugged in resignation and padded around a corner with her water jug. Dean followed her progress until she was gone from sight.

"Mebbe this place isn't so bad," he said softly, and settled down into a comfortable position against the wall to watch the street in the hope that she might return.

CROSSING THE CRACKED asphalt of what once had been the parking lot for the motel, Ryan found the

way into the building blocked by a mangy dog laying in front of the door, its pale tongue lolling from
the heat. Nudging gently with a combat boot, Ryan
got the dog to move and walked into the building.

As the one-eyed man pushed aside the door, the
rusty hinges creaked, and the cracked glass wob-
bled loosely in the frame. Waiting a moment for
his vision to adjust to the darkness, he then stepped
out of the afternoon sun into the lobby of the predark motel. It was somewhat cooler, although the
air reeked of sour sweat and rancid cooking grease.

Across the lobby, a stack of sandbags formed a
sort of front desk, flat stones on top serving as a
counter. Sitting behind that was a fat man wearing
a moth-eaten cowboy hat and no shirt, picking his
teeth with a thumbnail. Hanging on the nearby wall
was a baseball bat spiked with nails in the manner
of a medieval flail. Obviously a peacemaker to de-
ter any troublesome guests.

In the middle of the lobby was a fancy stone
fountain, the rocks bone dry and the drain clogged
with dust. A Dutch door marked Office was set
alongside a row of the empty phone booths, and
broken frames on the walls held only tatters of colored posters that once would have boasted about
local attractions.

Two sets of concrete stairs led to the second

floor, where dirty laundry was hanging over the iron lace railing. From somewhere deeper in the motel came the sound of soft snoring, along with the wet smack of flesh on flesh. But it was impossible to tell if it was folks having sex or a fistfight. In the corner, a dog looked up from gnawing on a bone, only long enough to growl at the companions.

Prying a bit of food from between his stained teeth, the fat man behind the sandbags inspected the morsel and popped it back into his mouth to chew and swallow. His splotchy face was marred with acne scarring, and his fingernails were shockingly long, with unidentifiable filth embedded underneath.

"We're not eating anything served here," Krysty stated flatly. "Even if it comes in a sealed can."

"I want to boil the air," Mildred added.

Scowling darkly, Ryan started for the desk. If this was where guests of the baron stayed, he wondered what the jail looked like. "You in charge?" he said gruffly.

"Yep, and you're the outies I heard about," the man drawled. "I'm Sparrow, and welcome to my place."

"Sparrow," Mildred repeated in disbelief.

"That's me!" He laughed, then paused to belch and scratch under an arm. "Shoot, and seven of ya at once! Never had the place so full. An' I see ya got your own sluts. Mind if I ride one when yer done? Might try the redhead myself. House rules, ya know. He-he. Sparrow rides free, ya know."

In cold fury, Ryan started for his blaster, but Krysty stepped in close to shove the snub-nosed S&W Model 640 under his chin and forced his head back until he looking at the ceiling.

"Want to try that again?" she demanded, grinding the muzzle into his flesh. "And get it right this time, feeb!"

"W-welcome t-to Rockpoint, madam," Sparrow stuttered, his greasy face damp with sweat. "Hey, I didn't mean nothing, just talking."

"Then shut your stinking mouth," Krysty ordered, removing the blaster and tucking it away. "Say anything like that again and the dogs will be chewing your bones."

"Yes, ma'am, sorry," he blubbered in apology, trying to force a grin.

"How did you know we were coming?" Ryan demanded, his hand still on the grip of the SIG-Sauer. The urge to kill was taking a long time to leave. He knew that his nerves were on edge from the lack of sleep, and it was becoming difficult to think clearly.

"Sec men sent a runner, told me to get some rooms ready. I chased out the lizards and put in a clean night soil bucket," Sparrow said in a rush of words. "Ya gotta empty that yourself, ya know. I run this place. Ain't got no slaves. Ain't allowed. Not enough water to spare."

"Hurrah for the baron," J.B. stated. On the wall was a honeycomb of letter slots, each with a hook for a key, but none was in sight. "Where are the keys?"

"Done need any," Sparrow said. "None of the locks on the first floor work. We had to bust 'em down to get in and never saw the way of fixing them."

"And what room were you told to prepare for us?" Ryan demanded.

"The big one on the first floor, way in the back, near the garbage dump," Sparrow said, rubbing a hand across his soft belly. "Now if ya want something better on the second floor, we got that. Door got a lock, and the window overlooks the barn so ya can watch your stuff. Curtains, nice and cool during the day. Best we got!"

There was a pause, then he added, "Of course, that costs more."

J.B. grunted at the news and Ryan narrowed his eyes. So that was it, eh?

"How much for the clean room?" he asked.

Smiling with greed, Sparrow said, "Half your water ration. We got a deal?"

"No," Ryan said, turning away and heading for the door. "We'll stay in the barn."

"But you can't do that!" Sparrow cried out. "The baron said ya gotta stay here!"

"And we shall be sure to tell him about your hospitality," Doc added. "Perhaps he would be interested in how you obtain extra water from travelers. I wonder if that falls into the category of stealing water?"

"Hey, now," Sparrow whispered, going pale. "No need for that. Man's got a right to earn a little water now and then. I was just, like, ya know... Help me Jed!"

There was a creak as the office door started to swing open, pushed by the barrel of a longblaster. Moving fast, Ryan fired twice into the wood, slamming it closed. There came a muffled cry of pain and a thump from other side.

"Don't move!" Mildred commanded, her .38 revolver pointed at Sparrow. The desk clerk froze motionless, his hand only inches from the club.

Krysty and Doc went back to watch the front

door and the balcony for the arrival of reinforcements.

With a low growl, the mutt started to rise and Jak pointed his Colt Python at the animal. "Call off," he said, cocking back the hammer on the blaster.

"Sit, boy," Sparrow said, shaking with rage.

Obediently, the dog stopped making noise, then turned around a few times before settling down with his bone once more.

Swinging around the Uzi, J.B. kicked open the office door and Ryan charged through, his blaster leading the way. Sitting on the dirty floor was another fat man, holding his bloody mouth. Next to him was a homemade blaster composed of a small-diameter bathroom pipe wrapped in layers of iron wire and bound to a wooden dowel. A cartridge was inserted into the crude barrel of the zip gun, two more rolling loosely on the linoleum.

"Kick it away," Ryan ordered and the man complied, the homemade gun skittering under a metal desk. "Now, move, fat boy!"

Slowly, the corpulent fellow rose to shuffle into the lobby and joined Sparrow at the sandbags. This close together, it was clear the two men were brothers, maybe even twins. Or else the gene pool of the ville was dangerously small.

"Damn, you folks are good," Sparrow muttered. "Haven't seen anybody move that fast, not even Hawk."

"Except for that bitch Kate," Jed added, trying to staunch the flow of blood from his split lip. "Damn, I think a tooth is broken."

"Tough," Ryan growled. "Who's Kate, the baron's wife?"

"Some slut who works for the Trader," Jed mumbled.

"Who? Oh, you mean Trader Kate," Ryan corrected. There were a lot of traders in the Deathlands, and they all used the word as a title, the way the barons did. Only the legendary Trader was known by the single word.

"No, just Kate," Sparrow corrected. "She's the sec chief for Trader."

"How do you know about the Trader?" Ryan asked, trying to control his words. The blaster felt big in his hands, as uncontrollable as a thrashing snake.

"I bought a predark med from him that saved my arm after a mutie bit me," Jed said, blood dribbling down his chin. "Didn't charge me anything what he could have."

"How long ago was this?" Krysty asked urgently.

Sparrow started to lower his hands, but at a gesture from Mildred he quickly raised them again. "I dunno," he said, scowling as if forcing a dim memory. "Maybe five months. Long time ago."

"Months," J.B. said slowly. "You gotta mean years. Five years, right?"

The fat man shrugged. "Whatever you say, you got the blaster," he replied. "But I ain't no feeb. It was less than half a year ago. He and the baron had a big fight about something, and the Trader ain't been back since. Used to stop by fairly regularly. Bought a lot of water."

"What's he to y'all?" Jed asked suspiciously. "Kin?"

"Describe him," Ryan demanded, feeling his heart pound in his chest. It was impossible.

The brothers exchanged glances. "The Trader? Hell, I dunno," Sparrow said. "Never saw the guy. He was always inside a big-ass tank, stays behind a blister of the military glass."

"How many wags?" J.B. demanded. "Describe them!"

Sparrow scrunched his face. "Well, there were three, one big wag and two others, each plated with metal and covered with blasters. Big stuff, cannons, mortars and rockets. Baron Gaza was scared to death of the guy. Hell, who wouldn't be with all his weapons.''

''More,'' Ryan said through clenched teeth.

Fumbling for a reply, Jed scratched his head. ''Well, I heard Kate call the big wag War Wag One. That help any?''

The universe seemed to go still at those simple words, as if it were breaking apart and rejoining in a new pattern, reorganizing itself on a most basic of levels.

''He's alive,'' Ryan stated. ''Trader is alive and back in business!''

Chapter Eleven

Mists of steam filling the air of the small marble room, Baron Edgar Gaza was sprawled naked in the shallow end of his large swimming pool, the clear mountain water flowing steadily around his hard muscular form from a feeder pipe. On the tiles near his head was a pile of dry towels and several loaded blasters. Laying at the bottom of the pool was a stiletto.

"I think they're spies sent by the Trader," Hawk said quietly, leaning against a marble pillar. His shirt was unbuttoned to the waist, the entire tattoo of the scorpion visible on his broad chest. "Best to chill them. Gather ten, no, make that twenty of our best men. We'll make this a night creep and garrote the bunch in their sleep."

Soaping his arms, Gaza gazed at his sec chief with saturnine calm. "The women, too?"

"Women we got," the sec man snorted angrily.

At the far end of the pool, the women of the baron's harem were slowly washing themselves,

the sudsy water carried away into another predark
pipeline. Where the dirty water went the baron had
no idea, but it was no place local so it wasn't a
challenge to his control over the ville. Once, the
wife of a blacksmith had given birth to a tiny baby,
and when the boy was ten Gaza equipped the child
with several bottles of air and flushed him down
the pipeline with orders to return and his family
would live comfortably for the rest of their lives.
A lie, but the boy eagerly accepted the challenge
and dived into the feeder pipe. He was never heard
from again.

The women stayed in this wing of the keep, their
tongues removed to stop any of them from talking
just in case one of them escaped somehow. Whenever one of them got too old, Gaza would brutally
kill her in front of the others saying she had tried
to escape, and then he would beat the rest as punishment for allowing her to try. Escape attempts
were few and far between.

It was something his father had taught him, keep
the slaves suspicious of one another and they become the guards. His father had been a very wise
man, the founder of Rockpoint ville. Wise and
hard. Edgar had been the youngest son of the baron,
and one day had been pitted against his older brothers in the Arena. Armed with knives and spiked

clubs, the boys were commanded to fight, the winner to be the heir to the ville. Edgar had offered to team with a sibling and share the ville, and when the fool accepted and turned his back, Edgar beat him to death and stole his knife. Now armed with two weapons, he savagely fought the others and won. But the eldest brother had gotten in a few good strikes before dying, and Edgar's badly broken leg had never healed correctly. He still limped to this day, the old break aching badly when the acid rains came in the fall.

"Well?" Hawk demanded impatiently. "What should we do, Baron?"

Washing lazily, Gaza looked at the desert giant. His loyalty was unquestionable, which was why the baron allowed the mutie to challenge his orders. Only a fool listened to bootlickers. Hawk had been found in the desert crawling with scorpions, stung a hundred times. Incredibly, the man lived and was proved immune to the deadly poison of the tiny killers. A useful skill that became their safeguard on the Scorpion God.

The sec men sometimes referred to him as the Big Scorpion, which amused Gaza greatly. The more the troops feared Hawk, the more authority the baron had over them. It was all a matter of control. Which was why he created the water short-

age. If he opened the pipes, the entire valley would
be flooded. But a simple twist of the valve and the
water slowed to the merest trickle. Now visitors
paid for the precious liquid with ammo and horses,
food, and sometimes their very lives. His troops
had the pick of the sluts, and his people believed
that he was their savior and only chance of life.

"We shall ace them, of course," Baron Gaza
said, slipping under the water for a moment, then
rising to push back his wet hair. The women waded
closer to their "husband," wrapping him in dry
towels as he walked from the pool.

"How is the matter in question," Gaza said, taking a clean robe from a marble bench and belting
a robe about his waist. "They have rapidfires and
a predark ammo. And the black hair man, Ryan,
has the look of a real fighter. I think it might be
best to let them stay for a day or two, sell them
water and then track them when they leave. Ace
them far from the ville and bring the blasters and
wag back for our private arsenal."

Padding naked past the sec man, a blonde looked
at the giant with no more interest than if he were
a chair, her full breasts swinging to the gentle motion of her young body. Hawk understood why their
tongues had been removed, but considered it a

waste. However, they could still be bent over a
bench. Didn't need a tongue for that.

"Chill them now, tonight," Hawk countered,
rubbing the scars along his neck with a palm.

Taking the stopper from a crystal bottle, Gaza
poured a goblet full of sparkling clean water, spill-
ing some onto the floor in the process.

"All right," the baron said after taking a sip.
"Send troops to the motel and ace the outlanders
in their beds. Then blame Sparrow and drag him
through the courtyard to the temple. He has been
stealing from me long enough."

"Nobody is above the law," Hawk agreed, rubbing his tattoo as he watched the women splash
about in the soapy pool. Already the currents were
flushing the suds away, leaving the water clear.

Noticing the direction of his gaze, Baron Gaza
fixed the man with a hard look. "Remember that,
old friend," he growled. "What scorpions can't
ace, the Scorpion God can."

IN THE LOBBY of the motel, the companions stood
transfixed, their minds trying to absorb the impli-
cations of the incredible news.

"The Trader and Abe are alive," Ryan repeated
softly.

"Mebbe," Krysty countered, then nodded at the two fat men. "We should continue this in private."

"Please," Sparrow begged, misunderstanding her statement and dropping to his knees. "Don't chill us!"

"Upstairs stupe," Ryan ordered, gesturing with the SIG-Sauer. "Jak, get the dogs."

The teenager nodded and started urging the hounds into the office with a soft whistle. The beasts followed him into the room and he closed the door with a sharp bang.

"My dogs," Sparrow cried. "Not my dogs!"

"Shut up and move," J.B. ordered, poking the man with the Uzi.

As they marched the fat men up the stairs, Jed tried to make a break and Ryan clubbed him to the floor with the barrel of his blaster. Trembling in fear, Sparrow did nothing, unable to speak. Going to the end of the corridor, Ryan shoved open a door to find a corner room containing only the barest essentials, a mattress on the floor, empty water pitcher and a night soil bucket.

Putting the men back to back on the dirty mattress, Ryan and J.B. kept them covered while Mildred cut some rope from the blinds and Doc expertly tied their feet at the ankles, and then each man's hand to the other's arm in a crisscross pattern. The brothers grumbled and complained, but didn't resist.

Coming out of the dark bathroom, Krysty ripped a paper-thin towel into strips and stuffed a wad of cloth into their mouths before gagging them tightly.

"Good job," Mildred said in approval. "They're not getting out of that."

Leaving the room, J.B. used his tools on the door and tricked the lock into engaging with a solid click. "That'll hold them for a while," he said, tucking the picks into his munitions bag.

Returning downstairs, the companions found Jak at the front counter, stropping a knife on a whetstone.

"Oh, no, did you kill the dogs?" Mildred asked.

"Nah," Jak drawled, sheathing the blade. "Locked in office."

"Good enough," Ryan said, holstering his piece, then rubbing his face. Fireblast, he was tired. But the sleep that had been so tantalizingly close was now faraway. "So, what do you think?" he asked aloud.

"Beats me," J.B. said bluntly, leaning against the sandbags and crossing his arms. "But it sort of makes sense. Where else could they get the ammo if not from a trader? There's certainly no ruins around here to scavenge."

"Might be just somebody using the name," Mildred suggested. "As advertising. You can trust me, I'm Trader, sort of thing."

"Never thought that," Jak growled. "Twisted."

The physician smiled. "No, my friend, you're just an honest man."

"Get lot enemies that," Jak added. "But make lot deals, too."

"However, there's a chance that it might actually be Trader," Ryan said slowly.

"Then again, it might just be some mercie who could have the Trader a prisoner," J.B. said, removing his glasses to clean them on a sleeve. "Forcing tech secrets about the wags and blasters to build an empire. Or his son, or a clone, or…"

His voice trailed off, the possibilities were damn near endless. And after what they had seen traveling the Deathlands, the man knew that almost anything was possible these days.

In reply, Ryan shook his head. There were too many questions and no bastard answers at all.

Darkness was starting to cover the ville, so Krysty lit a candle. Out the front windows, Ryan could see the bright light coming from the barn next door.

"Now what?" Mildred asked. "Somebody is

going to eventually miss those fools, so the sooner we leave, the better.''

"We can't leave at night," Ryan said, starting to pace. "Not without acing some folks, and then we'll have a war party chasing our asses across the desert.''

"Tomorrow should be good. Got to remove that sticking thermostat anyway," J.B. said, slipping on his glasses again. "A few hours of work could triple our speed across Texas. Six hundred miles is a long way to the next—" he paused and glanced up the stairs to the closed door "—to the next, ahem, waterhole.''

Stopping near the fountain, Ryan grunted at the discretion. They knew better than to even say the word redoubt among others. Some people knew of the legends, but the fewer that number stayed, the better.

"Engines have their use, madam," Doc rumbled. "But I have yet to see a car that can reproduce itself.''

Horses, eh? There was a thought. "How much ammo do we have?" Krysty asked, rummaging in her pocket. "I have a box.''

"Total of three more boxes of the .22 cartridges," J.B. replied. "More than enough to buy horses. The locals have plenty, so the price shouldn't be too high.''

"Unless the baron owns all of the horses.''

"Not going reach Grandee on horses,'' Jak said. "Need wag. Bad land down there.''

"Besides, we don't know how to find the Trader,'' Krysty stated bluntly. "His supply bases are secret, even if it is the same person.''

"We used to know them,'' J.B. added. "But he was always changing the locations in case of a traitor.''

Ryan frowned deeply. A traitor, that was something he hadn't considered until now.

"But how find?'' Jak demanded, brushing back his long snowy hair.

Pulling a map from his munitions bag, J.B. smoothed it across the counter and the companions gathered around, the combined candlelight almost making the document readable.

"Now we came from the east,'' Ryan said, "which leaves north, south and west. South of here is the Grandee, north is New Mex and the west is unknown.''

"Three choices, none of them guaranteed,'' Mildred said, using her butane lighter to start a lumpy candle on the front counter. The tiny flame constantly jerked as the fatty wax spit and popped.

"And a million combinations mixed in between those three. This is hopeless!"

"Damn straight. We need more info," Ryan agreed, smoothing out Texas with his hand. "Bastard lot of territory to recce blind."

"Sec men know truth," Jak grunted, glancing upstairs. "Those tubs lard might be spinning shitwebs." The teenager knew that he could easily force the two men to spill their guts with a hot blade, but that was something he would hold off doing until there was no other choice.

"Hey, we passed a gaudy house down the road," J.B. said, tilting his head. "There's always sec men there. It's only a couple of blocks away, and we do have free rein inside the ville."

Glancing out the door, Ryan started to speak, and Doc cut off the man. "I shall stay with Dean," the old man offered. "The establishment in question is too far away for any response from us to be of effective use if there was an altercation."

"Thanks. Save the MRE packs," Ryan ordered. "We'll bring you something for dinner."

"Anything but dog," Doc muttered, glancing at the silent office door.

Checking the street outside for any suspicious movement before leaving the motel, Ryan motioned the others forward and they split apart in the deepening darkness. As silent as a ghost, Doc melted into the shadows along the side of the building and was gone from sight. Krysty nodded in approval. The old fellow was getting good at that.

In the night air was a faint reek from the garbage dump behind the motel, but that faded as they crossed the street. From the roofed section of the ville, the lights from the windows were reflected off the rippling cloth, giving the streets a golden hue like something from an old vid. Now there came the aroma of frying peppers mixing with the clean smell of the desert salt. Somewhere a horse whinnied, and there came the crash of pots and pans, followed by raised voices marking a fight. The desert ville was full of life, and the sound of a whip was noticeably absent at the moment.

"It was this way," Mildred said, checking the map in her notebook.

The companions passed very few people on the streets, a young boy dragging a burlap bag full of sticks, an old woman bundled under a raggedy shawl limping along a side street. Muted voices came from behind the closed shutters, and something flew by overhead, its passage masked by the patched material roofing the ville. Steadily, the temperature dropped as night descended in full, slices of light beaming through the shutters and around closed doors, becoming brighter in the purple dusk. His boots slapping against the cobblestone street, a sec man walked down the center of the street with a longblaster slung over his shoulder, a hand tight on the faded leather strap. He looked hard at the companions, then slowly nodded, granting them passage and kept slowly walking.

Easing his stance, Ryan let go of his grip on the SIG-Sauer and Jak tucked the throwing knife in his hand back up the sleeve of his camou jacket.

"Lot of security here," J.B. muttered, taking his hand off his slung Uzi. "Everybody seems scared."

"If the baron is at war with the Trader," Ryan growled, "they bastard well should be."

"Roger that."

Skirting around the temple, the group heard the gaudy house long before they saw the place. Gales of laughter came from the second floor, shadowy figures ran past the louvered shutters, and there was actual glass in the lower windows, showing a roaring fireplace and tables of men eating and drinking. The few women moving through the crowd were scantily dressed.

A group of horses was tied to a stone hitching post, with a lone sec man leaning against it smoking a home-rolled cig. He watched the outlanders cross the street, but said nothing as they passed by, heading for the brothel.

"Must be the designated driver." Mildred laughed, and waited for a response from the others, then realized the joke was a hundred years out of date. Ah, well.

Stepping through the doorway, Ryan pushed aside a blanket hanging across the opening to help keep out the evening chill. Inside the building, the air was warm and heavy with the smells of food and wood smoke. From the bolt holes in the concrete floor marking where heavy machinery had once been anchored, it was obvious that the place had originally been some sort of factory, now gutted into a single huge room with bare steel beams supporting the second story. Clusters of candles hung from chains attached to the metal rafters, clay bowls underneath positioned to catch drippings so as not to lose a drop of wax. A roaring fireplace was near the wooden counter that served as a bar, with a bubbling iron pot sitting directly amid the crackling flames, the roasted carcass of something slowly turning on a spit.

The tables were mostly cut-down wooden spools that at one time housed industrial cable, the chairs a mixture of anything that could be sat upon, including a flat rock and some plain wooden boxes.

Incredibly, over in the far corner a stickie was stuffed and mounted on a wooden box, its eyes replaced with shiny glass marbles, its hands raised as if about to attack. The mutie was wearing pants, but its chest was bare, the mottled skin covered with the puckered scars of large bore bullet holes, along with a stitched slash on its neck that almost went completely across.

"Must been some fight," Jak muttered.

"Ah, that it was young fellow!" a drunk sec man called out, waving a wooden mug. "Buy me a drink and I'll tell you all the details. Lost ten men chilling the bastards, and nearly got caught by the Core!"

"Shut up, fool," another man hissed, grabbing the arm of his friend and squeezing so hard his knuckles went white.

The drunk went silent and bent over his mug to concentrate on his shine.

The Core, eh? Ryan filed that name away to check into if he got the chance. Maybe that was what the Trader was calling his people these days.

Now voices dropped as the companions made their way through the room heading for an empty table. Taking a seat, Krysty noticed an old brass plaque on the wall, the lettering barely discernable, buried as it was under the accumulation of grease and dirt.

"Rockpoint Nine Relay Station," Krysty read aloud. "Relay for what, I wonder?"

"No signs of any power lines," Mildred said, reviewing the ville in her mind. "Might have been a satellite base, or microwave transmission relay for telephones."

Placing his longblaster on the table in plain sight, Ryan left the table and went to the counter. The man behind the bar was tall and muscular, missing several fingers on his left hand, and his left eye was a marbled white, a long scar going from his forehead, across the dead orb and down to his dimpled chin.

"Lost it in a knife fight, eh?" Ryan said, gesturing at the man's white scar. "Me, too."

"But we're still here and the other fellas ain't." The bartender chuckled. "Nice to meet another brother of the blade. I'm Bart. So what do you want, outlander? No eyes for sale today."

Snorting a laugh, Ryan found himself immediately liking the man. "Just food," he said, then on impulse reached into a pocket and flipped the man a single .22 cartridge.

The bartender made the catch with both hands and stared at the round of ammo as if it were alive.

"Damn. Prime condition. Stew is on the fire, help yourself," Bart said, pocketing the round. "Got some roast lizzie, but not much left. If you ain't got a plate, use a hubber, but then you scrub it clean afterward. Or there's some flat bread. All you want."

A hubber, a hub cap for a plate. Glancing at the fireplace, Ryan now saw a battered plastic milk crate stacked with the ornate metal disks bearing car company logos. The companions had military mess kits, but again showing off their wealth in such a poor ville would only start a fight.

"We'll use the flat bread," Ryan decided.

A man stumbled at the end of the bar and thumped it with a fist. "Beer!" he called out, slurring the word.

"Smart choice on the flat bread," Bart said, pulling a chipped ceramic mug from under the counter and dipping it into an open barrel behind the counter. "Most people don't clean the hubbers so well, and some of them are kinda ripe."

"Is the bread fresh?" J.B. asked, joining them at the counter.

Sliding the mug down the counter to the waiting customer, Bart looked hostilely at the man's glasses.

"He's with me," Ryan said, twitching a thumb.

The sec man at the end caught the beer, slopping some of the pale fluid onto himself and the floor, then stumbled away sipping nosily at the mug.

"Fresh? Well, it wasn't made today," Bart admitted, wiping his mutilated hands dry on a wet towel tucked into his gun belt. There was no blaster, the holster containing a wooden cudgel instead. "But then, it wasn't made last moon either. Fresh enough to eat, if you got strong teeth."

"Anything to drink, Bart?" Ryan asked. This was a technique he had learned long ago. Chat with the bartender, get on his good side and slowly the man would spill the local gossip.

"Beer and shine," the man growled. "Only water here is reserved for sec men. Ain't none for sale."

"That so, brother?" Ryan asked, scratching at his leather eye patch.

Keeping a straight expression, Bart placed a scarred arm on the counter and leaned forward. "Well," he added softly, "if you pay double the price for shine, there might be water in the mug. Stranger things have happened."

"Sounds good. A round of shine for the table," Ryan reached into a pocket and placed a couple of .22 rounds on the counter.

"Nuke me, but you're packing brass," Bart said,

covering the rounds with a hand and sliding them out of sight. "What are you, the Trader's bastard?"

"Could be," J.B. said, resting an arm on the counter and briefly opening his fingers to expose a pile of cartridges. "And if we were looking to avoid that person, which would be the best direction for us not to travel?"

Bart arched an eyebrow at the man and clamped his mouth tight. "I'll have a girl bring the drinks," he said woodenly, all traces of friendliness gone.

"Well, that went poorly," J.B. muttered as they walked away from the counter.

"Gaza has these folks scared to the bone," Ryan agreed, glancing backward. The bartender avoided his look. "Mebbe we should visit the baron and see what we can learn from him directly."

"You mean, pretend we're mercies and try to hire on for the job of chilling the Trader?"

"We've done it before."

"Not always with success," J.B. stated flatly.

As they crossed the room, a group of sec men watched the companions closely and started to whisper among themselves. Ryan spotted them and marked the group as possible trouble.

Returning to their table, the men told the others what had happened. Just as they finished, some feminine laughter sounded from upstairs and the floor began thumping in a familiar pattern.

"Got idea," Jak said, inclining his heads toward the stairs. "Go talk girls. Never knew gaudy slut won't talk for extra jak and no sweating."

"They'd know everything," Mildred agreed. "Probably more than the baron does about what was happening in his ville."

"Food first," Ryan decided, pulling a box closer to the table. "Going to be a long night, no matter how this goes."

A girl who looked more like a gaudy slut than a waitress brought over a tray of mugs filled with water and left without saying a word.

"Wait a minute before drinking," Mildred said, taking a container and sniffing carefully. Lifting the mug to the flickering candlelight, she inspected the coloration of the contents, then dipped in a finger and placed a drop on the back of her hand, then touched the tip of her tongue to the drop.

"Clean," she announced at last.

"And clear," Ryan added, checking his rad counter. More than once, they had bought water only to find it hotter than the bottom of a glass lake.

After quenching their thirst, the companions got their food two at a time and settled down to eat. During the meal a few sec men wandered upstairs drunk, and a few came stumbling down the stairs fixing their pants and tucking in their shirts. A bald man stopped near the table and leered at Krysty, but she placed her revolver on the table and he moved off quickly muttering under his breath.

"If Jak gets nothing upstairs," Ryan stated, laying aside his wooden spoon, "we'll get back and start work on the wag so it's ready to leave at dawn."

"Leave for where?" Krysty said, chewing a mouthful of her stew. There was meat in the mix and some veggies, but also a lot of gritty corn. The kernels had to have been ground between pieces of sandstone. Or house bricks.

"Grandee," Ryan answered, taking the last chunk of flat bread and stuffing it into his mouth to chew it soft.

"We can use that place near the river as a base to start searching the Deathlands," he continued after swallowing, "until we find somebody who knows something."

"Gotta go there anyway," J.B. agreed, dipping his bread into the water to try to soften the stuff. The bread swelled a little and he chewed it carefully, finding more grit in the flat bread. Damn sand was everywhere. Had to be mighty uncomfortable for the girls working overhead.

"That seems to be our best plan so far," Mildred said, cleaning her spoon on a spare chunk of bread before tucking the spoon back into her jacket pocket. "I'll get something for Dean and Doc." Standing, she checked her blaster, then headed for the fireplace. A couple of the drunks watched her pass, but none of them got in her way.

As Mildred returned with cigarlike rolls of flat bread containing stew, a mature woman come over with a tray of wooden mugs.

"We didn't order a second round," Ryan said suspiciously.

As she placed the drinks on the table, he noticed the woman had eyes as blue as topaz, startling in their intensity of color.

"Here you are, sir. Sorry it took so long," she said loudly, then added in a whisper, "Bart is my husband."

"Something wrong?" Krysty asked in concern.

"Hell, yes," she replied quickly, taking the empty mugs and putting them on her tray. It was just a circle of plastic, but seemed to serve well enough. "In this ville asking certain questions get you sent to the temple to feed the Scorpion God. What you were talking about is top round in that mag. Ain't nobody here going to talk about that person you mentioned. Unless they're a feeb."

Well, that certainly covered those two at the motel. "Thanks for the tip," Ryan said. "Anything else?"

"Oops, sorry," the woman said for no apparent reason. Then pulling out a rag, she pretended to mop a spill on the dry table. When she took it away there now was a damp circle on the wood with a tail sticking out like the comet. Or a compass heading.

Krysty glanced up at that and emerald green eyes met those of ultrablue. "Understood," the redhead said, pressing a handful of spare rounds into the pocket of the woman's apron. "We'll stay low."

"Don't go upstairs, they're waiting for you. That wag caused a stir here like kicking a hornet's nest. Everybody wants it to try to escape," the woman said, turning to leave. "Sorry again. Anything else you need, just ask."

As the woman returned to the bar, Krysty wiped her hands across the mark obliterating if from the table. "South by southwest," she said taking a sip of her water, then reacted when she realized the mug was filled with shine. Mother Gaia, it was strong! They could use this to run the wag if necessary.

"Okay, got what we wanted," Ryan said, standing and hitching his belt. "Let's go."

The companions left the gaudy house and hurried up the street, pausing at the sight of the lighted barn, Dean standing in the doorway with a drawn blaster in his hand. Ryan slid the Steyr off his shoulder and worked the bolt. "Hey, Able," he called out, using their established code, asking if there was an ambush.

"No problems here, Charlie," the boy answered, giving the prearranged countersign.

The friends entered the barn and found the wag parked exactly where they left it, the nukelamp blazing away. High in the sky, lightning briefly flickered across the black storm clouds drifting among the thick patina of twinkling stars.

"Here you go," Mildred said, passing over the wrapped stew.

Without a word, Dean tore into it like a wolf and didn't speak for a few moments.

"Damn, that's good," he said at last, coming up to breathe. "Hot pipe, I was starving. What took you long enough? It's been over two hours, and I was starting to worry."

"Doc should have told you we were getting food," Ryan demanded sharply, glancing around. "Where is he, anyway? Taking a nap in the wag?"

Lowering his soggy sandwich, the boy blinked in surprise. "But he's with you," Dean said slowly. "I haven't seen Doc since you left."

Chapter Twelve

Stepping outside the barn, the companions listened to the ville around them, straining for the faintest cry from the missing man. But the silence was thick, no shouts or sounds of a struggle disturbing the night.

"The peace of a grave," Ryan spit, unholstering his blaster. "Somebody is playing us for fools. Mildred, J.B., stay here. Krysty, with me. We'll check the motel, see if Sparrow and Jed are still tied up. Jak, sweep the area for any traces."

As the man and the woman dashed out of the structure into the dark street, Jak grabbed a nuke-lamp from the back of the wag. Returning to the street, he started at the front door and began sweeping the blaze of light along the cobblestones.

"Pity we can't use the wag to search the ville," Mildred said, glancing longingly at the vehicle. "But that perforated muffler makes so much noise it would announce our presence to deaf people."

"Any chance you refilled the wag?" J.B. asked,

zipping up his leather jacket midway. Away from the canopy, the desert breeze blew strong, seeming to go straight down his collar.

"Sure, not much else to do," the boy answered while licking his fingers, then wiping his greasy mouth on a sleeve. "Mebbe Doc is just off at the shitters."

"For two hours?" Mildred shot back incredulously. "Damn well hope not."

"Could have fallen in," J.B. said with a frown. "Old wooden planks get weak and it happens sometimes."

The physician frowned. "Hell of a way to die. Drowning in a pit of shit. Stay here with Dean, and I'll go check."

"Nobody is going anywhere alone," J.B. stated forcibly. "We wait for the others to come back, then we check."

"He could die by then!"

"And it could be a trap. We go with what we know. I'd sure as hell hate to lose Doc, but I'm damn sure that I would rather keep you, Millie."

Just then, Jak appeared at the open doorway of the barn holding Doc's sword. The ebony sheath was missing, and the blade was darkly stained with blood.

"Night creep," the teenager stated. "Got him."

"Can you track them?" Mildred asked, pulling her piece. Suddenly the silence of the ville seemed to be the stillness of a waiting trap, with enemies watching from every shadow.

Jak shook his head. "Not on bare stone."

"Now we recce the outhouses," J.B. said, working the bolt on the Uzi. "Millie, stay with Dean. Let's go."

Jak and the Armorer charged into the night, their faces grim masks.

Pulling a metallic envelope from a pocket, Dean ripped it open and used the U.S. Army moist towelette to clean his hands of the grease from dinner, then checked over his Browning Hi-Power. His gut was starting to tell the boy death was on the move and coming their way.

"We didn't find him," J.B. reported ten minutes later, stepping into view. "And we did a once around the block in case it was just a mugging. Just some ville hardcases out to steal his blaster."

"He gone." Jak brandished the sword, the ebony stick now poking through his gun belt. "But we found sheath."

"Where?"

"Near shitters. Must have ambushed there."

"Well, don't sheath the blade!" Mildred advised. "We might need that blood."

"My very idea," Ryan said from the street, holding a dog on a leash.

Standing close by, Krysty had her blaster hard against the back of Sparrow. The man was shivering in the cold.

"Saw what was happening from the window," Ryan said with a scowl. "No sign of Doc from up there, so we brought some help."

"Your turn," Krysty said, nudging Sparrow forward with the muzzle of her blaster.

Ryan passed the man the rope leash. "Find our friend, and you keep breathing," he growled. "Run off, and we'll torch that pesthole with your brother still inside. Get me?" It was a lie, but Sparrow didn't know that.

"Sure, sure, no prob. Houston is a good tracker. We found lots of folks for the baron," the fat man sputtered, tightening his grip on the rope and scratching the animal behind an ear. "Just show him the blade."

Jak held out the steel and the dog approached it warily, then started to sniff, his tail wagging in excitement.

"Got the scent, boy? Good. Now go find the runaway. Find the runaway, boy!" Sparrow released the rope and the dog sprung forward, his nose checking the ground here and there, spreading across the street, then starting back again.

Mildred curled a lip at the wording. Runaway, eh? Sounded like the ville did keep slaves. Maybe they simply hadn't encountered them yet.

"What if this doesn't work?" Dean asked grimly, muted thunder rumbling on the horizon.

His father glanced at the keep rising above the ville just as lightning flashed, silhouetting the structure for a split second. "Then we grab the baron and trade his ass for Doc."

"If he's been aced?"

"Then Rockpoint gets a new baron," Ryan stated.

Over by the outhouses, the dog suddenly went stiff and lurched down a side street at a lope.

"He's got the scent!" Sparrow gushed, starting after the hound.

Moving fast, the companions raced along the cobblestones, following the dog through the maze of streets.

"Stay close. This could be an ambush."

"Good," Ryan snarled, working the bolt action on the Steyr.

Houston paused at an intersection, checking the ground several times before finally choosing an alleyway. People watched through closed shutters as the companions ran by, the adobe buildings going dark as candles were hastily extinguished. Obviously this was sec-man work and none of their concern.

Reaching a courtyard, the dog froze and growled at the darkness to the left, weird piles of things creaking in the wind, the jumble reaching higher than the wall surrounding the ville.

"What's over there?" Ryan demanded.

Sparrow shrugged. "Junkyard. Baron collects predark machines."

"I thought this place didn't have any wags?" J.B. said.

"None of them work," Sparrow replied. "Houston just don't like it there 'cause the baron guards the stuff with a couple of big cats he caught in the salt lands."

Gaza protected wags that didn't work with a couple of cougars? Sure. Ryan was starting to understand why the baron was on bad terms with Trader. It was starting to sound like Gaza was stockpiling weapons and wags for a major assault somewhere. A war was brewing in these sand dunes, which meant there had to be another ville nearby. Unless Trader was the target.

"Really hates those folks to the north of here, eh?" Ryan tried on a hunch.

"Ain't nothing to the north that I know about,"
Sparrow said, sounding puzzled. "Hey, there he
goes again!"

In a burst of speed, Houston scampered down a
broad street, then disappeared into a cross street.
Turning the corner, Ryan spied the dog running
past a group of sec men coming down the street
with crackling torches and crossbows in their
hands.

"It's the outlanders!" a sec man cried, starting
to level the crossbow. "Chill them!"

Releasing his grip on the Steyr, Ryan pulled the
SIG-Sauer and fired, the silenced blaster coughing
twice, the whispering 9 mm slugs tearing through
the soft tissue of the men's throats and the guards
fell, drowning in their own blood.

One of them got off an arrow that whizzed past
Jak, and he jerked an arm forward. The blade hit
the sec man in the chest dead center in the heart.
Still holding the crossbow, the man went completely still, then slowly toppled.

Another raised his longblaster and Dean flipped
his Bowie knife into the man's stomach, making
him drop the blaster. Then Ryan stroked the trigger
on the SIG-Sauer and the guard flipped backward
minus a face.

"Take the bows," Krysty directed, tugging a

quiver of bolts from the trembling arm of a corpse. "Once we start shooting, all hell is going to break loose."

"Has already," Ryan muttered, slitting the throat of a guard who was somehow still alive.

"A silenced blaster," Sparrow whispered. "You folks work for the Trader!"

"Close enough," J.B. stated, watching the windows along the street while Mildred took the other crossbow and a second quiver. The stock seemed to be whittled from a house beam, the cross hammered from a steel leaf-spring out of a car. She had seen similar homemade weapons before. They were crude, cumbersome and extremely powerful.

"Is he coming?" the man asked eagerly. "Going to do Gaza and Hawk? Be glad to help there."

"Go find your dog," Ryan ordered.

Moving around the sprawled bodies, Sparrow took off after the animal, with the companions close behind. Raised voices were heard in the distance, but they moved away from the group heading for the keep. Oddly, the area was starting to look familiar when Ryan saw the dog start for a redbrick building without doors or windows.

"Dark night, this is the rear of the temple!" J.B. said.

"Call him back now!" Ryan ordered brusquely.

Sparrow whistled and the dog stopped, looking back at his master, then turned and trotted back.

"So that's where he is," Sparrow said hoarsely. "They got him in the temple. Might as well leave. Most likely he's aced already. Or worse."

"What do you mean 'worse'?" J.B. demanded.

"Blood for water," Sparrow said, quoting the ville mantra. "But I also hear the Scorpion God likes it spiced with screams."

Doc was in a torture chamber? Shitfire. Ryan swung around his blaster until it pointed at Sparrow. In spite of the evening chill, the fat man started to sweat.

"You kept your part of the deal," Ryan said gruffly. "So we keep ours. Now leave before I change my mind."

Sparrow nodded energetically and took off at a run down the street, Houston tagging along behind his corpulent master.

"If he talks, we're dead," J.B. said, tracking their departure with the Uzi machine gun.

Ryan turned from the man and the dog. "He wouldn't do anything until he's set his brother free, and then they'll have to discuss whether they should side with Trader or Gaza."

"Say, fifteen minutes."

"Mebbe ten."

Staying in the shadows as much as possible, the companions moved around to the front of the building and studied the two guards at the door. Both were large men holding bolt-action longblasters, with a muzzle-loading pistol tucked into their belts. They were smoking cigs and appeared bored.

"No other doors," Krysty said, her hair a wild tempest of motion as her hands tightened on the crossbow. "We have to go in this way."

"No problem," Ryan said, removing the half-spent clip from the SIG-Sauer and gently inserting a fresh one.

Suddenly a bell began to ring from the keep and the guards jumped at the sound, casting away their smokes to slide their blasters off their shoulders and work the bolts.

"Shitfire, that must be the ville alarm," J.B. cursed, ducking lower into the shadows.

"A single shot from them, and we'll have the whole ville coming down our throats," Dean added, glancing around. Lights were appearing from behind closed windows. "Whatever we're going to do better be soon."

"We move on my mark," Ryan growled, steadying the SIG-Sauer in both hands. "Ready...go."

Stepping into plain view, Mildred clicked on the nukelamp, bathing the two guards in its blinding

light. Covering their faces, the men cursed as
Krysty and Jak used the crossbows. The bolts took
the men in the throats, neutralizing any chance of
them crying out in pain. Gagging on their own
blood, the guards staggered drunkenly about as the
companions rushed across the open courtyard and
finished the job with knifes. It was brutal and
messy, but there was no other choice.

Jak and Dean pushed the bodies against the wall,
while Ryan tried the door. It was locked tight. The
one-eyed man got out of the way as J.B. rummaged
in his munitions bag for some tools and got to
work. The rest of the companions nervously stood
around the man, watching the windows and side
streets for any movements. The alarm bell continued to sound from the keep.

"Barred from the inside," the Armorer said in
frustration. "No way to open this without using a
gren."

For a long moment, Ryan stared hostilely at the
door as if it were a living enemy. "Give me the
sword," he demanded.

Jak passed over the ebony stick. Unsheathing the
blood smeared blade, Ryan wiggled the point between the door and the frame. It took some muscle,
but he finally got the slim steel to slide all the way
through, then he pulled it upward in a hard jerk.

There was a crash inside and the door swung open a crack.

"Bring them," Ryan directed, slipping into the building with the SIG-Sauer leading the way.

The companions dragged in the bodies of the chilled sec men, leaving behind a wide crimson trail. But there was nothing they could do about that. Inside the temple oil lanterns burned in wall niches, illuminating a large empty room decorated with a wall tapestry of a blue scorpion. There was nothing else but a gate made of slim iron bars sealing off an arched doorway.

Reaching high, Mildred pulled down the tapestry and stepped outside to mop up the excess blood on the stoop, while J.B. went to work on the gate. As the physician came back in and tossed aside the gory cloth, there was a solid click and J.B. pushed open the gate.

"Hey, what was that?" a man called out from a dark corridor. "Who are you folks?"

Stepping through the archway, Ryan fired the silenced weapon directly into the unseen face. The blaster coughed, its muzzle-flash lighting the corridor for a heartbeat, and the man jerked backward as an explosion of blood and brains slapped against the brick wall. As the dead guard crumpled to the floor, the rest of the companions rushed past the gate, and J.B. locked it in their wake. That should buy them a few minutes, but not much more.

"From here on, it's chillin' time," Ryan said low and fast. "Ace anybody you see. All we're interested in is finding Doc."

Jak passed the crossbow to Dean. "Ready," the albino teen said, drawing a knife with each hand.

The brick corridor was lined with more tapestries that were barely discernible in the yellowish light of the hissing lanterns. A set of double doors closed off the end, and Ryan placed his ear to the wood. There were some muffled voices, a laugh and then the telltale crack of a whip followed by a cry of pain.

"That's Doc," Krysty stated, bringing up the crossbow.

Slamming open the door, Ryan withheld firing as Mildred clicked on the nukelamp, filling the next room with harsh white light. As the three sec men lowered their whips, the companions opened fire in unison with every weapon. The men reeled at the incoming lead and arrows, died on the spot torn to pieces.

Walking into the vast room, Ryan felt a shiver go through his bones. This was something new. It was a church from hell. The pews had been removed, leaving the center open for people to gather. A wooden railing stood before an altar at the back of the church, and a giant scorpion stood on a velvet-covered altar, a steady stream of water trickling from its open mouth into a stone basin on the floor. Surrounding the basin was a low stone wall filled with dozens of live black scorpions.

Set on either side of the altar were slanted tables, the left covered with a canvas sheet, the right supporting Doc. The old man had been stripped to the waist, his hands and feet shackled with chains and pulled tight, holding him motionless. His back was covered with welts and countless old scars, a few of them bleeding slightly from the cut of the whip, but his chest still rose and fell.

Keeping their every weapon on the motionless scorpion towering over them, the companions crossed the room, and J.B. got to work on the shackles.

"You okay?" Mildred asked, setting down the nukelamp and turning Doc's head to look into his eyes. The pupils dilated to the light. No drugs used this time, but her fingers found a hard lump on the back of his head that told the story. Hit from behind.

"I live," Doc whispered hoarsely. "Th-that is enough."

"Any more sec men around?" Ryan demanded,

taking the nukelamp and playing the white beam around the church. There were no other doors in sight, but that didn't mean a whole lot. Could be dozens of secret entrances.

Doc weakly shook his head while Mildred started to clean the cuts on his back with some of the precious med supplies from her satchel. The scholar winced at the application of shine, but said nothing. He had endured much worse.

"There were three," he croaked, "and three when we arrived. One is very big with a—"

"Got them," Ryan interrupted, taking the man by the shoulder and giving a hard squeeze. "We aced six."

"S-splendid."

"There," J.B. said with satisfaction and the mechanism disengaged, the chains dropping noisily away.

Krysty slid a shoulder under Doc's arm to help him stand, while Mildred helped the man slip on his shirt and coat.

"Think you can walk out of here?" J.B. asked, offering the ebony stick.

Fumbling to button his shirt, Doc stopped and took the stick. Extracting the blade, he inspected it in the white light, then held it out to wipe the steel clean on a sec man sprawled on the floor. The corpse had an arrow through its chest, and a slash along its neck that went from ear to Adam's apple, but not quite deep enough to open the big artery under the skin.

"If need be to leave here," Doc stated resolutely, closing the weapon with a solid click, "I can sprout wings and fly."

"What happened?" Dean asked.

Tucking the stick into his belt, Doc finished dressing. "I went to visit the outhouse, and they were waiting, not inside, but on top. I never even considered the possibility, but shall in the future. They knocked the LeMat away, but I got that man with my sword. Then I was struck from behind and awoke in this charming abattoir."

"Come again?" Jak asked, scowling in confusion.

"Slaughterhouse," Doc translated.

Doing a fast recce of the temple, Ryan walked closer to the giant on the altar. In the yellowish light of the oil lanterns the thing seemed to move slightly as if alive and watching. But starkly illuminated by the nukelamp, it was plain to see the thing was merely a statue covered with oil to distort the light. It was just a trick.

"So this is the Scorpion God," Ryan said in a

monotone. "A whole ville terrified of a statue from some predark museum or an amusement park."

"And this explains the blood for water we've been hearing about," Krysty said, studying the basin and enclosure. The scorpions reacted to her presence by running about and arching their deadly barbed tails, ready to attack. "Gaza must feed scraps of flesh to the scorpions so that the people can reach the basin and fill their water jugs."

"Literally, blood for water," Mildred muttered, tossing away a bloody cloth.

"Look at them go," Dean said in disgust. "Little bastards are expecting food."

"Getting oil, instead," Jak snarled. Going to a nearby niche, he removed the lantern and blew out the flame. Returning to the cage, he used the gun butt of his blaster to smash open the reservoir of the lantern and poured the flammable oil over the darting scorpions, then lit the wick of the lantern and dropped it. The fire whoofed alive, and the creatures started high-pitched squealing as they burned, scampering madly about and stinging one another in their utter lack of comprehension of exactly what was destroying them.

Checking the bodies, Dean took their blasters, ammo pouches and a folding knife. Not bad, but he had better. Then the boy paused. "I know this man," Dean said slowly. "He was the sec man who met us outside the ville gate."

"Said he would get back at us," Mildred said, wiping her hands clean, then tossing the damp rag away. "Guess he meant it."

"Indeed, he did, madam," Doc told her, starting to sound like his old self again. Using his ebony stick as a cane, he hobbled over, then stopped and forced himself to stand erect without assistance. Only the tightening of his mouth betrayed what the effort cost him in pain.

"By the way, how is the other prisoner? I heard him moan when I was being chained," Doc added. "I would suppose the noise reminded him of his own imprisonment."

Going to the other side of the altar, Ryan yanked away the sheet to expose the bloody remains of what had once been a man. His eyes were gone, as were his ears and nose. The sagging mouth held no teeth, and those were the least of the injuries. Both arms had been removed at the elbow, the stumps covered with horrible scars. His legs were missing at the knees, and there was only a tattered nubbin of flesh hanging between the naked man's scarred thighs.

"I wonder who he was," Mildred whispered, "and what he did to deserve this."

"Fuck her..." The tortured spoke, lifting his

horrible head. "Didn't fuck her, you bastard. We're in love! Don't care she was going to be your wife, ya got enough, Gaza! Bastard! Stinking, filthy bastard…"

Then a racking shudder shook the man. "Oh, God, please, no more. I'll tell ya anything you want to know. Where the Trader stores his fuel and weapons! Anything! But no more cutting. Please, stop cutting me up! No more!"

Thrashing feebly at his iron bonds, the prisoner began to mumble incoherently. Turning, Ryan gave Mildred a hard look and the physician sadly shook her head. With regret, Ryan placed the muzzle of his blaster to the mutilated remains of man and fired once. The head slapped to the side from the impact of the slug, and the moaning ceased as the man slipped into the sweet release of death.

"One of the Trader's men," J.B. scowled. "Did the local baron's bride and started a war. Damn fool."

"Love makes folks do crazy things," Mildred added softly. "I wonder what happened to the woman?"

"Hopefully long dead," Krysty said with a sigh. "And probably done a lot worse than this."

"Let's get moving before the same happens to us," Ryan said, heading for the front door of the temple.

Chapter Thirteen

The banded door to the keep slammed aside and Baron Gaza strode out of the structure, dragging a sec man by the throat. With a roar of anger, Gaza threw the man down the front steps onto the cobblestone street, where he landed sprawling before the waiting company of sec men filling the courtyard.

"My lord, it's true!" the man cried, rubbing his sore neck. "The people who saw the chilling claim that Ryan has a blaster that makes no noise!"

"Liar!" Baron Gaza shouted. "Find me those traitors and stuff them into the Black Queens!"

The sec men reacted badly to that order, and several openly stroked the grips of the blasters.

"But some of them were children," a sec man from the crowd said in a loud clear voice. Then almost grudgingly he added, "My lord."

Gaza turned on the man, but before he could speak, Hawk strode through the crowd leading his stallion by the reins.

"The children and women are spared, of course," Hawk said, striding through the crowd. "In fact, forget these liars until tomorrow. Tonight we concentrate on finding those murdering outlanders."

Murmurs of approval rose from the guards, and Gaza forced his rage under control. These weren't his wives, broken and beaten until they lived to serve, but armed fighters who he controlled only through fear. The ville was already twitchy enough about cutting off relations with Trader. If the stupe cattle knew his real plans, they'd probably revolt even faster than if they discovered the truth about the water.

"The outlanders are the top priority," Baron Gaza agreed loudly. "They aced sec men, a crime for which there is only one punishment. To become food for the god and earn this ville more water!"

Shouts of agreement came from the men, a mixture of revenge and greed crossing their dirty faces. Yes, he thought, they would like that idea.

"Except for this Ryan, who goes to the table!" Baron Gaza added as an afterthought. "Perhaps the knives can make him tell the secret of this silent blaster, eh?"

Now the sec man laughed at the foolish notion, his momentary outburst forgotten.

"Wall Sergeant Franz, Gate Sergeant Henny, double the guards on the wall," Hawk commanded. "Nobody leaves this ville tonight without the baron's personal authorization."

"And send off outriders," Gaza directed. "I want twenty men on patrol in the desert around the ville. If this Ryan gets outside Rockpoint, they're to bring him back alive. Chill the rest."

"But what about the night muties?" a man began, glancing toward the high walls.

"My lord, we can't double the wall patrols and send outriders while searching the ville," Hawk said quickly, walking his horse closer to the furious man on the stoop. "We don't have enough troops."

"Do as you think best," Gaza conceded, then sensing a loss of power quickly added, "But the man who captures Ryan alive can have his redhead as a reward. Permanently!"

The baron could see that the guards liked that idea. Pitiful fools. Norms were like horses—you needed a carrot and a stick to make them obey. Beat them once so they knew the taste of pain, then reward them often but always at the end of the stick so they would remember.

"However, I lay claim to the black woman," Hawk said, climbing onto his horse and gesturing at the men on top of the keep. "Even if she surrenders, I want her dead! Now to the walls! Let's find these coldhearts and show their guts to the stars!''

The alarm bell on the roof of the brick building started clanging once more and the sec men rallied to the sound, rushing to their posts on foot and horseback, waving their blasters and crossbows.

With only his personal bodyguards staying close, Gaza stood on the stoop of the imposing keep and looked across the roofed ville. The one location he ignored was the temple. Only feebs would dare to venture to that place. His secrets were safe there. Now where could the outlanders be hiding? Where?

From the barred windows of the keep, the wives of the baron watched the tableau below. Their fingers wove silent words to one another as they discussed what was happening, and how best to make it serve their needs.

PAUSING AT THE temple door, the companions checked their blasters before entering the corridor that lead to the front exit.

''Okay, got any idea yet how we're going to get out of the ville?'' J.B. asked, racking the scattergun to exit a shell and then thumbing it back into the feeder slot. It was a habit he had developed recently to spread the lubrication inside the weapon and make sure it was feeding smoothly when there was going to be fighting in the desert. He knew how badly sand and blasters mixed.

"We blow up the temple as a distraction," Ryan said, "then escape in the confusion."

"That should do it." The Armorer grinned and pulled out an implo gren. "I can rig all three to go simultaneously. That'll level this whole place."

"Save one to remove the gate," Krysty advised. "Blood is the only way they're going to let us leave."

"Gotcha."

"Wait a moment," Doc cried, feeling the empty holster at his hip. "Has anybody seen my LeMat?"

Dean gestured at the dead men on the floor. "They didn't have it," he answered, then pulled a big bore revolver from his belt. "Want one of their wheelguns? No reloads, but it's better than nothing."

"I suppose that would be wise," Doc stated, then frowned. "No, wait a moment. I remember somebody placing it inside a black statue, saying they would get it later."

"Statue?" Jak asked, glancing at the fiberglass scorpion dominating the altar.

"Hiding it from Hawk to keep for themselves, is what he meant," Ryan said, washing the light of the nukelamp along the side walls. ''There's going to be chilling, so we need every weapon. Let's find it quick.''

In the clear beam of the headlight, the companions started back for the giant scorpion, then noticed a series of shallow alcoves lining both walls. Normally in a predark church those were filled with statues of Christian saints, but held the squat somber figures of iron maidens. Resembling a metal statue of a fat woman, the iron shells were actually hollow and hinged to open like a clam shell, the interior covered with sharp spikes. When a prisoner was forced inside and the hatch closed, the spikes would only penetrate their flesh a little bit, making even the slightest move in any direction yield untold agony. The victims often went insane after only a few days and threw themselves at the spikes to end their lives but slowly bleeding to death. Both Mildred and Doc knew that even the legendary Torquemada had considered them cruel machines and only used the iron maiden on his worst enemies.

''Which one was it?'' Dean asked, studying the line of dark figures.

''That I do not recall,'' Doc rumbled. ''My attention was elsewhere.''

Feeling the pressure of the enemy outside the

temple, Ryan started for the closest device. "Dean, start on the left, Doc take the right."

Going to the first iron maiden, Ryan saw a pair of wrinkled eyes staring back from the viewing slit in the metal face. Dried and lifeless, the corpse inside was long dead. The next few held only skeletons. Across the temple, the others were having a similar lack of success.

Then peering inside an iron maiden, Ryan saw it was empty. What's more, the spikes weren't in evidence. Grabbing the handle, he twisted the locking bolt free and there was no sound, the metal well oiled. Suddenly alert, Ryan braced himself and was in front of the torture device when it started to swing aside. He stopped it purely as a precaution. A heartbeat later something slammed into the metal, knocking him backward. Even as Ryan drew his blaster, the door continued to swing open wide and a smashed wooden arrow fell to the floor with a clatter. Weighed on an angle, the oiled hatch swung closed once more with a muffled boom.

A boobie! The torture device was rigged with a trap to keep people out? What sense did that make? Unless it was a lot more than it seemed.

"Pass me the light," Ryan ordered.

J.B. handed over the second nukelamp, and Ryan opened the hatch just enough to slip the light inside on the floor. Then closing the door, he carefully put his good eye to a viewing slot and saw the back swing open wide for a moment onto a brick-lined passageway and then close once more.

"Found a hidey-hole," Ryan announced to the others. "I'm going to do a fast recce."

"At your back," J.B. said, leveling the shotgun.

Pulling open the door again, Ryan stayed well clear but no arrow was launched this time. Had to be a one-shot boobie. Retrieving the lamp from the floor, the man hunched over to fit inside the infernal machine and braced himself as the door swung closed. There was a subdued click, and the back opened wide as it had before and he stepped through into a room filled with boxes and barrels and crates. It was an armory, with racks of long-blasters lining the walls, and multiple shelves stuffed full of plastic jars of loose ammo, the rims sealed with wax to keep out the air.

On a table directly before the secret entrance was the LeMat pistol. Laying alongside was an empty crossbow, the trigger rigged with a copper wire feeding through iron guides thick with grease and leading to the iron maiden.

Then the device clicked impotently, trying to release an arrow that wasn't there, and the back of the maiden swung aside, admitting an Uzi machine gun held by J.B.

"You okay?" the Armorer asked, peering around. "Son of a bitch, it's the baron's private armory!"

"Looks like," Ryan agreed. He picked up the LeMat and tried to tuck it into a pocket, but the Civil War blaster was much too heavy, so he stuffed it into his belt instead.

"I'll rig this open and get the rest in here," J.B. said, slinging the Uzi and grabbing some rope from a peg on the wall. Then he realized it was sticky with some sort of glue and covered with black dust. It was a fuse! And just about the worst one he had ever seen. The local armorer had no idea what the hell he was doing. Just a rank amateur.

Ryan found extra arrows and placed them next to the crossbow while J.B. tied back the interior door, then opened the outer half of the shell and beckoned the rest of the companions over. Soon, they were spreading throughout the armory, looting the place of everything useful. The very best long-blasters were grabbed by Krysty, Mildred and Jak along with bandoliers of shiny brass ammo, while Ryan and J.B. smashed open the sealed jars and passed out handfuls of different ammo to each person. Dean kept his crossbow, in case there was

more silent chilling to be done, but he grabbed a
plastic predark quiver full of bolts with razor-sharp
tips.

After checking his LeMat for any damage or
tricks, Doc tossed aside the dead guard's crude
blaster and returned the Civil War piece to its holster, then began his own recce for ammo. However,
while there was a lot of black powder for the homemade scatterguns and muzzle loaders of Rockpoint
ville, there were no primers anywhere to be found.
Apparently they used rimfire cartridges to set off
their shotguns loads. A clever move, but useless for
Doc since he needed percussion nipples for the
LeMat. After filling his ammo pouch with a good
pound of black powder, cloth wads and lead balls
as a reserve, Doc then chose a massive Webley .44
revolver from the assortment of blasters on display.
He had used this type of wheelgun before and
found it to be a satisfactory substitute for the
LeMat. The bullets were loaded with black powder,
and the lead shiny smooth, showing it was also
homemade. Predark rounds were always steel-
coated, or copper-lined to prevent fouling the barrel.

Draping a gun belt over his chest, Doc flinched
as the leather pressed against his raw back and he
was forced to buckle the holster around his waist.

Oddly, with a gun on each hip he found the configuration quite comfortable.

"This must be a bolt-hole," Dean said slowly, testing the draw on the bow. "A place to stage a rally against invaders."

"Bad spot get trapped," Jak growled. "One door."

"Bull," Ryan stated, cracking his knuckles. "No baron would ever box himself in where he could be starved to death. There's another exit somewhere."

"Probably hidden like the door," Mildred said, laying aside a British made Hollands & Hollands .475 Nitro Express rifle.

The huge rifle had to have been the toy of some Texas millionaire and was in excellent condition, with a whole jar of the thick blunt-nosed cartridges. But the Nitro Express simply had too much power for the physician. Without most of the tools she had trained with in the predark days, the woman had only her bare hands to perform meatball surgery. Fighting to control the recoil of the .475 would strengthen her hands and lessen her delicate sense of touch. Killing enemies with the Nitro Express would render her able to save friends. The incredible irony of the matter almost made Mildred laugh and weep at the same time.

"Want to swap?" Krysty asked, proffering a .30-30 Remington longblaster. The barrel had been modified to receive a slotted bayonet at the front, the edge of the blade was feathered from a recent sharpening.

"Sure?" Mildred asked, accepting the lightweight hunting rifle.

Krysty easily worked the thick bolt on the heavy Hollands & Hollands and slid in a fat half-inch-thick round, closing the massive breech with a solid, satisfying clack. "Absolutely," she said grimly. She hated to chill anything, but when blood was necessary, Krysty did the job ruthlessly as any coldheart. It was a simple matter of survival.

"Dark night, we have enough stuff here to level this place," J.B. said, packing a coil of homemade fuse into his munitions bag, along with an assortment of items, including three predark grens. They were only concussion models, designed to knock out people with a deafening boom, not the deadly antipers that threw off bits of shrapnel. But anything would chill folks in the right hands.

"The baron has really been holding out on his troops if they're armed with homemades and he has blasters like this in storage," Ryan said, lifting the lid of a steamer wag to find it full of cedar wood chips and belted links of fat brass. "Check this—

25 mm belted ammo. I think the baron has a cannon somewhere.''

"Mebbe keep?'' Jak suggested, sliding rounds into the side port of the Winchester.

"Yeah, on the roof, most likely,'' Ryan agreed. "That's where I'd put it to get the best field of fire. Cover the whole ville from up there.'' Dropping the linked ammo, the man moved to a wall rack and started to rummage for 7.62 mm rounds for the Steyr, but so far nothing and he was dangerously low. He might have to grab that other Winchester.

Then Ryan saw the shockingly white stock of a U.S. Marine Corps M-14 and hurried closer. He knew the M-14 was a ceremonial rifle used in parades and military reviews for the predark prez. However, it used the exact same caliber as the Steyr SSG-70 sniper rifle. Pulling down the rifle, Ryan opened the 20-round clip and found it full of greasy hardball brass. Back in business!

Going over to the trunk full of belted ammo, J.B. pulled a knife and started to open the wide 25 mm shells to carefully extract the tiny C-4 charge inside the warhead. Some of the plastique was only a dried lump, but most of it was still soft to the touch, and still as volatile as the day it was made a hundred years ago. Soon he had a small mound of the material and started using his palms to press it into crude blocks. Pulling a shower curtain salvaged from the redoubt out of his backpack, Dean passed it over and the Armorer cut it into squares to wrap the C-4 nice and tight.

"We don't need to waste an implo gren now to get through the front gate," J.B. said confidently. "One of these blocks will blow that out of the wall like kicking a knothole."

"Prep one as a scuttle," Ryan said, slipping spare 9 mm rounds into the loops of his gun belt. "We'll get rid of that plastic scorpion and Gaza's private stash in one move."

"Make a hell of a distraction, too, if we time it right."

"Sounds good. Help me with that barrel of black powder, will you?"

While the two men got to work, Mildred continued sorting through some tools on a workbench, hoping to find a replacement for her lost scalpel, when she spied an ancient binder tucked into a shelf and blew off the dust to read the faded cover.

"Rockpoint Water Storage Relay Station Nine," the physician read aloud in amazement, flipping through the yellowed pages of the operations manual. "So that's why the ville is here. This used to be a pumping station for a major city. Water shortage my ass."

"Which means that isn't an artesian well attached to the fiberglass scorpion," Krysty said, practicing to reload the Hollands & Hollands. "There must be a feeder pipe somewhere."

"Not matter," Jak declared, checking the play of a Winchester lever-action rifle.

There had been a lot of .38 long cartridges for the short-barreled longblaster, and it was in prime condition without a sign of rust or corrosion. A lot of folks would fire weapons and then store them away without cleaning, only to return a month later to find the dampness in the air had combined with the residue of the powder to form a kind of acid that ruined a blaster. Mildred had told him the name of the chem, but it slipped his mind at the moment. Carbolic, or something. But there was none of that on the Winchester, which shone with oil.

"No, we can use that to our advantage," Ryan countered. "Let's find that feeder pipe."

Following a blurry map in the manual, Mildred led the group through the armory into a back room, the doorway damaged in spots where the door had been forcibly removed. Inside was a huge steel pipe rising from the ground and doubling back down again. There were some meters and a wheel valve on the pipe, along with a small diameter bleed rod that went into the brick wall and out of sight.

"Straight up the ass and out of the mouth of the Scorpion God," Ryan said. "Gaza controls the water from here, turning it on for the faithful, and off for the people he doesn't like."

"Surprised he hasn't declared himself a god yet," Dean said, showing a surprising understanding of the situation.

"Probably will someday," his father stated. "Bastard of a way to rule a ville. A brave man will charge blasters, but thirsty people will do anything to get a drink of water."

Checking a toolbox on the sandy floor, J.B. used a cloth to wipe the condensed moisture off a pressure meter. "Dark night! This valve is holding back over fourteen tons of pressure. There's enough water here to flood that whole ville. Wash it clean off the map."

"Over here!" Krysty cried out, waving.

In the corner of the pump room was a predark iron ladder bolted to the brick wall leading to a hatch set into the concrete ceiling.

"Let's check outside," Dean said eagerly, reaching for the ladder.

Pulling the boy back, Ryan said, "Remember, these folks like traps."

Using his panga to probe the way, Ryan found razor blades attached to the center of the first cou-

ple of rungs. Anybody grabbing in a hurry would
have sliced off fingers under their own weight.
Checking carefully every foot of the way, he
reached the ceiling and forced open the hatch. A
warm wind blew into the armory, carrying the
sound of the alarm bell still stridently ringing and
clanging, and raised voices shouting in the distance.
Crawling onto the roof, Ryan stayed low until he
was sure there were no guards present, then worked
his way to the edge and slowly stood to see the
whole ville.

Rockpoint was in turmoil, torches moving along
the top of the wall and cries rising from everywhere
below the rippling canopy across the ville. The
light of the wag could be seen from the top of the
temple in the distance, distorted shadows on the
adobe wall showing the barn was occupied. But
whether it was Sparrow looting the wag, or ville
sec men setting a trap was unknown.

"Everybody but the gaudy sluts out looking for
us," J.B. said, pulling out his Navy scope and peering through. "And I'll be damned if they might
also be hunting for us."

"Something sure put a round up the baron's
ass," Ryan agreed, leveling his longblaster. "And
Gaza doesn't even know about the temple yet."

"Might be because we have blasters," Dean suggested, joining the adults.

"Or type of blasters," Jak said, gesturing at the Uzi machine gun. "Some villes never seen rapid-fire. Only legend."

"That must be it," Krysty said softly, crouching low in the roof shadows. "Our blasters. They think we're spies for Trader."

Cradling the Steyr in both hands, Ryan scowled at the notion. "Fireblast! That makes sense. Okay, get back in fast before we're seen."

Quickly and silently, the companions scrambled down the ancient ladder back into the pump room, but as Krysty started to leave she felt compelled to look toward the keep rising above the ville, as if something were forcing her attention there. Then the urge was gone, carried away by the chill desert wind.

The last to leave the rooftop, Ryan left the locking bolt open to speed their escape. A plan was already forming in his mind, something he had never done before. But it seemed like their only chance to leave this pesthole without fighting Gaza and Hawk.

"Okay, new plan. Jak, help J.B. to rig the feeder pipe to blow when somebody enters this room. Krysty, Dean, buy us some time by using the shackles from Doc's table to chain the locking bar on the front door in place. Make it triple-hard for them to get inside. Mildred, give them cover.''

"And I, sir?" Doc demanded. The man hadn't joined them in the brief sojourn onto the rooftop, and was using his ebony stick as a cane when he thought nobody was watching. Ryan didn't blame the man. A whipping took a lot out of a person, left him feeling bruised deep inside as if he had rad sickness. It was a testament to the old man that he was up and moving.

"Sit and rest, Doc. We're going to be moving fast soon, and you will only get us chilled moving slow," Ryan directed, then saw a determined look of indignation grow on the scholar's face.

"Better yet, go make firebrands," Ryan said. "All you can, fast as you can. We leave here in five minutes."

"At once, my dear Ryan! I shall serve where Icarus failed."

"Shut up, ya old coot," Mildred chided, "and get cracking."

"What about you, Dad?" Dean asked, pausing in the open doorway of the pump room, one foot in the armory. "Going back up on the roof to do some sniping at the guards on the front gate?"

"Not yet," the one-eyed man answered, going to the master valve assembly on the feeder pipe and cracking the knuckles on both hands. "I'm going to set the Scorpion God free."

Chapter Fourteen

Going to a wall niche, Ryan removed an oil lantern, blew out the wick and very carefully poured a few drops of the mineral oil onto the base of the valve. Setting the lantern aside, he took the wheel in both hands, braced himself and started applying pressure. The wheel turned only a smallest distance then seemed to become stuck. The man knew that he had to do this gently, too much force too soon and the spindle could snap.

Dean started forward to help, but J.B. held the boy back. There was no room for another set of hands on the wheel; it was a one-person job.

Ryan's hands turned white, sweat appearing on his brow as he continued to exert himself more and more. One of his feet slipped and he almost lost his grip, but dug in even harder.

There was a terrible crack, and for an instant Ryan knew for certain that he had broken the spindle, then with a squeal of metal the wheel came free and began to spin easily. The meters swung high at the rush of water throbbing through the slim bleeder pipe, the length going into the wall shaking from the water coursing through it. Softly from the room beyond came a splashing sound as a torrent of water flooded the stone basin to overflow in only moments and then started to spread across the temple floor.

"It'll take awhile," Mildred said in the pump room, gingerly touching the bleeder pipe. It was already coated with condensation from the sheer volume of water going through. "But soon the temple will flood, and the excess will start seeping out the front door. The ville people will go insane."

"Good," Ryan panted. "The more confusion the better. Mebbe it'll start a revolt."

"Lots of folks would die in that."

"Lots of folks dying now," Ryan answered, massaging his wrists. "You better get moving before the water gets too deep in there to work."

Everybody but Ryan left the room, while J.B. knelt alongside the main pipe and pulled a block of C-4 from his munitions bag. Gently, he molded it under the arc of the pipe were it would be difficult for anybody to find. Then he disassembled one of the concussion grens and inserted the detonator and ring assembly into the soft claylike material of the plastique. J.B. had a few timing pencils in his bag, but those had a maximum limit of five minutes, which was much too short for the companions to get away from the temple.

"Along with the boobie, rig a secondary charge," Ryan directed. "I know how we can set this off from a distance."

"Got a radio detonator in your pocket?" the Armorer asked, packing the C-4 firmly around the core of the grenade.

"Better," Ryan said, and went back into the armory to return with a coil of the dirty rope.

"The water will be reaching here soon," J.B. scoffed, attaching a length of copper wire to the pull ring of the gren. "We can't trust that shit to burn when it's wet."

"Not a problem," Ryan said, looking at the ceiling.

REACHING THE FRONT DOOR of the temple, Krysty and Dean paused to listen as sec men shouted outside. Then somebody knocked hard on the door and demanded admittance.

The woman and boy drew their weapons as the person tried the lock several times, but after a while the guard went away. However, both of the companions knew the guards would return soon with tools and a lot more men.

Unraveling the tangle of shackles and chains from the torture tables, the pair wrapped three of the lengths around the wooden bar, locking the shackles onto each other to hold the knot tightly.

"Nobody is getting through that without explos," Krysty stated in satisfaction when it was done.

"Looks like we finished just in time, too," Dean said, looking down at the arrival of the first trickle of the water.

Expanding along the floor, the water puddled in front of the massive door, then began to seep outside. Almost immediately there were more shouts and somebody threw themselves against the door, rattling the chains. Then another joined the effort, their curses audible through the slim cracks along the jamb.

"What the hell is that noise?" a man cried out. "Sounds like chains."

"Why would the baron chain the temple shut?"

"He wouldn't, ya feeb. Get Hawk, we need a battering ram!"

Moving fast, the woman and boy retreated into the tunnel, and Krysty locked the iron grille while Dean keep guard with his crossbow. Then they both raced back to the temple, closed the set of double doors and looped the last chain through the handles.

Now Krysty held the first and last link of the chain on top of each other and placed a dagger from the armory through the loops. Lowering the crossbow, Dean drew his Browning Hi-Power and hammered the dagger into the wooden door in lieu of a stake. It wasn't much, but the knife would at least keep the chains from simply slipping off the handles when folks started banging to get inside.

They knew that none of these things would hold off a truly determined force, but all of this would buy them time and make the baron waste a lot of troops trying to get inside and capture them. Hopefully, that would be enough.

Returning to the armory through the iron maiden, Krysty closed the hinged hatch while Dean dragged over an empty wooden barrel. Together, they started to toss in any loose items available, tools, blasters, ammo, grinding stones, until the barrel was heaped high.

"Got to be a good half ton of junk there," Krysty said, dusting off her hands. "That'll slow them down some."

Busy at a worktable, Doc merely grunted in reply. The old man was busy making firebrands, using bits of stiff wire to attach short pieces of the rope fuse to crossbow arrows. Mildred was stuffing the completed products into a patched duffle bag

and Jak was nearby stringing a crossbow, a stack
of four more nearby.

"How did it go?" Mildred asked, cinching the
duffel closed.

"The door is solid," Krysty replied bluntly, "but
the sec men are already trying to get inside."

"So soon? Damn."

"Need any help?" Dean asked the people at the
workbench.

"Thank you, but this is the final batch," Doc
replied, handing Mildred the last arrow. "Especially since Ryan took the rest of the fuse."

Dean looked around to see the huge coils of ropy
fuses were missing from the wall pegs. "He took
all of it?" The boy frowned. "What for?"

"See yourself," Jak said, loading his arms with
crossbows. "But watch step!"

Heading for the pump room, the friends paused
as they spied J.B. on his knees playing a candle
along a piece of the copper wire stretched knee-
high across the open doorway. The flickering flame
was slowly turning the red metal a dark brown almost invisible in the dim recesses of the temple.

"Hold it," he directed, then turned off the nukelamp and the trip wire was gone, invisible in the
darkness.

"Okay," J.B. said, turning the lamp back on. "But watch your step."

"First person through that door is going to discover a world of pain," Dean commented, once on the other side of the trap.

Shifting her duffel bag of firebrands, Mildred snorted. "Yeah, for about half a second."

Glancing at the feeder pipe, Jak saw the wheel was wired to blow, as was the gren at the door. Whatever else happened, the water shortage in the ville was going to end this night, that was for damn sure.

"Where is Ryan?" Doc asked, stepping over the trip wire with exaggerated caution.

Tucking the candle into a pocket, J.B. jerked a thumb at the open hatch in the roof at the top of the ladder. "Making sure we can leave," he said. But interrupting those words was a fast series of soft chugs from the hatch. Drawing weapons, the companions scrambled up the ladder and onto the top of the temple. The last in line, Krysty caught the stock of the H&H Nitro on the hatch for a moment, and had to wiggle about to get through. The damn blaster was over five feet in length, much too long for such cramped quarters.

Standing in the shadows, Ryan was sweeping the edge of the building with the SIG-Sauer. He froze as a hand slithered into view near the corner, but did nothing until the head of the sec man rose into view. Instantly he fired, and the man fell backward with a bloody crater in place of a nose. Going to the edge, Ryan fired twice more and another man cried out briefly.

"Fireblast! Too bastard many people know about the roof hatch," Ryan growled. "And somebody with a brain is going to figure out why there's a pile of bodies in the street, at which point we're shit out of luck."

"Let's get to it," Jak said, passing out the cross-bows.

Overburdened with weapons, the companions dropped their backpacks to take the weapons and got busy nocking the firebrands.

"Think we can reach the motel from here?" Mildred asked, licking a finger to test the direction of the desert wind. Simple logic dictated what the plan was. She only hoped they could pull it off. They had been in tight scrapes before, but this was the first time they were doing a night creep on an entire ville. One wrong move would expose them, and then it was all over.

"The bows have the range," Ryan said, looking across the ville. "It's just a matter of can we hit the target."

Stepping on the crossbar of his crossbow to grab the string in both hands, J.B. pulled it upward until the cord caught on the tongue. Lifting the weapon, he slipped in a firebrand.

"Ranging shot," J.B. directed, touching the rope with his butane lighter. As the fuse sputtered into life, he raised the crossbow and pressed the trigger.

The flaming arrows arced over the ville to drop beyond the motel a dozen blocks away.

"Try ten o'clock, instead of eleven," he said, reloading and lowering the angle. "All together. Ready, shoot!"

The companions launched in unison, the flurry of arrows soaring high to plummet down into the open courtyard around the motel. Bursting from the building, Jed and Sparrow came running out with blasters drawn, both of their dogs baying wildly.

"Again," Ryan ordered brusquely, as tiny dots of light began moving along the top of the adobe wall. The sentries had spotted the firebrands. "Shift more into the wind!"

The crossbows were armed once more, and the next flight went over the motel, one arrow spiraling away randomly to disappear into the distance.

"The fuse came free and threw off the balance," Doc rumbled angrily.

Suddenly a chorus of voices rose from the opposite side of the temple, closely followed by a tremendous crash of splintering wood. Then it came again and again.

"Sounds as if the sec men are busting through," Dean said.

"Check the wires," J.B. commanded, running his fingers along the shaft of an arrow. "This volley has got to be on target!"

Locking his crossbow and reloading, Jak saw a man carrying a longblaster appear on a roof a few buildings away. Only a sec man would have a weapon like that, so he fired from the hip. The unlit arrow flew straight and hit the man in the stomach partially going through. Dropping the blaster, the man clutched the shaft sticking out of his belly and shrieked in pain.

Squinting in that direction, Ryan chanced two shots with the SIG-Sauer, but the wounded man was masked by the darkness and kept on screaming. Having no choice, he slid the Steyr off his shoulder, placed the crosshairs on the sec man's chest and put a 7.62 mm round through his heart, ending the cries.

But the crack of the sniper rifle rolled over the ville, and most of the voices on the streets stopped shouting.

"If they come to this side and find the bodies,

we're screwed. There's no canopy over here to hide the arrows," Ryan growled. "Load and fire at will, but hit that triple-damn wag right now!"

Fast and furious, the companions loaded and fired as quickly as possible, flaming arrows raining all over the area, setting fire to the roof of the motel and smashing to pieces on the streets. When the wind slowed for moment, they sent off the last flurry of arrows. Climbing high toward the stars, the firebrands curved sharply earthward and slammed all over the wag, penetrating the cab, the hood, and several going through the tattered canvas awning over the rear.

Only seconds later, a fire woofed out the back of the wag from the punctured fuel cans, tongues of flame licking from every hole in the canvas. Some sec man hidden behind the wag started running, but it was already too late.

The deafening explosion illuminated the entire ville in a blinding flash of light and rattled shutters for blocks in every direction. Caught near the blast, the sec men were slapped off the ground and sent tumbling through the air like burning rag dolls to hit the side of other buildings with lethal results.

Then from the boiling inferno of the barn came a series of sharp bangs and a new fireball boiled upward, spraying out debris as the cans of condensed fuel rocketed into the air and detonated above the ville.

By now every window was open and a dozen bells were ringing. Illuminated by the reddish glare of the rising fireball, the companions ducked low on the roof of the temple to try to stay in the shadows.

Blaster in hand, Ryan gave a short whistle and jerked a finger at the front of the temple. Dropping to his belly, Jak crawled to the edge of the roof, listened and then chanced a peek. Turning to face the others, he nodded and gave a thumbs-up.

"Okay, they're off to check the explosion," Ryan said aloud, rising to his knees. "That bought us time but not a hell of a nuking lot."

He paused as another detonation shook the ville, as the main forty-gallon fuel tanks of the U.S. Army GMC 6×6 added their destructive fury to the growing conflagration.

Still wary, Krysty was maintaining a close watch on the keep. When a guard appeared on the parapet with what seemed to be binoculars, she swung around the heavy longblaster, set the crosshairs on his chest and fired. The recoil kicked her hard in the shoulder, making the woman think she had missed completely, but the slug from the Nitro Express crossed the distance in a split second and the man flew backward minus a head, a splash of blood hitting the flagpole. Hopefully, Gaza would think it was shrapnel from the blast.

But as she worked the bolt, a woman dressed in white appeared briefly at a window in the keep, and Krysty got a fluttery feeling inside her head. Hastily, she raised the monster rifle, but the woman was already gone. Her heart pounding, Krysty suddenly knew she had aced the wrong target. The strange female was the source of danger, but whether she was a doomie or a telepath, Krysty had no idea.

"The baron might have a doomie," Krysty said aloud. "Hawk could be waiting for us at the horse corral."

Or the front gate. Breathing heavily in the darkness, Ryan said nothing at the news for a few moments. "Okay, too bad for him," he stated.

"J.B., check out the corral. Everybody else, clear the streets of any sec men!"

Standing in plain view, the companions went to the side of the temple and cut loose at a group of guards inspecting the bodies sprawled in the street. Side by side, they chilled every man, the continuing explosions from the wag drowning out the crack of their rifles.

"Corral looks clear!" J.B. announced, collapsing his Navy scope.

Holstering his piece, Ryan gathered up a thick coil of fuse from the roof and tied the end to the top rung of the iron ladder. Tugging hard, he decided it would hold and tossed the rest of the coil over the edge of the temple. With the others keeping watch, the one-eyed man slid down the rope in one fast motion, landing with his knees slightly bent to absorb the impact.

Instantly, he turned with the SIG-Sauer drawn and checked the street, but there were only the dead and the dying on the cobblestones.

Ryan whistled twice, and the rest of the companions descended one at a time, the process seeming to take forever, even though it was only a few minutes according to his wrist chron.

Once Doc was on the ground, Ryan lit the fuse with his butane lighter and watched it slowly start to burn upward.

''Let's get those horses,'' he growled, and started running through the maze of the ville with the others close behind.

Chapter Fifteen

As they raced through Rockpoint, a crackling noise steadily grew as flames began to spread across the ville following the canopy covering the streets. Soon the flames started to spread to the adobe houses, the compressed mud and straw bricks burning as easily as wood.

People were rushing into the street, clutching their belongings and staring about helplessly. A child got in the way of a running sec man, and he clubbed the little girl aside. With a cry of rage, her father smashed a water jug over the guard's head shattering his skull. As the body dropped, the rest of the family began kicking and beating the fallen man while cursing wildly.

"Looks like we've got that revolution," J.B. remarked as they ran past the scene. His last view was of the father yanking the blaster from the limp hands of the bleeding corpse and fumbling to work the hammer and trigger.

But as the companions took a corner, a group of

sec men were shouting orders to a crowd of people stomping out the burning embers on the ground.

"It's them!" a sergeant cried out, swiveling his longblaster and pulling the trigger. But the weapon misfired and only a feeble flame came from the muzzle.

As the sergeant feverishly worked the arming bolt, Ryan put a round into his chest, while J.B. fired the Uzi, the hail of 9 mm rounds tearing the other sec men apart.

"Head for the temple!" Dean shouted at the terrified people running about. "Water's everywhere!" But if anybody believed the boy, there was no indication.

Watchful of the side streets, the companions ran through the ville, shooting down any sec men who came their way. At a hitching post, a corporal stared in shock at their approach and raised his hands in surrender. Without remorse, Ryan blew him away and kept going, knowing full well the man would have started to shoot once their backs were turned.

The smoke was getting thick, blowing along the streets like mist in a tunnel, trapped by the canopy and adobe buildings. That was an unexpected bonus to hold down sniper fire, especially from that 25 mm cannon in the keep if it was working. Rising above the ville, orange flames were barely visible through the cloth and the dense clouds, then there came the sound of splintering wood as the roof of a burning tavern collapsed, sending sparks soaring skyward in a fiery whirlwind.

Needing to check his bearings, Ryan stopped at a gaudy house. The front door slammed aside, and there stood a bald man armed with an ax, along with a handful of raggedly dressed ville people carrying makeshift clubs. Behind them was a group of women in various stages of undress.

"By the Scorpion God, it's the outlanders!" the bald man yelled in triumph. "Chill 'em and the baron will make us sec men!" Like a pack of hounds flush with the scent of their prey, the rest yelled battle cries and charged.

Pausing for a full second to make sure Bart and his wife weren't among the gang, Ryan and J.B. then opened fire while Krysty braced for the recoil and stroked the trigger on the H&H Nitro. The longblaster thundered flame along the street, the big .475 slug blowing a gory hole through the leader only then to slam into the second and send him sprawling.

The noise of the longblaster startled the rest of the vigilantes, and they broke and run, tossing away weapons. Tracking the group for a moment, the companions then turned and hurried away, seeing no reason to ace the unarmed people.

"Fools," Jak muttered, thumbing rounds into the side port of the hot Winchester. When it was loaded, he yanked the crossbow off his shoulder and tossed it away. Damn thing weighed a ton and could serve no useful purpose now. The night creep was over, this was a straight firefight.

Screaming as he came, a sec man ran around a wooden cart loaded with loose bricks, shooting a homemade scattergun. Ryan dived out of the way just in time, and Mildred lunged forward to gut the man with the bayonet at the end of her blaster. The shotgun fell from a spasming hand as he tried to clutch the writhing nest of entrails pouring from his belly. Although still screaming, the guard was already dead, but Mildred couldn't stop herself from wasting a live round and firing the Remington into the man, ending his agony. There was only so far the physician would allow herself to abandon civilization, leaving a wounded man to die slowly was something she would avoid whenever possible.

By now the alarm bell stopped ringing, and people were running all over the ville, seeking cover, but also looting the buildings and the dead. Several fistfights had broken out, and once Dean saw a sec man shoot a corporal in the back. When the turncoat faced their way, the boy feathered him with the last bolt from the crossbow, then tossed the weapon away. Hot pipe, the ville was going insane, old scores between people being settled in the crimson heat of raw battle.

Doc discharged the Webley at an armed man on a rooftop. Although it was a predark weapon, the revolver was carrying bullets reloaded with black powder, and it boomed as if it had exploded, gushing forth a billowing cloud of acrid smoke. Yet even through the din, Doc saw the guard go over the side and fall to the cobblestones to land with a meaty crunch.

"Praise the lord and pass the ammunition," Mildred growled, then flinched as a slug hummed by so close she felt its warmth on her cheek. She turned quickly, but didn't see the source of the incoming rounds. Doubling her speed, the woman tried to ignore the itchy feeling between her shoulder blades of a crosshair marking her as a viable target.

Checking around a corner, Ryan whistled sharply at the others and held up a restraining hand. Listening to the growing noise of the fire and rioting fill the ville, the man watched the stables across the courtyard for any sign of activity. But he could only detect the natural motions of the horses, nothing fugitive suggesting hiding troops.

Taking point, Ryan sprinted across the open street to jump over a split-rail fence and hit the wall of the stable. Then he swung inside with his blaster, searching for enemies. But there were no guards at the corral, the adobe brick stalls containing only horses, mounds of hay and tack. The animals were shuffling in the straw on the floor, their eyes wide with terror. The animals were reserved for the baron and officers, so blasterfire would be well-known to them, but the thick smell of smoke stirred primitive fear response that no amount of training could completely overcome.

There was a movement near the fence, and Ryan almost fired until he saw it was J.B. covering his blind side. Good man.

The Armorer stood guard while Ryan gave the signal and the rest of the companions charged into the stable, grabbing blankets, saddles and bridles to throw onto the animals.

After her horse was saddled, Krysty looked around for anything useful to steal and spotted some sagging bags hanging from a wooden peg sticking out of the bricks. It took only a touch to realize they were water bags. Grabbing two, Krysty looped the first over the pommel of her saddle, then did the same for Ryan's horse. Finished with her own mount, Mildred saw the action and did the same, along with Doc and Jak. Dean searched for any feed bags for the horses, but couldn't find any.

During this, Ryan and J.B. had remained by the fence, ruthlessly chilling every sec man who appeared on the street, the bodies scattered along the surface like drunks after an orgy.

"Let's move out," Krysty called, guiding her frightened horse to the fence, with two more in tow by the reins.

Swinging open the gate in the fence, Ryan and J.B. climbed onto their animals, briefly checking the saddle and reins. Just then a sec man ran by, clutching the stump of an arm, blood spurting at every step.

"That's no blast wound," J.B. said, tightening the reins as a precaution when his horse reared in terror as a cougar lopped past the corral with a human hand sticking out of its fanged mouth.

"The lunatic!" Mildred cursed, fighting to control her mount. "Sparrow said the baron guarded the junkyard with some big cats. Cougars!"

"Must have released them to try and get us," Dean said, stroking the neck of his mare to try to calm her. The animal responded to his touch, but became jittery at the moment he stopped the sooth-ing caress.

"More likely they escaped, terrified of the fire," Ryan stated grimly, forcing his combat boots into the narrow stirrups. "But its still triple-bad for us."

"Look out!" Jak shouted, levering the Winches-ter with only one hand, the other tight on the reins.

Snarling and spitting, another cougar appeared from around a corner, chasing an armed sec man. The fellow fired blindly over a shoulder, and the big cat leaped through the black powder cloud to land upon the man, driving him to the ground under its weight. Then the man screamed as the cougar buried its fangs into the small of his back and sav-agely shook him, audibly snapping the spine, then cast him aside. In a blur of movement, the animal was gone, leaving a trail of bloody paw prints to mark its passage.

"We stay together!" J.B. commanded, inserting a fresh clip into the Uzi. "They're less likely to attack us in a group! Let's move it!"

The companions galloped through the billowing clouds of smoke, heading directly for the front gate. There was no more time to waste on subterfuge or tricks. The faster they got out of Rockpoint and into the desert, the better were their chances of staying alive.

Unexpectedly, the two cougars joined in the courtyard, snarling their blood-chilling cry as they padded through the smoky ville, attacking sec men and civilians indiscriminately. But anybody who discharged a blaster was brutally attacked by both animals and literally torn limb from limb.

Even as he fought to not get sick from the slaughter, Dean filed away the type of attack in his mind. The cats were a pair, male and female, working as a team. He had never seen animals do that. Most muties attacked in a mob but without any order, these killers weren't even eating the people they aced. Just chilling and moving on to find another. The very idea made the boy wish he had taken a longblaster instead of a crossbow from the temple armory, and he clenched his hand around the checkered grip of his Browning Hi-Power, privately wishing it was something more than a 9 mm pistol.

"They seem to be heading for the gate," Krysty said, struggling to keep her horse from bolting. The combination of fire and the cats was driving the animal into a frenzy.

"Stay behind the cats," Ryan ordered. "They'll clear the way for us."

"What if they turn?" Doc demanded, the Webley held in his right hand as he cocked back the hammer with a thumb.

"Left shoulder!" Ryan stated, holding the reins in his left hand, the right keeping the Steyr braced in his hip for immediate use. "Not the heart or head! And don't fucking miss!"

As if understanding the words, a cougar glanced backward to snarl at the mounted people, and the companions leveled their arsenal of weapons at the beast. For a moment, it seemed like the male cougar was going to charge, then the female sprang sideways and seized an old woman by the throat ripping away most of her neck. Gushing a horrible fountain of blood, the wrinklie fell to her knees, as the cougar mauled her with its front paws. Her high-pitched scream never stopped as the blood sprayed everywhere. Then she went limp and the cat raised its gore-streaked face to snarl at the sky.

At the sight, Krysty started to aim the Hollands & Hollands, but stayed her hand. The old woman was already dead, and they needed the help of the cats to reach the gates. Once there, she would blow their heads off with the Nitro Express.

Horses, dogs, civilians and sec men fled from the approach of the cougars, the chaos in the smoky ville increasing as the alarm bell began to ring

again from the keep. Or was it sending a message
to the sec men? There was no way of knowing.

With the bravado of ignorance, a sec man
jumped out of an alleyway firing two big bore
wheelguns at the big cats in a storm of lead. But
they dropped to the ground at the first round and
then leaped, the male seizing his gun hand by the
wrist and the female racking her claws across the
man's head, flipping over the scalp to fall across
his face. Bare white bone gleamed from the
smeared blood of the open head. As the guard tried
to shove his scalp back in to place, both cats sank
their teeth into his chest and ripped out vital organs.

That was when several shots rang out from behind the companions. Turning in their saddles, they
fired a volley at the group of sec men coming up
the street. The ten or so guards were moving from
doorway to alley, trying to always stay behind
cover as they closed in toward Ryan and the others,
the companions now trapped between them and the
big cats.

"Flank attack!" J.B. yelled, spraying the Uzi in
a figure-eight pattern, the 9 mm Parabellum rounds
ricocheting off the houses and streets in a hellstorm
of lead until the clip went empty. "Which way, the
men or the cats?"

"Fuck them both! Head down the side street!"

Ryan shouted, kicking his horse in the rump and urging it on to greater speed.

Galloping loudly on the cobblestones, the companions thundered past the snarling cats and down the side street. But the cougars followed, looping after the riders.

The stupe sons of bitches had to think the friends were running away in fear, Ryan realized in frustration, and instinct was forcing them to chase after them. That was when he saw the street was a dead end, terminating at the ville wall. Trapped again! Now there was no other choice. They had to ace the cats before the animals got underneath the horses and ripped out their bellies.

"Ace 'em!" Ryan ordered, reining in his mount and turning to shoot.

The barrage of rounds from the companions hit the cats everywhere, blood covering their muscular bodies. But the lead seemed to have no effect, and the cats leaped to turn in the air and charge at the mounted people, snarling with blood lust.

Trying to find the left shoulder, Ryan swung his rifle and both cats dodged. Fireblast, they were fast! Choosing a different target, the one-eyed man pumped a 7.62 mm round directly into the left eye of the male cougar. The animal jerked at the impact and shook its head to snap a bite to the left. But now their horses refused to advance and were backing away from the gate.

J.B. put a spray of 9 mm Parabellum rounds into the female and she turned toward them with eyes of green fury, her mouth scissoring the flapping piece of face.

Struggling with the heavy H&H rifle, Krysty fired just as her horse bucked, the heavy slug smashing into a burning adobe house and blowing a gaping hole in the mud bricks. Then Mildred fired four fast shots directly in front of the cougars, the lead glancing off the cobblestones, the noise and sparks making the pair retreat slightly.

Yanking on the bolt, Ryan yanked out the clip and stuffed in his last loaded spare. The big cats were too heavily muscled for anything but the .475 round to penetrate from a distance. The short Parabellum nines and the black-powder rounds just couldn't get in deep enough to reach any organs. The shoulder was the only really vulnerable spot. The muscle was thin there and a well-placed shot could reach the bone, blowing out a halo of bone splinters like shrapnel directly in the heart. But it was a bastard tricky shot, especially on an animal that could move faster than most wags could drive. Their speed was incredible!

Using both handcannons, Doc fired and missed.

Switching to the shotgun, J.B. hit the female and wounded her in the side, but nothing fatal. Krysty fired again, but it was only a graze. Dean banged away steadily with his Browning, making the male turn, and Ryan paused before firing again, hitting the cougar smack in the left shoulder.

The beast froze from the pain, galvanized for a half a heartbeat, and then it slumped to the ground. Puzzled, the female made a noise at its mate, then turned its attention to Ryan and worked its rear legs, hunching up for a charge when the sec men appeared at the mouth of the side street. The cat whipped around, startled by the intrusion of more people.

"We're wasting time and ammo!" Ryan shouted, as a shot hummed by his head. "Use a gren!"

Already with a sphere in hand, J.B. pulled the pin on the implo gren and threw.

Landing between the sec men and the cougar, the device activated on impact, generating its killing gravity field, compacting men, animal, street and buildings in a microsecond pulse of total destruction. As the dust cleared, only a mangled pile of twitching flesh remained at the bottom of a mirror smooth crater, none of the ooze could easily be identified as either man or cat.

"Good thing that worked," J.B. said with a sigh, easing his grip on another gren. "Only one of these babies left to use on the gate."

"Nuke that," Ryan said, studying the width of the steaming crater. "Use it on the wall right here."

"Here?" the Armorer repeated, looking at the imposing barrier. "If the grav field doesn't go all the way through, we're trapped for good."

"Better chance here than of us reaching the front gate alive," Ryan countered, the alarm bells starting to ring once more. "Those are for us, and I'm betting that they know where we're headed."

Nodding in agreement, J.B. galloped to the end of the street, set the timer and heaved the gren. His aim was good, and it landed on top of the twenty-foot wall with a clatter.

He was already riding back to join the others when a sec man appeared on the parapet of the wall holding the gren and raising it high to throw back down.

Chapter Sixteen

Watching from the window of the keep, it seemed to Baron Gaza that the sky was on fire, with pieces of burning cloth dropping into the streets everywhere, embers swirling thick as sand fleas over the adobe buildings. Several roofs were already smoldering, others blazing away, orange tongues licking at the stars.

For some reason, his wives were terrified of the outlanders and wouldn't allow him any closer than he was to an open window. As if somebody could accurately shoot a longblaster this high!

"They didn't breach my private armory, did they?" Gaza demanded, shifting uncomfortably on the stool.

He had caught a piece of shrapnel from the exploding wags, and a healer was cleaning the wound before sewing it shut. The old man was slow, but the best in the ville. Which was why Gaza had hobbled the man, cutting the tendons in his legs so he couldn't escape. Rockpoint ville had no slaves, but there were many different levels of freedom here.

His eldest wife, Allison, started to nod yes, then shrugged. Unlike the other wives, the blonde had a gift, a talent, a feeling for things that couldn't be described. Sometimes it was so haunting it was like trying to hold a moonbeam in your hand. Other times it was a slap in the face that something bad was near. This day had been such an occurrence, and while she didn't exactly know what it meant, Allison knew enough to keep her beloved husband under cover. And still he had been nearly chilled when the outlander wag exploded. Such a fireball!

The room was lush with furnishing, a wooden table covered with linen and silver bowls of cactus fruit. Bottles of aged shine, and sparkling clean water stood about for anybody to sample, and there was a huge roast of camel filling a center plate. Pictures adorned the walls and there were rows of books. Each of them lovingly preserved by the wives, and untouched by Gaza. Some bore the great name of Texas on the cover, but most spoke of things indecipherable.

"Black dust, it's like skydark out there!" the baron grunted, as the probe dug into his flesh.

The old man apologized, and the mute wives rushed forward to stroke their husband and show the healer how to do his job.

"Away with the lot of you!" Gaza shouted,

shoving them away. "I can't fragging stand it when you all hover around like I was made of glass. Get out and check on my horse. Take ten guards armed with rapidfires. I'll be there shortly after Hawk reports on the temple."

The slim redhead called Kathleen waved her hands in concern.

"Damn door is jammed and they had to smash through. I already sent sec men to climb onto the roof, so if the outlanders are inside, they're trapped with no way to escape."

Allison glanced at the burning ville and signaled that there was still much danger, and she didn't want to leave him alone.

"I'm fine, woman," Baron Gaza said, gritting his teeth from the pain. "Hawk is coming, and Darvis has been with me for a decade."

There were powders, even jolt to ease the pain, but those clouded the mind and Gaza needed to stay sharp. This Ryan was a tricky bastard, worthy of being a baron himself. Walked right in the gaudy house used by his officers to buy a meal. That took some major balls, or a hot steaming ton of stupidity.

Reluctantly, the women departed to do his will, taking the guards from the room, their steps echoing along the stone corridors until out of range.

Outside, there came the snarl of a cougar and the scream of dying men.

"Ouch! Careful, fool," Gaza muttered, turning on the healer. "Just because we're alone for a minute doesn't mean you can start rushing the job. That hurt!"

Then the baron stopped talking as he felt sharp steel pressing hard to his throat, the body of the healer warm against his back.

"Did you think I would forget, or forgive?" the wrinklie wheezed, forcing the knife harder into the flesh until a thin line of blood formed along the blade. "You took my daughter screaming to your bed, then sold her to the Devils as a gaudy slut when she didn't bear you a child."

"Please, no," Gaza begged, reaching for his blaster only to find the holster empty. Out of the corner of his eye, he saw the weapon laying on the table near the roast. When had the wrinklie taken the blaster?

"Let me live," the baron pleaded. "I'll give you anything you want. Horses, women, blasters! Anything you desire!"

Sliding the blade along the soft skin cutting new avenues of crimson, Darvis leaned in close and breathed on the baron's ear, sending chills down his spine.

"Anything?" the healer asked mockingly.

"Name it!" Gaza whispered pitifully. "Take my own wives!"

"Now that is a deal, my lord. What I desire," the healer growled, spittle striking the cheek of the trembling baron, "is to piss on your fucking grave!"

The knife started to cut in then for real, and Gaza screamed in terror when a blaster roared and something slapped against the baron with a wet sound, blood, hair and bits of flesh spraying onto the floor.

Staggering to his feet, Gaza saw Hawk walking in from the doorway, his blaster firing again and again into the limp body of the whitehair.

"Damn traitor, good thing I arrived when I did," Hawk said, kicking the dead man to make sure the job was finished. "Are you okay, my lord?"

"Th-thank you for saving my life," Gaza stammered, running his hands over his face, the fingers coming away streaked with pinkish brains and a sticky clear fluid. "Nuking hell, this is such a waste! It really is."

"He wasn't that good a healer, my lord," Hawk said, cracking open the cylinder and dumping the spent shells into a pocket for reloading.

Unexpectedly, there came the clockwork noise

of a hammer being locked into the firing position from the dining table.

"Not him, you. You are the waste," Gaza said softly and fired.

Hawk felt a searing white-hot pain in his chest and staggered from the blow, his weapon falling from numb hands. The baron fired once more, driving Hawk backward, and the man went out the window with a startled cry.

"Did you really think I would let anybody know I had begged a wrinklie for my life?" Gaza growled at the empty window, massaging his throat. "The healer may have been insane, but you were a fool, old friend."

"Such a waste," Gaza repeated, holstering his piece and shuffling from the room, holding his aching side. He still needed that wound stitched shut. This time he'd have the wives do the job. At least they could be trusted.

MOVING FAST, Ryan fired the Steyr without aiming, and the wall guard dropped the implo gren from his hand, the shattered wrist pumping blood from both sides.

A split second later there was a blinding flash, and the entire wall seemed to shake as wide cracks spread out like lightning bolts, making bricks tumble off.

Dust clouds rolled from the vibrating barrier, the horses rearing and whinnying in fright. Seizing the reins, the companions fought to stay on their mounts and the rumbles dissipated through the side street, rattling window shutters and shattering clay pots. As the aftereffects of the implosion slowly faded, Ryan could now see there was a gaping hole in the thick barrier reaching all the way through, only some glassy rubble covering the few yards of ground to the black desert outside.

"Walk them through," Ryan said, sliding off the horse and leading it through the dangerous wreckage. If the animals broke a leg at this point, the escape was finished before it began.

Everywhere on the streets, people were screaming, blasters firing, horses screaming.

"They're coming through!" a sec man screamed on the wall, his shaking hands dropping cartridges as he tried to load a scattergun.

Coming through? The feebs thought it was an invasion, not an escape, which gave J.B. an idea. While the others started traversing the littered passage, the Armorer rode to the mouth of the side street and tossed the last box of .22 cartridges into a burning pile of cloth where the canopy had collapsed. As he raced back to join the others, the bullets started cooking off, lead banging in every direction.

"Coldhearts are in the ville!" J.B. bellowed at the top of his lungs through cupped hands. "Cannies and muties at the front gate! Protect the keep!"

Incredibly, the cry was repeated by others and carried along. Soon the sec men on top of the gatehouse started shooting into the billowing smoke in mindless panic.

Meanwhile, the rest of the companions had reached the desert past the wall, only to discover outriders pounding toward the breach. Climbing on their horses, Ryan and the others peppered the enemy riders with blasterfire as the sec men on the wall started shooting crossbow arrows, the deadly hum of the barbed bolts chilling as they thudded deep into the sand.

Caught in the cross fire, the companions had no choice but to leave and kicked their mounts into action, sprinting for the safety of the night.

"We can't abandon, John!" Mildred yelled, moving to the motion of her mount.

"Not going to! Just drawing away their fire!" Ryan answered, clicking on the nukelamp.

The men on the wall shouted in surprise at the blinding beam, and Ryan leaned far over in the saddle and dropped the lamp on the sand as the companions kept galloping away. Thinking the outlanders had stupidly made a stand, the guards concentrated their weapons on the nukelamp until it was hit and darkness returned to the desert.

Already at the breach, J.B. started walking his horse through as fast as possible, when it tripped and caught a leg on a jagged pile of debris. Diving out of the way, J.B. just missed being crushed by the animal as it went tumbling. Scrambling to his feet, the Armorer saw the animal was crippled, its right leg bent at an impossible angle, badly broken in several places. Without hesitation, J.B. put a short burst from the Uzi into the horse, grabbed the saddlebags, then took off running. But the bags weighed more than he could carry, and the man reluctantly dropped the spare water and nukelamp.

Reaching the low stone wall of the boundary marker, the companions slowed their horses to take stock of the situation. The desert ahead seemed clear, but the outriders were still somewhere in the darkness, and the wall guards were getting better with those blasters now that they figured out it wasn't an invasion. If Gaza got his hands on J.B., he'd be aced on the spot. They'd have to make a stand.

"Doc, Jak, watch our backs!" Ryan ordered.

"The rest of us, let's start clearing off that wall and give J.B. some cover!"

"All for one, and one for all!" Doc said in a loud clear voice, drawing both of his huge pistols and cocking back the hammers.

Holding the reins in one hand, Dean gave a sharp nod at that advice as he pulled out the Browning. Never leave a friend behind, or a coldheart alive, as his father always said.

Dodging some loose bricks still falling from the smashed wall, J.B. hit the sand running and started to follow the hoof prints, holding tightly on to his munitions bag to keep it from flapping about and slowing him. Then a rumble sounded to the left, and he felt the ground shake as horses came thundering out of the darkness. Whistling loudly, J.B. headed toward them, thinking it was his friends. Then blasters started sparking in the darkness, a round tugging on his leather jacket. Mounted guards! Zigzagging in the night, J.B. opened up with the Uzi, the hardball ammo mowing down the first row of animals, the second row plowing into the dead. The shouts of pain were music to his ears, then the submachine gun jammed on a bad round and J.B. began laying tracks while jerking on the bolt to free the brass from the ejector port.

"Outlander!" a guard cried from above, and

crossbow bolts flew through the night thicker than a swarm of bees.

As the jam came free, J.B. raced for the desert, firing bursts over his shoulder until the Uzi was empty. Pulling a concussion gren from the munitions bag, he pulled the pin and released the spoon to flip the explosive charge high into the air. It detonated with a tremendous bang, the shock wave slamming sec men off the parapet to fall to their deaths.

At the sound of the gren, Ryan turned and squinted. There was a hellish light pouring through the breach in the ville wall from the burning buildings, and in the glow he could make out a running figure wearing a fedora and glasses.

"John got out alive!" Mildred cried in joy.

"We go back!" Jak stated firmly.

"We stay here!" Ryan commanded, reining his horse to a stop and sliding the Steyr off a shoulder. "Dean, get going son!"

The young Cawdor wheeled his mount and started for the ville racing across the sand, staying just out of the light washing through the breech.

Working the bolt, Ryan chambered a round and raised the sniper rifle to his eye for only a moment before firing. Silhouetted by the fire, a black shape on top of the wall cried out, the crossbow in his hands firing its quarrel into the guard beside him.

Leveling the .30-30 longblaster, Mildred began to slowly squeeze off rounds and sec men fell off the wall, then Krysty, Jak and Doc trained their weapons on the outriders as they appeared coming over a low dune. The mounted sec men had tried to outflank the companions, and paid dearly for arriving too soon.

Crouched low in the saddle, Dean urged the horse on to greater speed as he pounded across the flat open ground, his body moving in perfect rhythm to the massive animal. The distance between him and J.B. was decreasing by the second, and reaching behind, Dean released the lacings and the saddlebags slipped to the ground, making room for his passenger. This was why his father had sent Dean. He was the only person small enough to share a horse with J.B. and not fall behind from the weight of two riders.

The ground around J.B. was puffing dust as the ville sec men started to find his range. The Armorer was running in a zigzag to avoid offering a steady target, but he was starting to tire, and the range was too great for his shotgun, the last gren, or anything else he had. His lungs were burning from the frantic effort, and his precious glasses kept threatening to bounce off his face as he pounded the sand.

Reloading the Nitro Express, Krysty choked off a scream as an arrow went through her hair, cutting off several of the living filaments, and Jak cursed as he dropped the Winchester, blood flowing down a limp arm.

A buzz went by Dean, and he felt something wet trickling down his cheek. Blood? Hot pipe, that had been close! A half inch more and he would have been impaled on the shaft of the quarrel. Blasted locals were too damn good with those crossbows.

Reining the sweaty horse to an abrupt halt, Dean offered J.B. a hand, and the man scrambled on, kicking the beast hard in the rump with the heels of his combat boots.

"Light this candle!" the Armorer wheezed, holding on to the saddle for dear life.

Dean didn't bother to reply, just headed the horse into the darkness, kicking up the sand.

Creaking loudly, the front gate of Rockpoint raised and out stormed a dozen fresh riders, brandishing longblasters.

Now moving fast enough, J.B. hauled a C-4 block out of his bag, stabbed it with a timing pencil, broke off the detonator and tossed it behind.

"What was that?" Dean demanded, banking to

the left, and left again to confuse the enemy
marksmen.

"Protective cover!" J.B. said, reloading the Uzi.

The charge hit the ground and rolled a few yards
before violently exploding, throwing out a hellstorm of sand. Unable to see anymore, the guards
on the wall had to stop shooting out of the fear of
chilling their fellow sec men.

Not hindered by that consideration, Ryan and the
others filled the swirling sandstorm with lead, the
screams of dying men and horses a testament to the
accuracy of their shots.

Taking advantage of the distraction, Jak slipped
off his horse, retrieved his blaster and crawled awkwardly back into the saddle. Ripping open his shirt,
he stuffed the wounded arm into it as a crude sling,
then crammed the reins into his mouth and started
to fire the Winchester with one hand, throwing the
longblaster forward by the lever, then pulling the
trigger.

One of the horses coming their way was nicked
in the shoulder and veered sharply away from the
pain to collide into another. Mounts and riders
mixed and went crashing to the ground in a wild
jumble of limbs and blasters. The two sec men directly behind tried to jump the tangle of bodies but
only landed directly on the fallen men, crushing

them, hooves slamming into chest with pile-driver force, ribs shattering.

Half-blind from the swirling sand, the rest of the pack rode onward, unlimbering their weapons when the night was suddenly illuminated by a strident detonation within the ville. Seconds later a towering geyser of clear water rose like a fountain above Rockpoint.

"Somebody finally found the trip wire," Ryan muttered, his horse pounding over the hilly desert.

THE MEN on the walls stopped firing at the incredible sight, then held out their palms as a light sprinkle rained upon them from the rumbling geyser. Slowing their horses, the outriders did the same, staring in wonder at the fantastic, impossible sight. Water, clean, clear water, was gushing upward from the temple in the heart of the ville in unlimited amounts.

"Nuking hell, it was a trick!" a sec man shouted furiously. "Gaza told us there was barely enough water to keep us alive, while he was sitting on a hidden ocean!"

"Son of a bitch lied to his own sec men!" another man ranted, switching from looking at the ville to the escaping outlanders.

"Blood for water, my ass!" a guard snarled, rubbing old scars on his chest.

Reining in his mount, a sergeant brought the horse to a ragged halt in the sand. "Forget the outies," he commanded the rest of the troops. "Let's go get that son of a bitch Gaza and string him up by the balls!"

Waving their blasters, the sec men shouted obscenities and reversed direction to charge back into the ville, hellbent for bloody revenge.

Epilogue

Drenched to the skin by the falling water, Baron Gaza slogged through the ankle-deep puddles in the streets of the ville, heading for the junkyard. Again and again, he was approached by furious people screaming for revenge, and he ruthlessly cut them down with a rapidfire.

How could things have gone so bad so nuking quickly? He was an outcast in his own ville! There was only one conceivable way that the outlanders could have possibly found the pump room. Hawk had to have been right; they were spies for Trader.

Fortunately, the dried mud walls were softening under the presence of the water and soon the buildings would start to sag and crumble. Chaos was spreading through Rockpoint, and that alone was what gave Gaza the chance to escape with his wives. The silent women had expressed no wish to leave the man, and privately he was glad for their company. The more blasters covering his ass the better. Their sodden clothing clung to every curve, exposing a wealth of flesh, but the blasters in their hands were expertly balanced and swept the ville in a steady pattern. Gaza approved.

Reaching the junkyard, Gaza cut down two sec men waiting in hiding near the fence, then took the handcannons from their twitching fingers, along with an oil lantern. Damn fools.

Lighting the wick, Gaza held the lantern high as he maneuvered through the jumbled collection of junk and rusty cars, leading the five women at his back into a metallic cave formed by predark cars tilting against one another. The baron paused at one point, listening to the growing sounds of battle, punctuated by the groan of a collapsing building, before directing the women around a deadfall trap—an engine block attached to chains that would have swung along the middle of the tunnel with deadly force, a cast-iron pendulum that would have crushed any intruder into a bag of broken bones with one shot.

After a few yards more, the baron guided them past a pitfall, the bottom of the deep hole studded with pool cues, the long sticks sharpened and charred with fire to make them strong. The rotting remains of a curious sec man rested halfway down the pit, his desiccated corpse still suspended in the air from the wooden shafts jammed into his torso and broken limbs.

Once past that, Gaza kept his wives close as he paused to dig in the loose sand to uncover a wooden box. Lifting the lid, he cut a few wires inside, disabling a predark land mine, then started forward into the flickering darkness.

From overhead came the steady patter of the falling water from the towering geyser, and soon the hissing lantern revealed a ramshackle school bus sitting in the center of the dim tunnel, its rusty sides covered with corrugated steel, the windows barred, jagged knife blades jutting from the rim of each tire.

His wives bobbed their heads at the sight, and Della eagerly started for the vehicle, but he roughly pulled her aside.

"Leave it alone," Gaza directed impatiently. "That one's a boobie. No engine or fuel, and if anybody tries the ignition the whole thing blows."

The women smiled proudly in appreciation of the death trap and followed their glowering husband as he eased around the crumbling wreck to reach a large canvas-covered object just behind the bus.

Hanging the lantern on a pole sticking out of the hard-packed sand, Gaza ripped off the canvas to reveal the squat, angular box of a military wag.

Eight huge tires supported the APC, the armor a mottle of tans and creams, perfect camou for the desert. The hull was covered with closed blaster ports and hatches, with a big bore .50-cal sitting on top, a glistening link of oiled brass dangling from the breech.

"That's our ride out of here," he said triumphantly.

Gaza looked upon the vehicle with pride. He had found the war wag in a cave stuffed full of supplies, obviously some trader's secret cache. It had taken months of work to get it working again, and then after taking everything he could fit inside the vehicle, Gaza rigged the rest of the supplies to blow so that nobody could use the weaponry against him. He was miles away when the cave detonated, and upon reaching Rockpoint had proclaimed himself baron. The former baron had objected and got blown to hell for his troubles. What did bravery amount to against steel and blasters? Damn fool should have known better.

Going to the rear of the APC, Gaza checked a wax seal on the double doors to make sure nobody had entered the transport. When he was satisfied it hadn't been disturbed, he smashed the seal and shoved aside the doors with the squeal of stubborn metal.

"Inside!" he snapped, clambering into the darkness. "I'm leaving whether you bitches come with me or not!"

Hurriedly, the women scrambled into the APC and figured out how to latch the double doors shut just as there came a roar of power from under the floor and the vehicle lurched forward. Suddenly the interior was filled with white electric lights and they grabbed seats along the metal walls. The blinking lights of electronic equipment winked from racks above them, but the women ignored the display and fumbled to open some blaster ports, shoving through the barrels of their rapidfires.

Throwing the wag into gear, Gaza fed the big diesel engine's fuel and worked the steering levers to angle around the school bus, the sides of the LAV-25 APC squealing as its armored chassis scraped along the rusted pile of wrecks forming the slanted walls. Once past the bus, he stayed in the middle of the tunnel, easily jouncing over the pit and hardly flinching when the engine block slammed into the side of the military war wag, the strident impact making the steel hull loudly ring and rattle the bins of linked ammo.

A curtain of water blocked the end of the tunnel, and Gaza hit the gas as the APC roared from its hidden garage and onto the flooded streets. Water sprayed high behind the LAV-25 from the spinning tires, as Gaza directed the war wag directly into the crowds of people, plowing through the bodies as if they were no more than weeds. Needing both hands to drive, the baron could only laugh as the terrified people tried to splash out of the way and were crushed beneath the thick military tires. Galloping around the side of the temple, a group of sec men on horses charged at the wag, and Gaza surged through the center of the group, fishtailing the APC to smack them aside with crushing force. The sec men still alive fought to control their animals, and that was when the women cut loose with their rapidfires through the blaster ports, the barrage of small-caliber rounds finishing the job.

Dripping blood and entrails, the APC rolled through the downpour as the awnings ripped free, cascading down their accumulation of water. For a moment, Gaza was blind, and that was when from out of nowhere a Molotov crashed on top of the APC in an explosion of fire. But the deluge from the geyser quickly quenched the flames, and his wives retaliated with bursts of blasterfire.

Heading for the front gate, Gaza careened off the corner of a building, running down several people, their screams continuing to come from below the war wag but only for a few brief moments. Another

Molotov hit the vehicle's front prow, and as the
flames licked into the wag through the air vents,
Gaza frantically drove into an alleyway to dodge
any further firebombs. But unexpectedly, there was
no end to the alley, a wide breach going all the way
through the thick outer wall.

Suspicious as hell, the baron scowled at the sight.
Could this be some sort of a trick? No, there had
been no time for the sec men to arrange for such
an elaborate trap. This had to be how the outlanders
got out of the ville. Excellent.

Revving the big diesel engine, the baron charged
down the alleyway and roared through the crumbling gap, the APC riding rough over the irregular
chunks of masonry, dead horses and sec men. More
blasterfire came from the top of the wall, and then
Gaza was outside the ville on flat ground. Throwing
the war wag into high gear, the baron raced across
the desert sand into the night, and soon even the
sporadic sniper fire died away into the distance.

Easing off the bolt on her rapidfire, Della rose
from her chair and awkwardly walked to the front
of the APC to touch her husband on the shoulder.

"Yes, I have a plan. There are some ruins to the
north," Gaza replied to the unspoken question, then
paused for a moment as the badly stitched wound
on his throat began to bleed slightly. He mopped

away the blood and continued. "We'll hide there for a while and then move on to New Mex. I know of some villes there could use a strong baron."

Holding on to a ceiling stanchion, Della frowned and made a gesture with a fist.

"Yes, they have contact with the Trader," Gaza answered angrily. "But that homemade war wag of his can't possibly stand against us! Soon I'll be the Trader, and then I'll carve out an empire the likes of which nobody has ever seen before!"

The woman nodded in acceptance and carefully walked back to join the other wives. She had total faith in her husband.

Checking her blaster, Della stood guard at the rear blaster port, while Kathleen went to the front to ride shotgun, and the remaining women began checking over the hastily gathered supplies, each obviously content to do whatever was needed for the man they loved.

SLUGGISHLY, HAWK awoke into a world of searing pain. For a single chaotic moment, the sec chief thought he was still falling, then abruptly realized he was merely laying in a soft bed, his chest and left arm swaddled in bloody bandages.

"He's alive!" a sec man shouted across the

room, and others rushed closer to crowd around the wounded man.

Hawk grunted at their presence and tried to stand, but strong hands forced him back down onto the mattress.

"Easy, sir, don't tear open that stitching," a sergeant said. "We found the dead wrinklie who shot you, and his body has been thrown to the pigs."

The events replayed themselves in Hawk's mind, and he decided to accept the lie. "Where's Gaza?" he croaked weakly.

The faces in the room took on dark expressions.

"The nuking bastard ran away when the temple exploded!" a sec man cursed, tightening a hand on his gun belt. "There was some sort of well underground. We have a flood in the ville!"

Another sec man added, "Most of the buildings are melting."

Hawk understood. Yes, of course, sun-dried adobe mud bricks. He should have thought of that event.

"So how bad am I?" he asked with false calm. Death wounds often hurt less than minor scrapes.

The sec man serving as a healer snorted at that. "Merely flesh wounds, sir. The lead went clean through without hitting anything vital."

So the slug had missed anything vital and he

would live. Good. Gaza was going to die for that mistake.

"Get me a horse." Hawk groaned as he swung his boots to the floor and painfully sat upright. The barracks spun for a minute, then settled into place once more.

"The ville is dead," he continued. "Raid the armory and take every weapon. We ride tonight!"

"But your wounds..." a sec man said, frowning.

Baring his teeth, Hawk stood by a sheer effort of will. "Fuck them! I want both Gaza and those outlanders chilled by dawn!" he shot back angrily.

MILES AWAY in the desert, Ryan and the rest of the companions steadily rode on into the night. Ahead of them lay endless miles. At the end of their journey, hopefully, they'd encounter the mysterious person who just might be the Trader.

* * * * *

The heart-stopping action
concludes in BLOODFIRE,
Book II of THE SCORPION GOD,
Available December 2003.

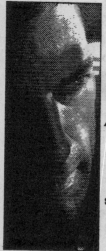

Stony Man is deployed against an armed
invasion on American soil...

ECHOES OF WAR

Facing an unholy alliance of Mideast terrorists conspiring
with America's most dangerous enemies to unleash the
ultimate—and perhaps unstoppable—bioengineered
weapon of horror, Stony deploys righteous fury against
this rolling juggernaut, standing firm on the front lines
of what may be their last good fight.

STONY MAN®

*Available in
October 2003
at your favorite
retail outlet.*

Or order your copy now by sending your name, address, zip or postal code, along with
a check or money order (please do not send cash) for $6.50 for each book ordered
($7.99 in Canada), plus 75¢ postage and handling ($1.00 in Canada), payable to Gold
Eagle Books, to:

In the U.S.
Gold Eagle Books
3010 Walden Avenue
P.O. Box 9077
Buffalo, NY 14269-9077

In Canada
Gold Eagle Books
P.O. Box 636
Fort Erie, Ontario
L2A 5X3

Please specify book title with your order.
Canadian residents add applicable federal and provincial taxes.

GSM67

Take
2 explosive books
plus a
mystery bonus
FREE